**Those Roguish Rosemonts**

*Three brothers with rakish pasts find love where they least expect it.*

Three brothers, three young men from a privileged, aristocratic background. All are expected to uphold the Rosemont family name—which means giving up their roguish ways and marrying well. But are they ready to make convenient marriages where love is second to duty? That is when they each meet a woman who challenges them and convinces them that love is the only way to find true happiness.

Read Ethan's story in
*A Dance to Save the Debutante*
Available now

And look for Jake's and Luther's stories
Coming soon

## Author Note

*A Dance to Save the Debutante* is the first in a new series, Those Roguish Rosemonts, and features the youngest of three brothers, Lord Ethan. Ethan's carefree existence is turned upside down when he meets Sophia Cooper, a debutante who is starting to discover that her season might not be the fairy tale she had hoped for.

I loved writing Sophia's story and exploring what the season must have been like for the young debutantes. Behind the glamor of the beautiful dresses and romantic balls, the season was a chance for families to make marriage deals and to try to advance their social status by marrying their daughters to men of higher rank.

Love rarely came into the matches, and they were sometimes made without the young woman's consent. That is the situation in which Sophia finds herself. But fortunately, she has a reluctant champion looking out for her in the form of Lord Ethan and is about to find she has undiscovered strengths of her own.

It always gives me pleasure to hear from readers, and I can be reached via my website, www.evashepherd.com, or my Facebook page, www.Facebook.com/evashepherdromancewriter.

# EVA SHEPHERD

---

## A Dance to Save the Debutante

ISBN-13: 978-1-335-40783-2

A Dance to Save the Debutante

Copyright © 2022 by Eva Shepherd

Harlequin Enterprises ULC
22 Adelaide St. West, 41st Floor
Toronto, Ontario M5H 4E3, Canada
www.Harlequin.com

Printed in U.S.A.

After graduating with degrees in history and political science, **Eva Shepherd** worked in journalism and as an advertising copywriter. She began writing historical romances because it combined her love of a happy ending with her passion for history. She lives in Christchurch, New Zealand, but spends her days immersed in the world of late Victorian England. Eva loves hearing from readers and can be reached via her website, evashepherd.com, and her Facebook page, Facebook.com/evashepherdromancewriter.

### Books by Eva Shepherd

### Harlequin Historical

#### *Young Victorian Ladies*

*Wagering on the Wallflower*
*Stranded with the Reclusive Earl*

#### *Breaking the Marriage Rules*

*Beguiling the Duke*
*Awakening the Duchess*
*Aspirations of a Lady's Maid*
*How to Avoid the Marriage Mart*

#### *Those Roguish Rosemonts*

*A Dance to Save the Debutante*

Visit the Author Profile page
at Harlequin.com.

To Brenda with love—no one could ever wish for a kinder, more caring sister.

## Chapter One

*London 1890*

Freedom was calling to him. It was promising fun and frivolity, a night of wine, women and song. He just had to leave the ball and it would all be his for the taking.

Lord Ethan Rosemont, the third son of the former Duke of Southbridge, looked around the crowded ballroom at his family's London home. His mother was distracted. Now was the perfect time to make his escape. He had done his duty. He'd put in the requisite appearance, made the required small talk. Surely no more could be expected of the feckless third son.

He edged his way around the side of the dance floor, careful not to make any sudden moves and draw his mother's attention. A few young women looked in his direction but were quickly brought to heel by their mothers. He would not be in demand until his two older brothers were married off and his fortune suddenly became of interest to the husband hunters. For now, he was safe. There was no point in chasing the third son when the Duke was still on the loose.

The Rosemont ball was the first of the Season, as was the tradition. Well, it had become a tradition since his father died ten years ago and his mother had made it her mission to find the next Duchess of Southbridge. And what better way to do it than to host the inaugural ball and give your eldest son first pick of the ripe new debutantes?

Ethan caught his older brother's eye and sent him a sardonic smile. Surrounded by a growing group of young ladies and their competing mothers, the poor man looked like a defenceless animal being pecked at by a flock of brightly dressed birds of prey. Once again Ethan gave thanks for being born third. Nothing had ever been expected of him, and nothing ever would be.

He could only hope that his brothers, Luther and Jake, took their time in finding brides. He expected that to be the case as they were as enthusiastic about the prospect of marriage as he was. At twenty-eight his eldest brother was still unwed. According to Ethan's reasoning, that meant, at the tender age of twenty-three, he would not have to shackle himself to a wife and children for at least five years. Five more years of freedom, of which he planned to enjoy every minute. And he couldn't do that while stuck in the constrained atmosphere of a Society ball.

He passed through the French doors and commenced humming a tune he'd heard a few nights ago at the Lambeth music hall. The tune brought to mind the rather delightful chorus girl he had met that night, and the tantalising private dance she had performed for him when she had finished entertaining the masses.

Antoinette, Annette, Angela... What was her name again? Whatever it was, the young lady was certainly worth a second visit.

The sound of crying interrupted his reminiscence of what Antoinette, Annette or Angela could do with that lithe body of hers and halted his progress.

Damn it all. He knew exactly what the problem would be. Mrs Hawden, the housekeeper, had recently hired a young maid. She couldn't be much older than fifteen and he had heard it was her first time away from home. She had looked so miserable as she went about her work, and he doubted Mrs Hawden would be helping the situation. The woman wasn't exactly known for indulging the staff or showing much compassion for their personal problems.

He looked up and down the hallway. There were no servants in sight, no one who could offer comfort and reassurance to the young girl. They would all be too busy performing the tasks assigned to them and making sure the ball went off with its usual military precision.

With a resigned sigh he turned the handle and entered the library. The source of the crying was hunched up in a leather chair, almost buried in piles of blue taffeta, and it was most definitely not the maid. Her blonde head rose. She looked up at him with red-rimmed blue eyes, gasped and swiped at her face in an attempt to undo the damage.

He wished her good luck with that. It would take

a bit more than a few desperate wipes with a sodden lace handkerchief to repair those tear-smeared cheeks and swollen eyes.

'I'm sorry… I was just… I didn't mean to…' she spluttered, tears still coursing down her cheeks as she attempted to stand and straighten out her gown.

He signalled for her to sit and moved to the seat across from her. She sat back down and twisted her handkerchief into a ball. 'I'm sorry. You must think me frightfully foolish.'

'Not at all,' Ethan said, not sure what he did think about finding a crying debutante, but knowing he could not leave her, not when she was this distressed. 'Do you want to tell me what the problem is?' he asked, making his voice as gentle as possible. 'Maybe I can help.'

She twisted the handkerchief even more tightly. 'It's all just so horrible.'

Ethan nodded. Judging by the tears it most probably was. 'What is so horrible?'

'This is my very first ball.'

He nodded again and waited for her to continue.

She drew in a deep breath, which turned into a hiccup when she exhaled, and her tear-stained cheeks blushed. 'I had dreamt of it being like a fairy tale, but it's been horrid.'

Ethan suppressed a sigh. It was a familiar story. Didn't all young women expect their first Season to be like a fairy tale, where some handsome prince would sweep them off their feet? The reality was more like a cattle market, where the men on the hunt for a wife assessed the available young women, weighing up their attributes and the flaws to try and maximise the return on their investment, while the mothers fought a polite battle to seize the man with the highest title and greatest wealth for their daughter.

Ethan shuddered. A nightmare would be a more apt description.

'What went wrong?' he asked, having a reasonably good idea what the answer would be.

'My intended has all but ignored me all night,' she said, then gave a loud sniff.

'Oh, I am sorry.'

She looked down at her scrunched-up handkerchief. 'Mother said that he would dance with me tonight, possibly several times, and the next day he would probably send me flowers and ask to walk out with me, and then he would woo me throughout the Season, but he has hardly spoken to me all night.'

She glanced up at him, those blue eyes appealing to him for understanding. The fright she looked at the moment, it was no surprise her beau was avoiding her, but presumably she had not had puffy red eyes when she arrived at the ball.

'I see,' Ethan said, and he did see. This courtship appeared to be one arranged between the families. Possibly the poor young man had as much to say in the matter as the debutante. 'Has he expressed any interest in courting you?' he asked, trying to keep any judgement out of his voice.

'Oh, yes,' she said with an eager nod. 'He visited my mother when we first came down to London. She said he was quite taken with me and that he would make an excellent husband.' She sighed. 'But he's spent almost the entire night with his chums, talking and laughing. He had one dance with me when I first arrived and then he just returned me to my mother and left me completely alone.'

She was so forlorn, and Ethan was so torn. He did not want to get involved. This was not his problem, but his heart went out to this young woman. She was caught up in a system she did not seem to understand and he could see it was breaking her innocent heart.

He could see what was happening here and had seen it before. An arrangement had been made. The parents had given their consent. No real courtship was required. Instead, the man could enjoy his remaining months as a bachelor by larking about with his friends. Meanwhile, this poor young thing, who had been looking forward to her debut for years, who had been trained for it, had dreamt about it, was reduced to tears because life was not a fairy tale.

'Perhaps your beau needs to think that there is a rival for your hand.'

Her swollen eyes opened a little wider. 'What do you mean?'

'If you danced with another man, he might realise he needs to make more of an effort to court you.'

She crumpled further in her chair. 'But that's the thing, you see. No other man has asked me to dance.'

That too was to be expected. If the other men knew she was spoken for, what would be the point of trying to attract her interest? She was effectively off the market.

'I'm another man. If I dance with you, then that

might be enough for your beau to try harder to win your fair hand.'

He looked at her hands, which were indeed fair, although right now they were clutching that rather damp, twisted handkerchief.

'Oh, would you? Would you do that for me?'

'I'd be honoured.' Antoinette, Annette or Angela would just have to wait a bit longer.

Sophia rubbed her handkerchief across her eyes to wipe away the last of her tears, then returned the drenched knot of lace and linen to her reticule. This handsome stranger was going to save her. It wasn't quite what she had envisioned for her first ball, but it was certainly better than being abandoned, left to cry all on her own.

And hopefully he was right. Once they had danced together the Duke would become her Prince Charming and her Season would be just as she had dreamt it would be. Unlike the other debutantes, because she didn't have a title, she had not been presented to Queen Victoria for her coming out, which was a disappointment. But as her mother kept reminding her, she was already a greater success than all those aristocratic young ladies because no less than a duke had expressed his interest. But so far there had been nothing successful about this ball, and right now she felt like a complete failure.

'This really is kind of you,' she said, pleased that the wobbly tone had left her voice. She sent him a grateful smile. He smiled back at her.

Oh, yes, he most certainly was a handsome stranger. Even, dare she admit it, more handsome than the man she hoped to marry. His brown eyes contained so much warmth that staring into them was raising her body temperature, and despite the growing heat of her skin she found it impossible to look away.

Instead, she continued to stare at his lovely, smiling eyes. The way they crinkled up at the corners was so endearing, showing he laughed often. He was so obviously a kind man, otherwise she would feel uncomfortable being alone with this stranger, but she felt safe with him. In contrast to his warm eyes, his black hair reminded her of the sky on the darkest midwinter night. She wondered what it would be like to touch. Would it be silky, allowing her to gently run her fingers through it, or would her hands get caught in those tousled curls? And what of that dark stubble on his chin, what would that feel like? Rough to the touch, she imagined.

She quickly lowered her eyes when he inclined his head and raised his eyebrows in question. She had been staring at him for far too long and heaven knew where those inappropriate thoughts had come from. Midwinter skies and silky hair? For goodness' sake, what was wrong with her?

'Yes, very kind indeed,' she mumbled, gripping her reticule tightly.

'So, shall we?' Those brown eyes were still smiling but he did not appear to be laughing at her.

She waited, unsure what he was asking. Was he suggesting she answer her own questions by running her fingers through his hair and along his strong jawline to discover for herself what stubble felt like?

She giggled at the absurdity of that notion, then bit her bottom lip to halt her outburst. She had already made herself look foolish with all her tears. Did she need to act even more like a giddy young girl by giggling senselessly?

'But before we return to the ballroom and drive your beau wild with jealousy, perhaps we should introduce ourselves,' he said, standing up. 'I'm Lord Ethan Rosemont.'

She rose to her feet and bobbed a quick curtsey. 'How do you do? I'm Miss Sophia Cooper.'

'I'm very pleased to make your acquaintance.' He made a formal bow. 'And I would be honoured, Miss Cooper, if you would grant me the next dance, but perhaps you'd like to freshen up first.'

'Oh, yes, I suppose I should,' she said, and then to her mortification hiccupped. Her hand shot to her mouth, but he merely smiled at her, as if she had done something sweet rather than extremely gauche. She lowered her hand and smiled back in gratitude.

'I'll wait for you by the French doors just inside the ballroom.'

'Oh, yes, of course,' she muttered, embarrassed that she had got distracted and actually forgotten what they were planning to do.

'When you enter, I'll be so dazzled by your beauty that I'll simply have to dance with you immediately. That should make him sit up and take notice.'

She gave a little laugh and departed for the ladies'

room. It was all make-believe, but for the first time since the Duke had abandoned her she really did feel like the belle of the ball about to embark on an exciting adventure.

That illusion was shattered the moment she looked at her reflection in the mirror. No one would be dazzled by the blotchy cheeks and puffy eyes of the woman staring back at her.

It was amazing that Lord Ethan hadn't run out of the room at the sight of her. She could only further admire his kindness, or, at least, appreciate his ability to take pity on a dishevelled wretch like her.

But her appearance made one thing abundantly clear. Lord Ethan was only interested in helping her gain the attention of another man. Looking how she did, he most certainly would not find her attractive.

She suspected when he was a child, he would have been the sort of boy to rescue abandoned puppies and cats and give those bedraggled strays the care they so craved. And right now that was just what she looked like, a stray, dishevelled animal that nobody wanted.

She splashed water on her face but it made no difference. She splashed some more and tried to reorganise her hair.

'Perhaps Madam would like to use some powder,' the attending maid suggested, holding up a powder puff.

'Oh, yes, thank you, and anything you can do to make me look respectable would be wonderful.'

Normally, Sophia would eschew cosmetics, but she was desperate and was sure, under the circumstances, a little powder would not hurt. It wasn't vanity, she told herself. She just did not want to embarrass Lord Ethan by looking as if she'd been dragged through a hedge.

She sat in front of the mirror and the attendant fixed her hair and applied a light dusting of powder. Her eyes were still red-rimmed, but it made a vast improvement.

Thanking the attendant, she returned to the ballroom. Ethan was standing by the door as promised. He turned to look at her. His gaze locked onto hers with an intensity that caused her heart to flutter and her stomach to perform a peculiar little jump.

He placed his hand over his heart, as if his too was beating like a bass drum, stepped towards her and sent her a quick, almost imperceptible wink.

She giggled, embarrassed at her silly reaction. This kind, handsome stranger, this Lord Ethan Rosemont, was doing her a favour. He said he'd pretend to be dazzled by her beauty and that was all he was doing. He was play-acting and that was no reason for her body to react in such a foolish manner.

She wasn't Cinderella. He wasn't her Prince Charming. Even if he was decidedly charming. This was all just a ruse to get the attention of the man she wanted to marry.

He took her gloved hand in his and bowed over it, his lips hovering inches above her hand, then looked up at her, his eyes still feigning desire. 'I know it is forward of me to ask you to dance before we have been formally introduced, but I simply cannot help myself. I must dance with the most beautiful woman in the room.'

'Oh, and who would that be?' Sophia said, aiming

for flirtatious nonchalance but ruining it when another embarrassed giggle escaped.

'Why, you, of course, and you wouldn't be so cruel as to say no, would you?'

'No, I mean, yes. I mean, no. I wouldn't be so cruel as to say no, but… Oh, let's just dance, shall we?'

'Good idea.'

He took her hand and escorted her out onto the floor. The orchestra, seated in the alcove above the dance floor, began to play a waltz. His arms surrounded her and they glided across the parquet floor. Why did it not surprise her that he was a superb dancer?

'We need to give your beau a show,' he whispered in her ear. 'If he thinks another man is smitten with you, then that green-eyed monster is sure to raise its head, and before you know where you are he'll be courting you for all he's worth.'

She nodded, trying to focus on his words, not on his cheek, so close to her own, not on the arms holding her, or the hard wall of his chest.

'So, you'll excuse me if I do this.' His hand slid further round her waist and pulled her in towards his body. This was not how her dance instructor had taught her. He was so close she could feel the warmth of his body. So close all she would have to do was lean forward slightly and they would actually be touching.

It was somewhat inappropriate, but it did feel nice. Yes, very nice indeed.

He looked deep into her eyes, causing Sophia's heart to beat that little bit faster. Now that they were mere inches away, she could see that his eyes weren't just brown, but contained a hint of gold, like polished amber. It was a shade that was both warm and captivating, just like the man himself, and Sophia continued to stare into them as if mesmerised.

'How's this for a look of adoration? Do you think your intended will think I'm entranced?'

Sophia nodded as if to break a spell of her own making. If the Duke didn't think they were entranced, then there was something wrong with him because it felt very real to Sophia.

'Well, in case he still isn't convinced, let's really make him worry.' He smiled at her, that lovely, enchanting smile. Thank goodness this was all pretence, otherwise she was sure that smile would have her swooning in his arms.

'Excuse me while I do this.'

He pulled her so close they were now actually touching. Sophia gulped but put up no objection.

'I know it's too close for propriety's sake, but nothing frightens a man more than the thought that another man is after his beloved.'

'Hmm, yes,' Sophia said, trying hard to ignore the way her breasts were almost skimming his chest.

But that was asking the impossible. As if unable to resist temptation, she moved in even closer. Her hand slid along his shoulder until it moved to the back of his neck. It was as if they were about to embrace. A thought that caused Sophia's heart to pound hard and fast, to its own frantic drumbeat.

'That's it,' he murmured in her ear. 'You're getting into this play-acting now. I'm sure once we leave the dance floor that foolish man will take you in his arms and never let you go. Tomorrow he will shower you with flowers and cards, and before long he'll be down on bended knee begging you to marry him.'

Sophia pulled back from him and moved her hand to the edge of his shoulder. Had she forgotten that she was supposed to be thinking about another man, the man she wanted to marry with all her heart? She really was becoming addle-brained. She'd only just met this man. He was merely showing her a kindness. There was no need to become all mushy and forget who she was and what she wanted.

The waltz came to an end and he led her off the dance floor. 'Thank you, Miss Cooper,' he said with a bow, as if she had been the one to do him a favour. 'You are a sublime dancer.'

'Thank you,' Sophia replied, unsure if this was still part of the play-acting or whether he really was complimenting her. And was that why he was still looking at her with adoration in his eyes? Whether it was play-acting or not, it was lovely.

'I believe the next dance is mine,' a man behind her said.

She turned to see the Duke of Ravenswood. He was talking to her but staring at Lord Ethan.

'Shall we, Miss Cooper?' he said, extending his arm, still scowling at Lord Ethan, who was returning his look of disdain.

It had worked, exactly as he said it would. She should be excited to finally have the Duke's attention. She *was* excited. Of course she was.

'Rosemont,' the Duke said.

'Ravenswood,' Lord Ethan replied, in a manner which almost sounded like a sneer.

He looked at her and inclined his head towards the Duke, his question clear. *Is this your beau?*

She nodded slightly, smiled her thanks, then placed her hand on the Duke's extended arm. He covered her hand with his own, still staring at Lord Ethan as if proving that she was his and no one else's.

The Duke led her out onto the dance floor and they reeled around in an energetic polka. Lord Ethan remained watching them for a moment, then strode across the room towards the French doors. It had all worked out perfectly. Thanks to Lord Ethan, she had what she wanted. She was in the arms of the man she had set her heart on, but as the ballroom doors swung closed she couldn't help but feel she had just lost something precious.

## Chapter Two

It was not his problem. It most definitely was not his problem. But bloody hell. Ravenswood. That innocent, naïve young thing was going to marry *him*. Ethan signalled a hackney cab driver and gave instructions to take him to his club. He no longer had any interest in the theatre, or chorus girls, or any other diversions. Seeing that sweet Miss Cooper in Ravenswood's arms had soured his mood.

It was not his problem, he repeated to himself as he walked up the stairs of his club and nodded to the footman who took his hat, coat and gloves. Young women married inappropriate men all the time. When members of Society were bargaining for the best marriage deal, they rarely considered the character of the man, particularly if the man in question was a duke.

*But the Duke of Ravenswood.*

What on earth had her mother been thinking? But then, like Miss Cooper, there was no way the mother could truly know the real Duke of Ravenswood.

Women lived in a different world from men. They knew nothing of what went on in the bawdy houses, gambling dens and other places of iniquity.

Even though it was not Ethan's business he was tempted to return to the ball, pull her out of that man's arms and...

He stopped walking and turned up his hands, as if indicating to an invisible audience how hopeless it all was.

What was he going to do? Marry her himself? That was a ludicrous idea. He didn't want a wife, any wife, and he would never be interested in an innocent debutante. He liked his women experienced, fun-loving and not interested in dragging a man up the aisle.

No, he would cease thinking of little Miss Sophia Cooper and the Duke of Ravenswood and concentrate on what he did best: enjoying himself.

He entered the billiards room and asked a passing servant for a brandy. Perhaps he should have tried to distract himself with Antoinette, Annette or Angela after all. He downed his brandy, ordered another and racked up the billiard balls.

He took his shot, the cue ball hitting the other balls with an almost violent thwack and causing them to scatter to the four sides of the table. A howl of approval went up from the other men in the room as several balls slammed down the pockets. He walked around the table and assessed the lie of the balls. This is what he should be concentrating on. Not thinking about Sophia Cooper and her dreams of a fairy-tale courtship.

He gave a snort of disgust. She would be getting

a fairy tale with Ravenswood, of that he was certain. Unfortunately, it wasn't going to be Cinderella and her prince. Instead, she was more like Little Red Riding Hood, about to be eaten alive by the big, bad wolf.

Ethan remained at his club, playing endless games of billiards and drinking far too much brandy, until he was sure the ball would be well and truly over, the guests would have departed and it would be safe to return to his family home.

The next morning, he awoke still determined to put all thoughts of Miss Cooper and Ravenswood out of his mind. Instead, over breakfast he made what he hoped was a discreet enquiry.

'I see you invited Ravenswood to last night's ball,' he said to his mother as she poured a cup of tea and passed it to him.

'Yes, dear. I know none of you boys particularly like him, but he's apparently courting Miss Sophia Cooper. She's the only child of Ambrose Cooper, that Yorkshire industrialist who died a few years ago. Her mother is a friend of the Ashencrofts and they suggested I invite Miss Cooper, and as the Duke is said to be courting her I thought I had better invite him as well.'

She paused and sent a pointed look down the table at Luther. 'And it is so nice to see a duke taking his responsibilities seriously and actively seeking a duchess.'

'Was she the girl you were dancing with?' Luther asked, in what Ethan knew was less curiosity than a desire to get their mother off her favourite topic of trying to find him a wife.

'What?' Jake said, looking up from his plate, heaped

high with eggs, bacon, sausages and an assortment of other food, all chosen for their ability to counter the effects of last night's overindulgence. 'Did Ethan actually dance with someone he wasn't forced to? When did this happen?'

'I believe you had left by then,' their mother said, sending Jake a disapproving glare, which he handled in his usual manner by ignoring it.

'So, Luther, did you manage to find the perfect future duchess?' Jake asked, causing Luther to scowl at his smirking brother.

While their mother commenced listing all the attributes of the various young women at the ball and attempted to get her eldest son to show the slightest interest in at least one of them, Ethan went back to trying to not think about Miss Cooper and Ravenswood.

By the time breakfast had finished, he had made a decision. He didn't have much of a conscience, but what he did have was never going to let him rest until he took some action. He needed, somehow, to warn Miss Cooper that she was making a big mistake. But how do you warn a young woman that a duke, a man who is at the very peak of British Society, will not make a good husband? And how do you do it while at the same time making sure the young lady does not think that you have any designs of your own in that way?

He could hardly shock the young lady by letting her know Ravenswood was a notorious lecher who seduced every woman that came his way, no matter what damage he caused. That he was an inveterate gambler who lost more often than he won, and hosted wild parties at his Derbyshire estate, the behaviour at which could almost make Ethan blush.

There was no point revealing all those gruesome details. He wanted to save her from a disaster, not destroy her innocent, trusting nature.

This was unlike any problem that Ethan had ever had to solve, so he would just have to work it out as he went along.

Arriving at the Coopers' Mayfair town house, he presented his card to the footman and asked if Miss Cooper and her mother were at home. He was certain they were at home. The question was, were they at home to him?

The footman returned and informed him that Miss and Mrs Cooper were indeed at home and would be happy to receive him. He entered the drawing room wishing he had a clear idea of what he was going to do and how he could achieve the impossible of convincing these two women that they should not set their sights on a duke.

Miss Cooper smiled up at him from her seat beside the unlit fireplace. Mrs Cooper greeted him and indicated that Ethan should take a seat. She pointed to one adjacent to her, but far removed from her daughter. Ethan smiled at both women and sat down, then took another look at Miss Cooper.

Overnight, she had been transformed. Without tears streaming down her cheeks, without swollen red eyes, she was rather more attractive than he had realised. Her bright blue eyes were no longer dulled by tears but were lively and intelligent. Last night her skin had been mottled and blotchy. Now it was more akin to delicate porcelain.

While she wasn't the type of woman to whom he was usually attracted—far too fresh-faced for his liking— she was certainly pretty. Pretty enough to attract a man's attention, which must surely make it easier for him to achieve his goal. If he could direct her towards another man, one who would treat her with the respect and tenderness she deserved, perhaps she would forget all about wanting to be the Duchess of Ravenswood.

'What brings you to our humble home so early in the morning, Lord Ethan?' the mother asked while the footman served the tea.

There was hardly anything humble about their richly furnished home in an exclusive part of London, and as it was nearing midday it was also not exactly early, but then, polite conversation never put much emphasis on accuracy.

'My mother wished to pass on her regards and wanted me to enquire whether you enjoyed our ball last night,' he said to Mrs Cooper. It was the perfect excuse for his visit and not entirely a lie. If his mother had known he was calling on the Coopers, she was sure to have asked him to say those very words.

'Sophia had a delightful evening,' the mother answered, smiling at her daughter. 'She danced several dances with the Duke of Ravenswood. Such a refined, handsome man. Isn't he, Sophia?'

Miss Cooper nodded and smiled back at her mother, causing Ethan's heart to sink. He had heard other women describe Ravenswood as handsome, although he couldn't see it himself. Every time he saw that man he was reminded of a slippery eel, and he almost expected him to be surrounded by a waft of sulphur.

And as for refined, that was a joke. If they saw the way he behaved at the Venus Gentlemen's Club they would know he was a boorish oaf who treated women as if they were playthings designed solely for his base enjoyment.

'Sophia is as good as promised to the Duke,' Mrs Cooper continued. 'It's quite an honour to have a duke paying her so much attention,' she added, with an expression that could only be described as self-satisfied.

'And has the Duke visited today, sent flowers or his note?' Ethan asked, hoping the answer would be no.

The mother's smile pinched in tightly, then returned as bright as before. 'Not yet, but the day is still young and he did say he was looking forward to seeing Sophia at the next ball.'

That was a good sign. Both mother and daughter would be disappointed that the Duke was not being more attentive. But the mother's reaction was also a bad sign. She was so eager to hear from Ravenswood that if he did eventually deign to send his card, they would be so grateful they would excuse any past slights. The man was a duke, and unfortunately dukes would be forgiven anything.

Ethan suppressed a sigh. This was going to demand more ingenuity than was usually expected of him.

'I believe the Duke goes riding each day in Hyde Park. Perhaps that is where he will be today,' Ethan said, trying to formulate a plan as he spoke.

The mother tilted her head in interest. 'He does?'

'Yes, I believe so.' Ethan knew no such thing, but if he could get Miss Cooper alone, he might be able to talk some sense into her. Although what he would say to her, he still had no idea. 'I too am planning to go for a ride in the park. Perhaps your daughter would like to accompany me and we might meet the Duke there?'

Sophia looked at her mother, her eyes appealing.

'I'm not sure if that would be appropriate,' the mother said, her lips once again becoming pinched. 'As I said, Sophia is promised to the Duke.'

Ethan nodded. 'Yes, if the Duke saw her in my carriage, he might get the wrong idea and think that your daughter is being wooed by another man.'

The mother nodded her agreement.

'And that would never do, would it, Mother?' Miss Cooper added. 'Last night, when Lord Ethan danced with me, the Duke was most put out. After that, he danced with me many times so no other man could do so. We wouldn't want to upset him like that again.'

Miss Cooper's face portrayed its usual wide-eyed innocence, but it seemed there was a bit of unexpected cunning behind that gentle facade. Ethan stifled a smile as the mother digested this piece of information.

'Yes, Miss Cooper is correct,' he added, feigning a frown. 'It's so much better if the Duke knows he has no competition for your hand.'

'Well, perhaps a ride in Hyde Park would do Sophia the world of good,' Mrs Cooper said as Ethan and Miss Cooper exchanged quick smiles. 'She needs to get some fresh air.'

Mrs Cooper looked at her daughter, who quickly adopted a serious expression. 'Off you go, dear, and tell your lady's maid you wish to wear your new pink dress and for her to restyle your hair before you leave.'

'Yes, of course.' Miss Cooper stood up, gave her mother a quick kiss on the cheek, sent Ethan a fleeting smile and rushed out of the room.

He looked towards the door through which she had departed. She did have rather a pretty smile, he had to admit. But if she married the Duke, he doubted she would do much smiling. He knew exactly what effect marriage to that man would have on such a delicate young woman. As time passed, that smile would be seen less and less frequently. Her innocence would soon be destroyed and she would eventually become hardened and bitter. He had seen it in many a young woman forced to marry reprobates like Ravenswood, and he would hate to see it happen to Miss Cooper.

As soon as the door clicked shut, Mrs Cooper turned to Ethan, her face severe. 'I hope I don't need to remind you that my Sophia will be marrying the Duke of Ravenswood and no other.'

'Yes,' Ethan said slowly, taken aback by the sudden vehemence in the woman's words.

'He has made it clear to me he wants her hand. He is a duke, and I will be expecting Sophia to settle for nothing less than being a duchess.'

Ethan chose not to reply.

Her expression hardened further. 'I hope you realise my daughter will not be marrying a man who is merely the younger brother of a duke. And if you were hoping to convince me otherwise, you will be wasting your time. My daughter is a good, obedient young lady and will do whatever her mother tells her to do.'

'Believe me, Mrs Cooper, I will not be marrying anyone any time soon, and I only have Miss Cooper's best interests at heart.' It was an unusual discussion. Usually, a young man would be trying to convince a mother that his intentions were honourable because he *wanted* to marry the young lady. It was also a true statement. Ethan only had Miss Cooper's best interests at heart, but he suspected that he and Mrs Cooper would differ over what that actually entailed.

They drank their tea in silence, Mrs Cooper continually sending Ethan stern, pinched looks, the intent of which was so clear she could be shouting that he would not be marrying her daughter. He might serve his purpose in attracting the Duke's attention, but that was all he was good for.

Miss Cooper returned to the room, along with her lady's maid, and Ethan stood up.

'Beautiful, my dear,' her mother said. 'When the Duke sees you in that dress, he will be enchanted. Don't you agree, my lord, that the Duke will be enchanted?'

Ethan smiled at her. 'What man wouldn't be? You look lovely, Miss Cooper.'

She blushed a sweet shade of pink. If Ethan was looking for an innocent young woman to marry, he was sure she would be top of his list, but he was neither interested in innocent women nor wanting a bride.

'Shall we?' he asked, taking her arm. 'Good afternoon, Mrs Cooper.'

'Good afternoon, my lord,' she said, indicating to the footman to show them out. 'I'm so pleased we were able to have our little conversation and we are in agreement.' She kissed her daughter on the cheek and pushed a few strands of her blonde hair off her face. 'When you get home, you must tell me if you saw the Duke and everything that he said to you.'

'Yes, Mother,' she said quietly, her eyes lowered, like the obedient daughter she was reputed to be.

Sophia forced herself not to smile like a silly fool. She kept her face as composed as possible as they left the drawing room and walked down the hallway, followed by her lady's maid, who was to act as chaperone.

Even when Lord Ethan helped her into his open-topped carriage, she merely nodded her thanks and stopped her lips from doing what they wanted to and curling into a happy smile.

'I'm so pleased you called,' she said, only slightly annoyed that she sounded as if she was gushing. 'When you left the ball last night, I thought that would be the last I would see of you.'

She sent a quick glance at her lady's maid, reminding herself that Maggie would be taking note of everything she said and did so she could report it back to her mother.

'I was concerned about you,' Lord Ethan answered.

'Oh, yes, all that crying.' Heat came to her cheeks

at that memory. 'Well, you don't need to worry. I had a lovely time in the end.'

Sophia knew that wasn't entirely true. She'd had a lovely time when she had danced with Lord Ethan, and it was wonderful that they had attracted the Duke's attention, but she had been so disappointed that Lord Ethan had left. Which was somewhat confusing because she really did want to marry the Duke. Wasn't it every young woman's dream to marry so well? Of course it was, and she should not be thinking about other men.

Her father had often told her he wanted her to grow up to be a princess, and to have everything she could possibly desire. He had been born into poverty but had worked hard and built up a business that had made the Coopers one of the wealthiest families in England, even wealthier than many aristocrats. As her mother regularly reminded her, he had done it all for Sophia. He was determined that no one would ever look down their nose at his little girl just because of her background. Now she could repay him for all he had sacrificed by becoming a titled woman, just as he had hoped.

And she was so close to achieving her own dream and her parents' dreams. It was essential she do nothing that might put achieving that in jeopardy.

'Does the Duke always ride in Hyde Park in the mornings?' she asked.

'Many members of the aristocracy exercise their horses in the morning, before it gets too crowded.'

'It will be good to see him again.' Sophia wasn't sure whether that was entirely true, but now was not the time to question her confusing thoughts, not if it interrupted the pleasure of riding through the streets of London with this rather dashing man.

'So, our ruse paid off and the Duke danced with you last night, several times,' he said.

Sophia sent a quick look at her lady's maid, then nodded. 'Yes, we danced quite a few dances. Mother was so pleased.'

'And what about you, Miss Cooper? Did you enjoy dancing with Ravenswood? Were *you* pleased?'

She looked at him, baffled by his question. 'He is the man I am hoping to wed.'

'That wasn't what I asked.'

She shrugged and stared out of the carriage at the passing houses. No one had ever asked her whether she enjoyed the Duke's company, whether she liked dancing with him. It was what was expected of her and he was a duke. Having his attention was surely pleasure enough.

'Yes, of course I enjoyed dancing with him,' she replied, knowing it was the correct answer but not sure if it was an entirely honest one. 'But I did enjoy our dance as well,' she added. *Enjoy* was perhaps not the right word, but it would have to do. She had no words to describe how she had felt when in his arms. She certainly could not tell him how shivers had run through her body, how her skin had felt alive, as if she were being gently caressed by soft feathers, and the memory of his touch had continued to linger, long after they had parted. No, she most definitely would not be telling him that.

'It was all my pleasure,' he replied quietly, causing that irrational shiver to once again ripple through her.

She smiled her thanks, even though she doubted he was telling the truth. No one would enjoy dancing with a woman looking the way she had last night.

'I must apologise for the way you found me. It really was bad behaviour. I don't usually burst into tears, but I think the excitement of my first ball had overwhelmed me. Mother was frightfully angry with me. She gave me such a telling-off when I got home. She said she could tell that I had been crying and she was sure the Duke could as well.'

'Did the Duke ask you what had upset you?'

'No, and Mother said that was a good thing. She said it showed how gracious he was that he didn't mention it and was not annoyed, even though I had risked shaming him.'

Lord Ethan said nothing, merely raised his eyebrows in question.

'Mother said that dukes have to keep up appearances,' she rushed on, unsure why the Duke's behaviour needed defending. 'She said it did not look good for him to be dancing with a young woman who had been crying. By ignoring it he showed the high regard in which he holds me, and I should be grateful that he *did* dance with me when I was in such a frightful state.'

Her mother had to be right about that. Wasn't she always? But the Duke *had* said nothing, while Ethan had been so considerate and caring. All the Duke had done was give her a disapproving look, as if her appearance somewhat repulsed him.

'And is that how you felt?' he asked. 'Did you think that, by not enquiring as to the cause of your tears, the Duke was showing his high regard for you?'

She stared at him. It had been a while since anyone had asked her what she thought or felt. Not since her father had died two years ago. Her mother had told her it was the duty of a young woman to obey first her father and then her husband, that they were the ones who should instruct her on what to think, on what her opinions, beliefs and tastes should be. And, as Sophia no longer had a father, until her husband took over that responsibility it was up to her mother to instruct her.

'I'm sure if it is what the Duke did, then it was the correct thing to do,' she replied in the manner of which her mother would approve.

He gave her a long, considered look, causing her to squirm and nibble on her lower lip.

'I would never contradict anything your mother has said. But if I can be so bold as to offer my advice, I would suggest you should make up your own mind about what you think and feel. Not everyone is what they appear to be, and sometimes people put their own interests before those of others.'

She tried to make sense of what he had said and formulate an answer. What did she need to make up her mind about? Her mother cared about Sophia's future and often reminded her that everything she did was for Sophia's benefit. The Duke had said he was interested in courting her. Surely Ethan couldn't be suggesting that either of them was putting their own interests ahead of hers. How could they be? They all wanted the same thing, didn't they? For her to be married to the Duke and to be a duchess.

They entered the park as she tried not to think about who should be instructing whom, who had a right to opinions, thoughts and feelings. Instead, she focused on the beauty of the surrounding trees, resplendent in their late spring foliage. She tilted back her head as they drove under the soft green canopy, loving the way the filtered sun played on her face. Looking around, she spotted a yellow-and-white carpet of daffodils and, beyond that, soldiers in their bright red uniforms drilling on the open grassed areas.

It was a perfect day. This was what she wanted to think about and enjoy. She turned to Lord Ethan. 'Thank you so much for suggesting this ride. It really is most kind of you.'

'My pleasure,' he said with one of those lovely, lazy smiles.

It was too early for the park to be crowded, and only a few fashionably dressed young ladies were promenading along the paths, but quite a few men in top hats and tails were out exercising their horses. She should be looking to see if any of the men on horseback were the Duke, but that could wait for now.

'Would you mind if we walked?' she asked. 'Mother says that when I'm a duchess, I will have to conduct myself with unruffled dignity and never let anyone think I was ever an untitled girl from the provinces.' She smiled, knowing that he would understand and not criticise her for her lowly origins. 'But I'd love to stroll through the park. I haven't felt grass under my feet since I came to London.'

'And what you wish for, you shall have,' he said, reaching out to signal the driver to halt.

'I think it's going to rain, madam,' the lady's maid said, looking up at the sky.

Lord Ethan and Sophia followed her gaze. Grey clouds were indeed converging ominously on the horizon.

'If your lady's maid is worried about getting wet, she can remain here,' he said, causing anticipation to swell within her breast. 'She'll be able to see us wherever we are in the park, and if it does rain, the driver will put the top up and we'll hurry back.'

Maggie narrowed her eyes and looked from Lord Ethan to Sophia and back again.

Sophia was tempted to send him a conspiratorial smile, but she was sure that would not be missed by her lady's maid, so her expression remained completely impassive. 'It will be all right, Maggie. I promise we won't go far.'

Lord Ethan helped Sophia down from the carriage, while Maggie went back to frowning at the clouds, as if the force of her disapproval could cause them to disperse immediately.

They strolled along the path and she was almost tempted to skip. She hadn't felt this way for such a long time, not since she was a child. It was wonderful to be free of her mother, free of her lady's maid, and free from the constant talk of what she should and shouldn't do to capture the heart of the Duke. She would just enjoy the moment. Thoughts of the Duke and her future marriage could wait for another day.

## Chapter Three

'Don't tell Mother, will you?' Sophia said as she took Ethan's arm.

Ethan had no intention of telling her mother anything. 'Would she not approve?'

She sent him a smile that he could only describe as cheeky. 'Mother never stops reminding me of the correct way to behave and says it's going to be even more important when I become a duchess.' Her lips pinched together in an impersonation of her mother. 'A duchess has to set the standard, so you must conduct yourself with dignity and grace at all times.' The pinched expression turned into a smile. 'But I'm not a duchess yet.'

And Ethan hoped she never would be, not if it meant her marrying Ravenswood.

'So are you looking forward to your marriage?' he probed as they strolled along the path.

She stopped and turned to look at him, her brow furrowed. 'That's a funny question to ask. He's the Duke of Ravenswood.'

'Yes, I know that. I've known him a long time, before he inherited his title. So, do you want to marry him?'

The furrows on her brow deepened. 'Of course, he's the...' She smiled. 'You know what I was going to say, don't you?' She gave a little laugh. It really was a pleasant laugh, one he would like to hear more of, but for now he intended to have a serious conversation. He wanted her to think carefully about what she was about to do, because once she married Ravenswood, there would be no going back.

'It will be wonderful to be a duchess,' she continued.

'I didn't ask you if you wanted to be a duchess. I asked you if you want to marry the Duke of Ravenswood.'

She slowly shook her head, as if not understanding what he was saying and why he wasn't just accepting her answer.

'The Duke is more than his title,' he said. 'He's also a man. Do you want to marry the man?'

She chewed on the edge of her bottom lip and continued walking. 'Yes, of course,' she said eventually, her voice once again formal and precise, as if giving the answer that would be judged correct.

'Why? What is it about him that makes you want to be his wife?'

The chewing on her lip intensified, and he worried that she might be about to do herself some damage.

'Well, he's rather handsome,' she said with a tentative smile, looking over at him.

'If you say so.'

'Well, he's not as handsome as you, of course.' Her cheeks flamed red and her hand shot up to cover her mouth. 'Oh, I shouldn't have said that. It was rather forward.'

Ethan laughed. 'Not at all. No man will ever take offence at being told he is handsome. So, what else do you like about the man who bears the title Duke of Ravenswood?'

She recommenced gnawing on her poor bottom lip. 'Well, he's also a very accomplished dancer.' She sent him another of those delightfully cheeky smiles. 'But I'm sure you won't take offence if I tell you he's not as accomplished as you. I did so enjoy dancing with you at last night's ball.'

He smiled back at her. 'As I you.'

They held each other's gaze for a moment, then she looked down as if being caught doing something she shouldn't, and they recommenced walking in silence.

'So, Lord Ethan... Will I be seeing you at future balls?'

He gave a short snort of laughter. 'No, I rarely attend balls. Last night I had no choice as my mother was the hostess, but generally I avoid such events like the plague.'

She halted and frowned at him, as if he had suddenly started talking in a foreign language with which she was unfamiliar. 'But how will you meet your future bride?'

His laughter became louder. 'That's another good reason for not attending balls.'

Still frowning, she tilted her head in query.

'I have no intention of marrying any time soon. My eldest brother, Luther, inherited the title and will be expected to marry soon and provide an heir, then there's my other brother, Jake, but as the spare's spare there's no pressure on me to find a bride.' Thank goodness, he wanted to add.

'And you see this as a good thing?'

'A very good thing.'

'But do your parents not wish to see you wed?'

'My father passed away many years ago and at the moment my mother is more interested in finding a bride for Luther, so there is no family pressure.' Even if his father had lived, Ethan doubted he would care if, or when, he married. His father had never concerned himself with any aspect of Ethan's life, had hardly noticed his existence. It wasn't personal. It was just the way it was. Why would his father waste his time on the spare's spare? However, despite all but ignoring his third son, he had thankfully left Ethan a generous settlement in his will, enough so that Ethan could live well and never have to worry about money. That, he suspected, was more because his father would not want to see anyone with the Rosemont name living in poverty than because he had any regard for his third son.

'I'm so sorry,' she said, and he was unsure whether she was expressing her condolences over his father's passing or her pity that he would not be expected to marry. He waved his hand to dismiss both concerns.

'Unlike you,' she went on, 'I'm an only child, so my mother's entire focus is on my future, and my father only ever wanted the best for me.' She smiled up at him. 'He always said he wanted me to be a princess. We used to talk about it often, how I would be living in a castle with my handsome prince. It was silly, really, and something that could never happen, but becoming a duchess is almost as good. In fact, it's even better, because it is the highest title a non-royal can achieve.'

Ethan cringed. She was living in a fantasy world, and if she did marry Ravenswood it would make reality even harder to bear. 'You need to think of what *you* want, not your parents.'

'What I want is to make my mother proud of me and to honour the memory of my father.'

They walked further along the path, while Ethan tried to think of a way to tell her that she would not be honouring her father's memory by marrying a degenerate who would never make her happy. He could think of no other way than listing all the vices in which the man indulged, and explaining the horror to which she would be subjected when she married, but talking of such things with an innocent young woman would just not do.

She came to a sudden halt and placed her hand on top of his. He braced himself, hoping against hope she was going to tell him she would not be marrying Ravenswood, that the mere thought of that man made her recoil in disgust.

'Promenading along the path is lovely, but can we walk across the grass? I so miss the countryside, and really, while we're in London for the Season this is the closest I'm going to get to meadows and fields.'

Her smile was so infectious that he couldn't help but

smile back. 'As you wish, my lady,' he said, leading her off the path. 'Although I'm afraid I can't supply you with sheep and cows.'

'Thank goodness for that. They would make such a mess of this glorious park.'

'Do you and the Duke plan to live in London after you marry?' he asked, trying to lead the conversation back to his real reason for walking with this sweet young lady.

She shrugged. 'Oh, I don't know. I suppose that will be up to my husband.' If Ethan knew the Duke, and he believed he did, she would be stuck on his Derbyshire estate while he continued to spend his time indulging in all that London had to offer.

'But where would you like to live, Miss Cooper?'

'Well, I do love the countryside, but I also love London, at least what I've seen of it so far, which to be honest is not very much.'

'You have five months left in the Season, or until you marry, to see and do everything you want to in London. So, what do you hope to do?'

She looked at him as if he had suggested something scandalous. 'Until I marry, I will do what my mother allows.'

'Like this walk across the grass.'

She nudged him in the side in a playful manner.

'Hopefully she won't find out, although she has spies everywhere,' she said with a laugh, and looked back at the lady's maid, sitting in the carriage, her unflinching gaze fixed on them.

It was a joke, but he suspected it held a great deal

of truth. The Secret Service really should recruit more lady's maids if they wanted to gather detailed information on what went on in the households of the wealthy and influential.

'But if you *could* do what you wanted to, what would you do?' he asked.

Again, her brow furrowed, as if this was a question she had never pondered before. 'I don't know.' She thought for a moment. 'Well, I did enjoy last night's ball.' She looked up at him and smiled. 'Well, not the crying bit, of course. But once we danced, it was such fun. And then the Duke danced with me.' Her smile faltered. 'But then he left. I suppose he doesn't like dancing as much as I do.'

Ethan had a good idea where he would have escaped to. The Venus Gentlemen's Club was his usual haunt and was not too far from the Rosemonts' home.

'So, what else do you think you'll enjoy doing while you're here in London?' he asked.

'I don't know. You said you've known the Duke for a long time. What does he enjoy doing?'

Ethan winced, then coughed to cover his reaction to her question. Gambling and whoring were the activities that immediately came to mind, but they were hardly things he could mention to a young lady, especially one who thought she was about to marry a dashing duke who would turn her childhood daydreams into reality.

'He attends a lot of events on the racing calendar. I'm sure this year he will attend Derby Day, Ascot, the Grand National and various other smaller events. Do you enjoy horse racing?'

'Father always said that gambling is a vice and has been the ruination of many a prosperous man,' she said with a frown. 'But I suppose if someone like the Duke attends races, then it must be all right.' She looked to him for confirmation.

Perhaps now was the time to tell her that the Duke loved not only horse racing but also every other form of gambling, and had debts throughout the land. Ethan suspected that was the very reason he was interested in marrying her. As the daughter of a wealthy industrialist, she would come with a sizeable marriage settlement. Everyone knew there was no other reason a high-ranking member of the aristocracy would marry a woman who did not come from a family with a long pedigree.

'And what does your mother say about gambling?' Ethan asked.

'Well, when Father was alive she agreed with him, but I don't know what she'd think if she knew the Duke gambled.'

Ethan was beginning to suspect the mother wouldn't care, as long as he was a duke and he made her daughter a duchess.

A few spots of rain blotted his shoulder. He looked up at the dark grey sky. 'I think your lady's maid was right. It's starting to rain. Perhaps we should return to the carriage.'

'Oh, can we walk for a while longer?' She gazed at him with those appealing blue eyes that he was becoming increasingly incapable of resisting. 'A few drops of rain never hurt anybody.'

They exchanged a conspiratorial smile. 'Why not?' he said, taking off his jacket and placing it over their heads.

More rain splattered the path, turning the gravel from light brown to mud-coloured. The park became a hive of frantic energy as men on horseback spurred their horses from a trot to a canter, and the promenading women rushed towards their carriages, their lacy parasols of no use in even the lightest of downpours.

'Cowards,' she said, laughing at their haste.

Then the sky opened up, sending a torrent of water descending from the heavens. Ethan grabbed her hand, and they ran, the all-but-useless jacket flapping above their heads.

They reached the nearest place of refuge, a bandstand, raced up the steps and came to a panting halt.

'Don't you love it when it rains?' she shouted above the pounding of rain on the tiled roof. 'It's as if everything bad gets washed away and you can start again.'

He stared at her for a moment. Instead of being upset, or worried about the state of her clothing or hair, as he would have expected, she was laughing. He had assumed he would have to once again console her, but she was happily enjoying the moment.

She really was a delight. And she certainly looked delightful right now, with raindrops in her hair, her cheeks flushed from the exertion of running and her breath coming in rather suggestive little gasps.

'Don't you just love the way everything smells when it rains, so fresh and renewed?' She closed her eyes and inhaled deeply, and Ethan followed her example. Yes, he could smell the trees, the leaves and the damp soil, but there was something else, something much more enchanting, a sweet, feminine scent, with a surprising underlying spiciness.

Spreading her arms wide, she did a small twirl, her skirt flowing out around her.

Caught up in her joy, he also laughed. He'd never found rain funny before, had always seen it as a mild inconvenience, but she was right. It did make everything smell fresh. It made you feel more alive somehow, and he could almost believe they had been given a clean start.

She spun to a stop and smiled at him, a smile that was almost wicked. 'And what's even better, my lady's maid won't be able to see us through this rain.'

He looked in the direction of the carriage. The driver had pulled up the covers. It was unlikely she could see much of anything at this distance through the small windows, even if it wasn't raining.

A sinful thought crossed Ethan's mind. They were alone, with no supervision. If he caused a scandal, if the Duke believed she was no longer an innocent, untouched young lady, would that result in his calling off their courtship? Would that save her from an intolerable fate?

He dismissed that thought as quickly as it occurred. For so many reasons, it was a bad idea. A very bad idea. Firstly, he did not ruin young women's reputations. He had never done so before and he wasn't about to start now. Despite having had many women in his life, not one of them could be described as innocent and none of them gave a fig about their reputation. Secondly, if he did the unforgiveable, the only way Society would actually forgive him, and the only way he would forgive himself, would be for him to marry Miss Cooper. And that was something he simply would not do.

Although here, alone with her in the rain, with her tresses dishevelled, her face glowing and that entrancing, almost naughty smile on her face, doing what he knew he must not *was* a tempting proposition.

Sophia felt free. She was happy. It had been a long time since she had experienced those wonderful, uncomplicated emotions.

She swung around the pillar and laughed again, loving the feel of the fresh rain on her face, loving being able to behave in such a childlike manner.

Her mother would disapprove. But her mother wasn't here now. She swung back round the pillar one more time, the light breeze catching her hair and further loosening some locks.

Sophia could hardly remember the last time she had laughed like this. She had expected her Season to be full of fun and laughter, but so far it had all been extremely serious. Securing her marriage was more like a business negotiation than a courtship. And Sophia was constantly reminded that the Duke was yet to formally promise her anything. He had merely expressed his interest, had informed her mother that he admired her. As her mother pointed out, that did not yet mean he intended to marry her. She still had to prove to him she would be the perfect Duchess of Ravenswood, so he would offer her his hand.

And being caught in the rain, spinning round like a child and laughing out loud was certainly not the behaviour expected of a future duchess.

But the Duke was not here either. She could behave like Sophia Cooper, and not the future Duchess of Ravenswood.

'You know, I think I prefer getting caught in the rain to attending a ball,' she said, watching Lord Ethan shake rain off his jacket.

'Perhaps I should advise my mother to host her next ball in the middle of a rainstorm.'

She laughed, still hanging off the pillar. 'That would be such fun. At the last ball hardly anyone seemed to be laughing, at least not the women, and even the smiles seemed forced and polite.' She shrugged. 'Although, I suppose that's the way people are supposed to behave in Society.'

Hadn't her mother told her, repeatedly, that ladies laughed quietly and covered their mouths when they did so? They smiled a lot, but made sure their lips were never too wide, and they should always avoid showing their teeth. A polite upturn of the lips was enough to express pleasure and approval.

She smiled at Ethan, showing all her teeth, and he smiled back at her, not in the slightest bit shocked by such disgraceful conduct. If only he were a duke and not the younger brother of a duke. She was sure the woman he married would be allowed to smile, to laugh, to even be playful if she wanted to, just like they were doing today.

But she *was* to marry the Duke. She would fulfil her father's wish and give him everything he had hoped for, a daughter who was a titled lady and at the very pinnacle of Society. Everything she hoped for as well, she reminded herself.

She looked down at the rain splatters on her dress. Her mother had insisted she change into this new dress for her ride in the park. The silk brocade, with its lace and ruffles, was more ornate than one would usually wear for such an occasion. Sophia knew why her mother had pressed her to wear it. To impress the Duke. Not just because it was a flattering design, but because it showed off the family's wealth. And now the gown, designed in Paris and made by a leading London dressmaker, was covered in wet splotches.

'Mother is going to be so angry when she sees me.'

He stopped shaking his jacket and joined her beside the pillar. 'She can hardly be angry with you because it rained. You don't control the weather.'

'I don't think Mother will see it that way.' She knew her mother would be furious at her for taking such a risk. What if the Duke had seen her in such a state? she imagined her mother saying. He would be mortified, would maybe even have second thoughts about whether she would make a suitable duchess. Her mother was probably correct.

She brushed her hands over her skirt, then decided to ignore that problem for now. This might be her last chance to just enjoy herself. Once she was married to the Duke of Ravenswood, she would have to conduct herself in the impeccable manner befitting a duchess. She gave an involuntary, inexplicable shiver at the thought of that future.

'Are you cold?' he asked.

Before she could explain that her shiver had nothing to do with the temperature, he lifted her hair, his fingers lightly touching the back of her neck, and draped his jacket over her shoulders. It still contained the warmth of his body. She wrapped it tightly around herself and snuggled into it, as if she were being embraced by his strong arms, and drew in a deep, contented breath. This time it wasn't the smell of rain-drenched leaves she inhaled, but his deliciously masculine scent. It was intoxicating, spicy, like something exotic and forbidden. She took in another deep breath and briefly closed her eyes. Another shiver rippled through her, but this one was both delicious and strangely melancholy, as if she was yearning for something she would never have.

She opened her eyes and found him staring at her. Despite the cool air, heat rushed to her face. 'Thank you,' she murmured, trying to collect her thoughts and push out any inappropriate reactions to the touch and smell of his jacket.

They looked out at the now empty park, the dripping trees and the falling rain.

'Don't worry about your mother being angry,' he said. 'I'll tell her it was all my fault that we got caught in the rain. I'll also apologise for not seeing the Duke and say I should have known that he wouldn't be riding in this weather. Your mother can shower all her wrath on me over that as well.'

'Does the Duke not like the rain?'

'He is not a lover of the outdoors.'

This surprised Sophia. 'But he has an extensive estate in Derbyshire.' Her mother had often mentioned the estate that had been in his family for countless generations, the one that would be inherited by Sophia's firstborn son, and her mother's first grandson, along with the title Duke of Ravenswood.

'Yes, and an extensive house, where he entertains frequently.' His jaws clenched together and a dark shadow seemed to cross his face, which caused her to wonder, Why would he have any reaction to the Duke entertaining—surely that was a wonderful thing?

'Yes, Mother has prepared me well for hosting large dinner parties and balls. She said that the Duke is a friend of the Prince of Wales himself, and I might have to host dinner parties where he and his entourage attend.'

'Yes, quite possibly.' His face still dark, he turned towards her. 'Miss Cooper, before you agree to marry the Duke, I do think you should get to know him better. You need to know whether he really is the sort of man you want to spend the rest of your life with.'

'What on earth can you mean?' she asked, trying to give one of her practised smiles. 'He is a duke, one of the most influential and respected men in the country. Any woman would be more than happy to marry him. I'm a very lucky young woman indeed to have been singled out for his attention.' She repeated the phrases her mother had said to her many, many times.

'But is he the right man for you?'

'Of course. He's the best man in the world for me.'

'All I'm saying is, I think you should take a bit of time to get to know the Duke and then decide for yourself whether that is true.'

This conversation was no longer fun, it was uncomfortable. 'I think we should be getting back.'

'Of course.' He smiled at her and she rather wished he wouldn't. If his words were disconcerting, that smile was even more so. He really was sublimely handsome. Her gaze moved from that warm smile, the one that was making her mushy inside, to the strong outline of his jaw, then swept up to cheekbones that looked as if they had been carved by an expert sculptor. Then, as if under a force over which she had no control, her eyes moved back to his lips, those full, soft and—dare she think it?—tempting lips.

'Before we go, I think you had better tidy up a bit, so your mother isn't too angry with me for leading you astray.' He said it with a laugh, but if he had read her thoughts he might not have found jokes about leading her astray quite so funny.

He reached down and retrieved a linen handkerchief from the pocket of his jacket and lightly dabbed the rainwater off her face. Sophia stared up at him, unable to move, unable to think, unable to breathe, as the cloth gently caressed her cheeks.

'There, that's much better,' he said, standing back to observe his handiwork. 'But we'd better tidy up your hair as well.' Her heartbeat went from thumping rapidly in her chest to pounding throughout her entire body as he reached over, lifted the strands of her hair that had become loose and clipped them back into the bun behind her head.

While he was concentrating on her hair she was concentrating on his face, and the touch of his fingers gently rearranging the escaped locks. He was so handsome, masculine, yet also kind and gentle. That jawline, which she had wondered about touching last night, was strong and firm, while his lips were so soft and inviting. Her gaze lingered on his mouth. What would those lips feel like if she stroked them lightly with her fingers?

'That will have to do,' he said, and her gaze shot back to his eyes.

He stood back once more to observe his work. 'It's perhaps not as good as your lady's maid would do, but I'm sure it will pass muster with your mother. You might have to say that it was somewhat windy in the park today.'

She nodded, unable to speak.

'It looks like the rain is starting to ease off,' he continued. 'Perhaps we should take the opportunity to make a dash back to the carriage.'

She removed his jacket from around her shoulders and a sense of loss swept through her as she handed it back to him.

Placing his arm around her shoulder, he held the jacket over their heads. 'Right, Miss Cooper, let's face the elements together.'

As one, they raced down the steps and across the now sodden grass. Once again, Sophia laughed, loving the freedom and the wildness of what they were doing. Oh, how angry her mother would be if she could see her now, and how disappointed the Duke would be. This was most certainly not how a duchess should behave, but it was such fun.

The driver opened the door and they burst into the carriage, bringing the cool, fresh air with them. Her laughter died when she saw Maggie's frown.

'It rained. We got caught in it, and it was windy as well,' she blurted out, as if she needed to explain herself to her lady's maid.

Maggie crossed her arms, a gesture that said as clearly as words, *I said it would, didn't I? And a future duchess should not act in such a reckless, ungracious manner.*

Sophia knew her lady's maid was right. Going for a walk when it was raining *was* reckless and not very decorous. But surely she was entitled to one last taste of childlike freedom, to run, laugh and enjoy a simple pleasure. Of course she was. The Duke had not seen her, so no harm had been done.

She smiled at Lord Ethan. He smiled back and then, like a sudden premonition, a thought occurred to her. Perhaps running across the park with another man, her hair dishevelled, her dress spattered with rain, *would* get back to the Duke and it would destroy her chances of ever becoming the next Duchess of Ravenswood. That would be terrible. Wouldn't it? Yes, of course it would be.

# Chapter Four

Lively conversation and laughter continued throughout their return journey. They were like old friends who had enjoyed a pleasant outing, which was exactly what they had done. It was fun, and Sophia wished their time together would never end.

They turned into her street and she saw another carriage parked outside her home. It bore the Duke's coat of arms on the side, and a footman and driver, seated up top, were dressed in his livery of gold and purple.

Her good mood evaporated.

What was wrong with her? She should be excited. If the Duke was paying them a visit, then presumably he had come to court her. That was what she had wanted so badly she had been reduced to tears at last night's ball. But that was before she had met Lord Ethan.

She dismissed that thought immediately, shocked that she had even entertained such an idea. Spending time with Lord Ethan had been enjoyable, but it was the Duke she wanted to marry.

When they received their first visit from him, both Sophia and her mother had almost jumped up and down with excitement. A duke, no less, paying them a visit, and expressing his interest in Sophia, a young lady with no title, and no connections. It was more than either of them could have hoped for from her first Season.

Now she just had to regain that initial excitement. He was interested in courting *her*, little Sophia Cooper, a nobody from the provinces. It was a dream come true. How could she not be beside herself with excitement?

With that in mind, she forced herself to keep smiling and tried to ignore the tightness in her chest and the uncomfortable quivering of her stomach. That must be nerves, that was all. And how could she not be nervous when a duke had come to call? It was only natural, wasn't it?

Being with Lord Ethan had been fun, but that was all it was, a bit of harmless fun that meant nothing.

The carriage came to a halt, and the footman opened the door and lowered the steps. She alighted with her head held high, as if she was indeed a duchess already.

'Will you be joining us, Lord Ethan?' she asked, her voice sounding oddly formal after their previous familiarity, but that was the way she should address this man who was not a relative and hardly even a friend of the family. Her mother would be rightly horrified if she had heard how they had spent the morning laughing together and talking as if they had known each other for many years and not just met for the first time last night.

She could only hope that the Duke never found out. That would ruin everything.

Lord Ethan was staring at the Duke's carriage. He nodded slowly, his face once again dark, as if a shadow had passed over it. 'Yes, thank you, I will.'

Relief washed through her. That too was quite irrational, but for some reason she knew she would feel less nervous in the Duke's company if she had Lord Ethan with her.

They entered the house. She asked the footman to show Lord Ethan into the drawing room while she rushed upstairs with her lady's maid to mend the damage that the outing had caused, not just to her hair and clothing, but to her demeanour as well.

With great haste, Maggie helped her out of her dress and into another gown, one she hoped her mother would approve of, then fixed her hair.

Sophia stared at her reflection in the mirror, trying to remember all the lessons her mother had drilled into her regarding how a future duchess must behave. Stand up straight, shoulders back, chin lifted, like you owned the world and were the superior of all you encountered. It was not a pose that came naturally to her. She often thought she was superior to no one, but it was one she was going to have to force herself to adopt. So much was depending on the Duke finding her acceptable.

'There's no need to worry, madam,' Maggie said, inspecting Sophia's hairstyle from each angle to reassure herself it was perfect. 'You look beautiful, and the walk in the park has brought such lovely colour to your cheeks.' She gave a small laugh. 'Or is that pink tinge due to seeing the Duke again?'

She looked up at Maggie's reflection. She had

puffed herself up, and unlike Sophia had no difficulty standing with her shoulders back and her chin high. It seemed Maggie also had aspirations and was hoping to soon become the lady's maid to a duchess.

'Yes, perhaps,' Sophia replied. 'Yes. This is so exciting, isn't it, Maggie?' she said with more enthusiasm, as if trying to convince both herself and Maggie. 'I can't wait to see him again.'

She remained seated.

'Then, madam, shouldn't you return to the drawing room? Your mother and the Duke will be waiting for you.'

'Yes, of course.'

She stood up and quickly inspected her clothes and hair in the mirror to ensure all was as it should be, then walked down to the drawing room in what she hoped was a sufficiently stately manner as befitting a future duchess.

If her mother asked why she had changed her clothes, she would say it was in case the Duke had seen her in the park. She would tell her she wanted him to think she had dressed to please him and him alone. It wasn't exactly a lie. She would never tell an outright lie to her mother, but there was nothing wrong with not telling her the entire truth, especially if the entire truth would upset her.

She also did not need to know that Sophia had run across the grass in the rain with Lord Ethan's arm around her shoulders, both of them laughing like a couple of happy-go-lucky children.

She entered the room and the two men rose from

their chairs. As she took her seat she forced herself not to look at Lord Ethan, but to have eyes only for the Duke, and to smile in the manner she had been instructed. A small upturn of the lips, no teeth. Then she lowered her eyes, as expected. Her mother had repeatedly told her that lowering one's eyes was the correct behaviour for a modest young woman.

'I was just telling His Grace that you had gone in the carriage to the park, hoping to see him,' her mother said.

She nodded to her mother, then looked over at Lord Ethan, who was staring intently at the Duke, his jaw clenching so tightly she could see it flexing under his skin.

''Fraid you wouldn't have found me there,' the Duke said with a booming laugh that filled the large drawing room. 'Not much one for exercise, especially so early in the day.'

'Then you honour us by paying a visit so early, Your Grace,' her mother said.

'Yes, this is rather early for you, isn't it, Ravenswood? Normally you'd be getting home about this time, wouldn't you?' Lord Ethan's words caused Sophia's smiling mother to frown, but the Duke only laughed louder as if it were a joke.

'Nothing wrong with burning the candle at both ends before a chap settles down,' the Duke said. His gaze moved to Sophia, and she was forced to lower her eyes again. Not from modesty this time, but due to the manner in which he looked at her, as if she were a tasty morsel he was keen to devour.

'So you plan to settle down when you marry, do you?' Lord Ethan said, causing the Duke to laugh again. Did this man laugh at everything, whether it was a joke or not?

'Indeed I do.'

Sophia looked at her mother, who was beaming fit to burst, then over at the Duke, who was staring straight at her. She knew what she had to do…what her mother had told her she must do. She sent him her practised smile, the slight curl at the edges of the lips that most definitely did not show any teeth.

'No point chasing about town for what you can get at home,' he said, his gaze moving slowly up and down her body.

His comment should have been reassuring, even flattering. Wasn't he saying that when they married, he would be a devoted husband? But the unpleasant way her skin prickled in reaction to both his words and his look was far from reassuring.

'And what would that be?' Lord Ethan said, his narrowed eyes fixed on the Duke, his words terse. 'Mutual affection, respect, admiration? I assume that is what you would offer your wife.'

The Duke drew in his chin and frowned as if Lord Ethan had said something preposterous. 'What's come over you, Rosemont? Not like you to be so sentimental.'

'It's not like me to talk about marriage at all, but I believe those are among the qualities that make a happy home life.'

The two men stared at each other, while her mother looked from one to the other with a strained smile.

'Hardly any of your business, is it, Rosemont?' the Duke said with a sneer.

'No, but it should be yours,' Lord Ethan said, his words clipped, his steely eyes never moving from the Duke's. 'A man who believes himself to be a gentleman would never talk about marriage as a means of getting what he'd otherwise have to chase around town for.'

'Perhaps I need to repeat myself,' the Duke said, slowly enunciating each word. 'What business is it of yours, Rosemont?'

They continued to glare at each other, chins lifted, tense jaws jutting forward, hands gripping the arms of the chairs, reminding Sophia of how stags looked moments before they locked horns in a battle for supremacy.

She was unsure what the conversation was about, or what had caused such a level of tension between the two men, but she had the feeling Lord Ethan was defending her honour over something the Duke had said. But that couldn't be right. Shouldn't it be the other way around? Shouldn't her honour be defended by the Duke?

'Thank you for visiting, Lord Ethan,' her mother said, standing up and pushing the bell to summon a servant. 'We won't keep you any longer.'

Lord Ethan rose from his chair, but the Duke remained seated.

'Yes, Rosemont,' he said, his lips curling back into a smile more akin to a snarl. 'You should take your leave. You need to learn when you are not welcome.' He looked at Mrs Cooper, who nodded vigorously.

'Charles, would you show Lord Ethan out?' Sophia's mother said when the footman entered. 'He will be leaving us. Right now.'

Lord Ethan released a long, slow breath, bowed to Sophia and her mother, then looked back at the Duke. 'We can continue this conversation when we next meet at the club,' he said through clenched teeth.

'No need,' the Duke replied, stretching out his legs. 'I have better things to do when I attend the club than discuss marriage.' He gave another loud laugh, causing Mrs Cooper to smile, a wide smile that actually showed teeth, as if what the Duke said was highly amusing.

'Of course you do, Your Grace,' Mrs Cooper simpered. 'And whoever you marry will be a very lucky young lady indeed, and one who I am sure will always be prepared to show her gratitude to you for providing her with such an elevated position in Society.'

'Yes, an elevated position is one I'll no doubt consider on my wedding night,' he said with another laugh as he winked at Lord Ethan.

Lord Ethan stepped towards the Duke, his chin jutted forward, his fists clenched. 'You b—'

'Goodbye, Lord Ethan,' Sophia's mother said, stepping quickly between Lord Ethan and the Duke. 'Thank you for passing on your regards from your mother, but we won't detain you any longer.'

'Yes, goodbye, Rosemont,' the Duke said, a satisfied smirk on his face as if he had just won a victory.

Lord Ethan turned to Sophia and bowed again. 'Good afternoon, Miss Cooper. And if I can be of service to you at any time, please don't hesitate to ask.'

'That won't be necessary,' her mother said, ignoring the servant and taking Lord Ethan's arm and leading him to the door. 'Goodbye, Lord Ethan.'

Without waiting for Sophia to answer, and before she could stand and curtsey goodbye, her mother shut the door behind Lord Ethan with a decisive click.

She then turned to the Duke and smiled. 'I must apologise, Your Grace. We would never have invited that frightful man in if we'd known he'd behave like that.'

The Duke waved his hand in dismissal of all that had happened, still not bothering to stand while her mother took her seat.

'It looks like little Sophia has made a conquest there,' he said, smiling in Sophia's direction. 'Perhaps I should be a tad jealous.'

'Not at all, Your Grace,' her mother said with a trilling laugh in her voice. 'He's the third son of a duke. I'd hardly call him competition.'

'Indeed. Still, does a man good to know he's getting something that other men want.' His gaze once again swept slowly over her, and once again that unsettling prickling feeling crept up her skin. 'Does him good indeed.'

'Well, my Sophia is a beautiful young woman. It's not surprising that other men are paying her attention.'

'Not too much attention, I hope,' the Duke said, no longer smiling.

'Definitely not,' her mother said in a rush, her hands extended almost in supplication. 'Lord Ethan merely escorted Sophia round the park in the hope that she might see you out riding, and her lady's maid was in attendance at all times.'

She looked at Sophia, smiled and placed her hands over her heart, as if making a solemn declaration. 'Sophia is not a flirt or a coquette. She is an innocent, modest young lady and her reputation is entirely unsullied.'

The Duke laughed. 'I'm sure it is. And as I said, a fellow doesn't mind if he has a bit of competition. Makes a gal an even more attractive catch, and it's especially heartening to see your daughter has caught the eye of Lord Ethan. He's a bit of a one for the ladies, that one.'

Pain gripped at Sophia's stomach and she took a few deep breaths to release the tight clenching. Why should she care if Lord Ethan was *one for the ladies* or not?

'Then of course Sophia will see no more of him,' her mother said. 'And if he doesn't realise that already, he will be informed that his visits to this home are no longer welcome.'

*No*, Sophia wanted to call out. Nothing happened between us. We just went for an innocent walk together. But was that entirely true? She remembered how she had reacted when he'd placed his coat around her shoulders. How she had closed her eyes and savoured the lingering heat of his body and his intoxicating scent. Could that be honestly described as innocent? Was it really acceptable behaviour for a woman who wished to marry another? Was her mother right that it was best if they saw no more of each other? Perhaps. But she so wanted that not to be so.

'You can rest assured,' her mother continued, smiling at the Duke, 'my Sophia always does as she is told and is a true homebody, most definitely not the type to flirt or try and catch a man's eye. She is the sort of young woman who on her marriage will find contentment in making a home that any man would be pleased to come back to.'

Sophia wondered if that was entirely true. She'd had many lessons on how to run a large estate, how to manage servants, how to prepare a household budget, to organise a dinner party and a ball, but she wasn't sure if she'd say she *found contentment* doing it. It was merely what was expected of her.

'Isn't that so, Sophia?' her mother said.

Sophia looked at the Duke and nodded, then quickly dropped her gaze again, her cheeks burning. Why did he keep looking at her like that, as if he was a hungry young boy staring through the window of a cake shop?

'I'm sure she does, and it's nice to still be able to make a young lady blush,' the Duke said, then boomed out a hearty laugh. 'Been a while since I've been able to do that.'

'Isn't that what you'd expect from a young lady as modest and as innocent as my Sophia?' her mother said.

'Mmm…' he responded, his gaze once again slowly scrutinising her, then he turned his attention back to her mother. They continued to chat together, while Sophia kept her eyes lowered, as was expected. She couldn't help but wonder why the Duke had bothered to visit, as he had paid her little attention, apart from looking at her in that disconcerting manner. He seemed not the slightest bit interested in talking to her or getting to know her any better, as one would expect if you were looking for a wife.

After a few more minutes, and after the Duke had declined the offer to take tea, he rose. 'I will see you at Lord and Lady Wilton's ball next week, Sophia,' he said in a manner that suggested it was a statement, not a question.

'Of course you will, Your Grace,' her mother replied for her. 'Sophia is looking forward to it.'

'Then I shall see you both there.' The two ladies curtsied low, and with a quick bow of his head the Duke departed.

The moment the door shut behind him, her mother's smile disappeared and she turned to Sophia, her eyes blazing.

'What was the meaning of that behaviour?'

Sophia shook her head, unsure of what she had done wrong.

'You were sitting there pouting with your chest caved in as if you'd just received disappointing news.'

'Oh, you told me to look modest at all times. I thought that was what I was doing.'

'Modest, yes. Petulant, most decidedly not. You need to look as if, while you are an innocent young lady, you are eager for the Duke's attention and interested in everything he has to say. Perhaps keep your head slightly tilted to show that his conversation fascinates you, and keep your eyes fixed on him at all times, to show how much you are attracted to him. Just lower your eyes when he looks at you, after first holding his for a second or so, as if you can hardly bear to look away but know you must. That way he knows you are reserved, but, well, that you'll be amenable when you are married.'

'Amenable?'

'Yes, amenable. The Duke will instruct you on what that means on your wedding night.'

Sophia winced. Was it natural for a young woman to be so perturbed by the thought of her wedding night?

'Well?' her mother asked. 'Do you understand how you're supposed to behave in the Duke's presence?'

'Yes, Mother,' Sophia replied, wondering whether she would be able to remember when to look modest, when fascinated, and how to appear amenable but reserved at the same time. Especially as she didn't feel any of those things when she was in the Duke's company.

'The blushing was good, though,' her mother continued. 'Try to do more of that, especially when the Duke makes comments about your future life together as man and wife. He seems to like that.'

Had the Duke made her blush? Sophia couldn't remember. She knew that Lord Ethan had caused her to blush frequently. Also, traitorously, she suspected she looked at him as if interested in what he had to say, and possibly stared at him as if she found him attractive, but that was because she *did* find him attractive. Perhaps, when in the Duke's company, she should pretend he was Lord Ethan.

That thought sent heat rushing to her cheeks. How

could she even think such a terrible, disloyal thing about the man she hoped to marry?

'Yes,' her mother said, nodding her approval. 'Like that.'

The heat on her cheeks increased. She was deceiving her mother, something she knew to be wrong, especially as all her mother was trying to do was ensure she made a good marriage.

'And for goodness' sake, do not look at that Lord Ethan so much. During that ridiculous altercation you kept looking at him and not the Duke, as you should have been. The Duke should be the one to command your complete attention, and your concern.'

'What was the altercation about, Mother?'

Her mother waved her hand in dismissal. 'It was nothing, but the Duke handled it all with such graciousness, as you would expect from a genteel member of the aristocracy.'

It didn't seem like nothing to Sophia, but then, surely her mother would not lie to her.

'Sophia, I know this is confusing for you.' Her mother moved over to sit next to her on the sofa and took hold of her hands. 'But we are so close to achieving our goal. We must do nothing to upset the Duke. He has still not asked for my permission to formally court you, merely shown that he is interested in you. You must do everything you can to encourage his attention. Do you understand?'

Sophia nodded.

'Today's visit was significant, but you have to remember that as a young lady without a title you have to try even harder than the other debutantes. You have to make sure that it is you the Duke wants to marry, and no other.' She gently stroked the side of Sophia's head. 'You will try harder, won't you, Sophia? You will do exactly what I tell you to do?'

'Yes, of course I will, Mother,' Sophia responded.

'Because we don't want the Duke to get the wrong idea about you. You must let him know with everything you do and say that nothing would give you greater pleasure than to be the Duchess of Ravenswood.'

Sophia nodded again. 'But did you mean what you said about Lord Ethan not being able to pay any more visits?' she asked, her breath catching in her throat as she waited for the answer.

Her mother's hand dropped from stroking the side of her head and her lips pinched together. 'Of course I did. Have you not been paying attention to what I've been saying?'

Sophia shook her head, then nodded. 'Yes, Mother, of course I have been.'

Her mother's expression softened, and she took hold of Sophia's hands. 'Yes. You are a good girl, but your innocence and trusting nature could be misconstrued. I know you have no interest in Lord Ethan, but the Duke might not see it that way. It is good that his attentions have made the Duke see you in a more favourable light, as someone other men are attracted to. After all, we wouldn't want him to think that you were an easy catch, but enough is enough. We must do nothing to discourage him. Competition is good, as long as he knows he is going to be the victor.'

She released Sophia's hands and sat upright. 'No, you will not be seeing Lord Ethan again and he will not be welcome at this house.'

A tight band of pain gripped her chest, making it hard to breathe. She wanted to see Lord Ethan again, wanted it more than she knew she should, but her mother was right. She dragged in a shaky breath. If she was to marry the Duke, then it would not do for her to be spending any time with another man, especially one about whom she was having such inappropriate thoughts.

Ethan should have punched him. Despite being in the presence of Miss and Mrs Cooper, he should have taken Ravenswood by the scruff of the neck, dragged him outside and beaten the life out of that pig of a man. How any man, even one as debased as Ravenswood, could sit in a young lady's drawing room and make all those inappropriate innuendos he would never know.

And as for the mother... Ethan paced up and down his bed chamber, his fists clenching so tightly nails were digging into flesh. The mother knew exactly what the Duke was alluding to when he had said there was no point chasing around town for what you could get at home. The woman had even smiled, as if the man was making a polite joke, rather than saying something degrading about her daughter. And how could she just sit there, simpering and smiling when the Duke had joked about being in an elevated position on their wedding night? It beggared belief.

No woman should be treated like that, especially

one as innocent and trusting as Miss Cooper. If Ravenswood had made such crude innuendos in the presence of the women he usually associated with he would have got an equally ribald response. But Sophia was different.

Ethan stopped pacing. *No woman should be treated like that.* Was he any different from the Duke? Like Ravenswood, he'd had countless women in his bed, moving from one to another with hardly a backward glance. Was he any better than the man he despised?

Yes, he *was* different. Unlike Ravenswood he had no intention of marrying an innocent debutante. And he would never subject her, or any other woman, to insulting comments. Nor would he ever trick a young woman into a marriage that could bring her only unhappiness.

And that was what would happen if Ethan didn't act to stop this marriage.

He commenced pacing. He had made a mistake. He had left quietly, telling himself that a brawl in the middle of the drawing room would not do, but after what Ravenswood had said, and how the mother had reacted, even such uncouth behaviour would be understandable.

He stopped pacing once again and looked out of the window, seeing nothing of the street below. At the time the temptation to let Ravenswood know what he had thought of his scurrilous innuendos had been all but overwhelming. Even the mother's intervention had done nothing to temper his fury. If he hadn't caught sight of Miss Cooper, sitting there in trusting innocence, not knowing what had been said about her, he would have given full vent to his anger. But he would not expose her to such barbarous behaviour as two men fighting like uncivilised ruffians.

But the next time he saw the Duke he would not use such restraint. He would give that degenerate a thrashing he would never forget. He would learn that he needed to treat Miss Cooper with respect. She might not have understood what was being said about her, but that made it even worse. Had Ravenswood actually expected Ethan to join in on a ribald joke at Miss Cooper's expense, the way her mother had?

He went back to pacing the room, wearing a path down the middle of the oriental rug. Then once again stopped and stared out of the window at the quiet street below, unsure whom he was now most angry with, Ravenswood or Mrs Cooper.

Until today, he had assumed that Mrs Cooper was as naïve to the Duke's actual character as her daughter, but now he knew differently. She was fully aware of what Ravenswood was like and didn't care. She was more than happy to throw her daughter at that degenerate, a man who would treat her daughter in a despicable manner, all because he possessed a title. It was abhorrent.

Miss Cooper had no one looking out for her interests. No one except him. She now needed him more than ever, even if she didn't realise it.

The problem was, how was he going to look out for her? He stared out at the street scene below, as if searching for inspiration.

As much as he wanted to tell Mrs Cooper in no uncertain terms what he thought of her, and as much as he was itching to give Ravenswood the beating that low-life deserved, neither actions would help Miss Cooper.

He went back to his ineffectual pacing, still contemplating the beating he wished he could give Ravenswood. But apart from making Ethan feel a lot better, it would serve no other purpose.

But one thing he most definitely would be doing was preventing this travesty of a marriage from ever taking place. Somehow, he would have to convince Miss Cooper that this marriage was wrong, the Duke was wrong, her mother was wrong, and, despite what she claimed, that becoming the Duchess of Ravenswood was not the best way to honour the memory of her father.

And he had to do that while avoiding any entanglement that might result in him having to marry the girl himself.

How he was to achieve this he had no idea. All he knew was that it was a lot to ask from a man who had shunned responsibility his entire life and was an extremely unlikely, not to mention reluctant, knight in shining armour.

## Chapter Five

Sophia tried to summon up some enthusiasm. It was her second ball of the Season. She should be bubbling over with excitement, the way she had been before her first ball.

She held on to the bedstead as Maggie gave her corset laces one last, forceful pull, then held up her arms so her lady's maid could lower the ball gown over Sophia's head. Her lady's maid seemed excited enough for both of them and she was all but singing as she went about her task of making her mistress look attractive.

It was hard to believe her mood could be so different from how it had been when she was getting ready for the last ball, just a week ago. When Maggie had dressed her for that ball, Sophia had been full of nervous anticipation and looking forward to seeing her handsome duke again. She had imagined descending the stairs into a magnificent ballroom. He would gaze up at her from the foot of the stairs, wonder and admiration sparking in his eyes. She would float down towards him and he would greet her with a kiss on her hand. Then, ignoring all others, he would sweep her onto the dance floor and they would dance the night away.

That night, her illusions had been quickly shattered. He'd done none of those things. Instead, after one dance he had abandoned her, and returned to his laughing friends. It had been humiliating, and she feared that tonight would be no different.

Maggie fastened the line of small buttons running up the back of her gown, then asked her to sit so she could finish styling her hair.

As Maggie made the final touches to her appearance, Sophia reminded herself of everything her mother had told her. She had insisted that tonight's ball would be different. The Duke would be different. He might even make his intentions towards her clear. After tonight, it might be official she was being courted by the Duke of Ravenswood.

That certainly was something to get excited about. So why did she feel so nervous, and not in the manner of anticipating something wonderful? The churning in her stomach resembled fear. It seemed she was frightened of the man she was hoping to marry. That could not be natural. Could it?

Something else that would be different about tonight was Lord Ethan. He would not be present. If the Duke abandoned her, there would be no one to save her from the humiliation of standing on the side of the dance floor like a wallflower.

Lord Ethan had told her he rarely attended balls, had only been present at her first ball because his mother was hosting it. If she knew he would be in attendance tonight, she was certain she would not be so jittery. Unlike the Duke, Lord Ethan was not someone she feared. She felt safe with him, protected. She sighed lightly, remembering his warm jacket around her shoulders, the pleasure of running through the rain with his arm around her, of their laughing together, and of the way he had looked at her when they had danced together.

Maggie's reflection smiled at her, causing Sophia to move uncomfortably on the embroidered bench in front of the mirror. Her lady's maid presumably thought she was sighing over the Duke, not a man whom she shouldn't even be thinking about.

She stood up, and Maggie picked up her elbow-length gloves and her fan from the dressing table and handed them to her.

'That gown looks lovely on you, madam,' she said, scrutinising Sophia's appearance with a critical eye.

'Yes, thank you, Maggie. You've done a wonderful job, as usual.' And she had. Sophia's hair was piled on top of her head in the fashionably voluminous style, and Maggie had artfully woven in a cascade of curls so they tumbled gently around her face and neck. And the dress was indeed beautiful. Yet another Parisian design, made in the most expensive embroidered silk available. Her mother had told the dressmaker that, while the pale pink fabric had been chosen to depict her youth and innocence, she wanted the style to accentuate Sophia's curves, and that was exactly what the gown did.

'The Duke will be very impressed,' Maggie added, brushing out the gown's long train. 'I'm sure you'll be a duchess soon.'

'That will be all, Maggie.' Sophia's words came out more tersely than she intended. 'Thank you,' she added in a softer tone.

Maggie was only saying what Sophia knew to be true. The gown, with its figure-hugging style and low-cut neckline, *was* designed to draw the Duke's attention, to tempt him, as if she were being offered up to him like a sacrificial maiden.

She shuddered and pulled at the neckline, trying to lift it up above her décolletage. She did not want the Duke looking at her in the unsettling manner he had when he had visited. For a moment she wondered about changing into something more demure, but there was no time, and this was the dress her mother had selected for her, so really she had no choice.

With a resigned sigh, she pulled on her gloves and walked down to the drawing room, where her mother was waiting.

Her mother stood up, took hold of Sophia's hands and smiled. 'My dear, you look beautiful. That gown is perfect. You look just like the duchess you soon will be.'

Sophia's stomach clenched, and she tried to swallow down the lump in her throat. Her mother's compliment, and her obvious pride, should be making Sophia happy, but the pain gripping her did not feel like happiness.

'Mother, is it normal to feel…?' She tried to order her thoughts.

'What, dear?' her mother asked, lifting one of the curls falling over Sophia's shoulder and smiling.

'Is it normal to be frightened of the man you hope to marry?'

'My dear, it's perfectly natural,' she said, flicking her hand to indicate that the lady's maid should leave them. 'Sophia, darling, you are an inexperienced young lady, as you should be, and the Duke is an experienced man of the world. I would be shocked if you weren't a little frightened of him. But all you have to do is follow his lead. He knows more than you about what is right and proper. And when you do marry, you don't have to worry about anything. He will know what to do on your wedding night. Just make sure you do everything he asks of you.'

Sophia swallowed again, her stomach clenching tighter.

'But I am pleased that you raised the subject.' Her mother gently stroked the backs of her hands. 'After his recent visit, I feel certain that the Duke will soon make some sort of declaration.' She stood back and smiled at Sophia. 'And I'm sure that tonight he will not be able to resist you, looking as you do.'

Her face became serious. She stepped forward and gripped Sophia's hands tightly. 'It is important that you listen to me, Sophia. If the Duke does take you aside tonight, make sure you behave in an agreeable manner. Do everything I told you to do. You must never forget he is a duke and has the power to make you a very lucky young woman indeed. It is essential that you please him.'

Sophia nodded as she struggled to draw in a breath.

'Keep that thought in your mind at all times when you are with him. Your role is to please the Duke and make him see that you will be a good wife and a perfect duchess. You must let him see you are everything he expects you to be.'

All Sophia could do was nod again.

Her mother patted her hands. 'Good girl. I know you will make a wonderful duchess. We just have to prove that to the Duke. But that will not happen if we don't get to the ball. So come along, we mustn't keep your future husband waiting.'

Throughout the journey Sophia remained quiet, her anxiety growing the closer they got to the Wiltons' home, while her mother chatted animatedly. So much was expected of her tonight. At the first ball she had assumed all she had to be was herself, that the Duke had expressed his interest in *her*, so she did not need to perform, or convince him to marry her. But now, it seemed she did. It was essential she capture the Duke's attention, show him how perfect she was for him, and what a perfect duchess she would make. And if that didn't happen, she knew how disappointed her mother would be, knew that she would not be fulfilling her father's dreams for her.

The carriage arrived, and the footman lowered the steps. Before she could leave the carriage, her mother took a firm hold of her hand. 'Remember, you must conduct yourself like the sophisticated duchess you will soon be,' she said, her face stern. Then she smiled, put her hand under Sophia's chin to tilt it up. 'And remember to smile. You need to show the Duke that you are capable of enjoying yourself, like the lovely, carefree girl you are.'

Sophia forced a smile onto her face, unsure how she was to follow those contradictory orders, how a carefree girl who is also a sophisticated duchess actually did behave.

They entered the ballroom and waited at the top of the stairs along with the other guests waiting to be announced. Sophia tried to relax, to smile, to feel the required excited anticipation. And she should be excited. She had looked forward to her Season for many years, had prepared for it, dreamt about it. Now she really should be enjoying it.

The footman announced Mrs and Miss Cooper and they descended to the ballroom. Then Sophia saw him. Looking up at her from the bottom of the stairs. The weight pressing down on her shoulders suddenly lifted. It was as if she was floating on a cloud. Music filled the air, elegant couples swirled around the highly polished dance floor and the sparkling chandeliers suspended from the ornate ceiling sent glittering light over the room. It was all so enchanting.

And Lord Ethan was staring straight at her. She smiled. He smiled back, looking more handsome than ever. He was dressed in the same black, swallow-tailed evening suit, white shirt and white bow tie as every other man in the room, but he was so much more elegant. Elegant, handsome and just divine. If only he were a duke, then he really could be her Prince Charming and she could get her fairy-tale Season.

'I can't see the Duke anywhere,' her mother said, interrupting her foolish fantasy. 'He said he would come tonight.'

'Perhaps he's late.' *Perhaps he hasn't come at all.*

'No, there he is, over in the far corner.'

The sudden tension in her mother's voice caused Sophia to look in the direction she was indicating. She expected to see the Duke surrounded by his friends, just as he had been at her first ball, but he was talking to a young woman. A tall, elegant woman in an exquisite gown, diamonds and an array of other gems sparkling from her necklace and earrings, and pearls woven intricately through her hair.

Her mother gripped her arm. 'That's Lucretia Hawksbury, the American heiress,' she all but hissed under her breath. 'She's rumoured to be seeking a man with a title. This is a disaster, Sophia. A complete disaster.' She turned to Sophia and quickly scanned her appearance. 'You must draw the Duke's attention away from that American.'

Sophia had no idea what her mother expected of her. She was following all the rules drummed into her by her sergeant-major deportment instructor—head up, shoulders back, chest out. What else was she supposed to do, slip on the train of her gown and tumble down the remaining stairs? Sophia stifled a giggle. That would certainly get the Duke's attention, along with that of every other guest, but she suspected that was not the sort of entrance her mother had in mind.

They reached the bottom of the stairs, where Lord Ethan was waiting.

'Miss Cooper, Mrs Cooper,' he said with a bow.

Her mother scowled at him, then looked back to where the Duke was standing.

'You look beautiful tonight, Miss Cooper,' he said quietly.

She smiled at him. Under his gaze, she did indeed feel beautiful. She no longer felt the ball gown exposed too much flesh, was cut too low in the front, clung too closely to her waist and hips. It was as if she had dressed for him, so he would admire her, so he would be attracted to her.

'I'm surprised to see you here,' Sophia said, trying to remember not to sound too enthusiastic and draw her mother's displeasure. 'I thought you said you did not enjoy balls.'

'I made yet another exception, as I was hoping to see you again.' He tipped his head towards her mother, who was still staring in the Duke's direction. 'The Wiltons sent me an invitation, so no one can prevent me from seeing you here.'

'I'm so pleased you accepted,' she said, suddenly unable to stop smiling.

Her mother turned back to Lord Ethan, still scowling, then her expression slowly softened.

'Why, Lord Ethan, how lovely to see you here.' She extended her hand to him, which he took, and bowed his head.

'How delightful—the orchestra has already started playing.' Her mother clasped her hands together in what was obviously feigned pleasure. 'You two young people go and enjoy yourselves. We've only just arrived, so Sophia's dance card is yet to fill up.'

Sophia could almost see her mother's mind working. If dancing with Lord Ethan had got the Duke's attention last time, perhaps it would work again tonight. But she cared not a bit what her mother was thinking, if it meant she could dance with Lord Ethan.

Her mother's gaze then returned to the Duke and her smile died. The Duke was still talking to the American woman, causing that scowl to return to her mother's face.

'But don't monopolise her attention all night,' Sophia's mother added, not looking at Lord Ethan. 'Once you've danced one dance, return her to me, as I'm sure there are other men who will be eager to take her hand.'

Ethan followed the direction of Mrs Cooper's gaze. It was no surprise that her attention was fixed on Ravenswood. And the reason for her disapproving look was equally predictable. Ravenswood was talking to another woman. It seemed Miss Cooper had competition. Strong competition, in the form of an American heiress. Lucretia Hawksbury's family was said to have an unrivalled fortune, one that a man like Ravenswood would be desperate to get his hands on. Unlike Miss Cooper, Miss Hawksbury was a sophisticated, worldly young woman, and she too was in search of a title. Surely she would make a better wife for Ravenswood. She had the necessary income to settle his debts and, with such a powerful family behind her and a formidable father, she would be more capable of keeping the Duke in line than Miss and Mrs Cooper would ever be.

This was good news indeed. With any luck, it would mean Ethan would achieve his goal of rescuing Miss Cooper from a disastrous marriage without actually having to do anything.

He turned his attention back to her. 'Miss Cooper, would you do me the honour of this dance?' he said with another bow, hoping she would realise that the decision was hers and hers alone. She did not have to dance with him just because her mother told her to. Nor did she have to be a pawn in this woman's or the Duke's game. She was free to make her own choices.

'Yes, I would be delighted to dance with you,' she replied, sending him that angelic smile that crushed his heart. Why did she have to be so innocent? But how could he blame her for being exactly the sort of woman she had been raised to be? It was just a shame it made her so vulnerable, especially to predatory men like Ravenswood.

He escorted her onto the dance floor and, damn it all, he could see that the mother's ruse had worked. The Duke had already seen them. He excused himself from Miss Hawksbury's company and made his way across the room towards Mrs Cooper.

It seemed his time alone with Miss Cooper was to be limited, so Ethan decided he must make full use of it and not think about her beauty, her unfortunate innocence or her vulnerability.

He placed one hand on her slim waist and took her other hand in his, noticing the white skin of the underside of her slender arm and the interlacing of blue veins. It looked so pure and defenceless, just like Miss Cooper herself.

He continued to stare at the flawless skin. Was that why he wanted to save her from Ravenswood, because she was as yet unsullied by the harsher side of life? Had her vulnerability elicited some primal, protective instinct in him, an instinct he had previously been unaware of? Why else would he be here at another infernal Society ball? But why her? Why now? This was not his first Season and she was not the first innocent young woman to be married off to an inappropriate man.

'I am so sorry about the way my mother treated you when you visited,' she said, drawing his gaze back to her face and that sweet smile still curling her pretty lips. Those lips were possibly the loveliest he had ever seen. So full, so soft. Would they taste as sweet as they looked?

He quickly looked away. What on earth was he doing, thinking of her in that way? Was he as bad as Ravenswood after all?

'Do not apologise,' he said. 'How I am treated is of no matter.'

He looked over her head towards Ravenswood. That was why he was here. That was all that mattered. He had to save this young woman from that bully.

His gaze returned to those big blue eyes and once again his heart seemed to dissolve in his chest. She was like a leaf, caught up in a swirling wind over which she had no control, being blown in whatever direction suited the ambitions of her mother, and the financial needs of the Duke.

He had an overwhelming urge to enfold her in his arms, to protect her from the world and cherish her the way she deserved to be cherished.

Music filled the air and they circled the room. If he did hold her closer than propriety might demand, that was merely his primitive, protective instinct taking over again, nothing more. After all, only a brute like Ravenswood could feel anything other than protective towards such a naïve young woman. And, while he might have many flaws, Ethan liked to believe he was no brute.

'But at least she's letting us dance together now,' she said.

'I suspect that is for no other reason than that she hopes it will once again get the Duke's attention.' They both looked in the Duke and Mrs Cooper's direction. Their heads were close together, and they were talking intently.

'Oh, yes, I believe so,' she said quietly, then smiled. 'But I don't care what the reason is. I'm just pleased you decided to attend this ball and am so happy you asked me to dance with you again.'

For a woman who was schooled to be constantly modest, it was a bold statement, particularly as it was directed at a man whom she was not expected to marry. He had seen that spark of rebellion in her as they'd run through the park and here it was again. Perhaps it was something he could kindle so she could break free and become the woman she wanted to be, rather than the one her mother had made her.

'And I too don't care why we're dancing together, just that we are,' he replied, and they exchanged smiles.

'Hopefully Mother will want us to dance together all night long, to really attract the Duke's attention.'

He laughed, enjoying this surprising defiance. 'I'd like to hope there is some other reason you want to dance with me.'

'Oh, there is, of course,' she blurted out. 'I love... I mean, I thoroughly enjoyed dancing with you at our last ball, and I enjoyed our time together in Hyde Park as well.'

'As did I, Miss Cooper.' That too was the truth. Even though he was playing the role of a reluctant knight in shining armour, he did enjoy being in her company. Perhaps more than he should.

'So, are there any other young ladies you plan to dance with tonight?' She looked up at him from under thick black eyelashes. 'I wouldn't want to keep you from them.'

'Not one. You are the only young lady I wish to dance with.' That too was an honest answer, although his reasons were perhaps somewhat less than honest, even if, to his mind, they were eminently honourable.

But he would not want her to get the wrong impression, and he might not have much time, so he needed to stop complimenting her or gushing about how pleased he was and get down to the real reason he was here. 'Miss Cooper, I need to talk to you about the Duke of Ravenswood.'

Her lips pursed, and her brow furrowed. 'Oh, let's not, please. The Duke is all my mother ever seems to talk about. Let's just enjoy this dance. Once I'm married, I'm sure I won't be allowed to dance with any other men but my husband.'

'But is marriage to the Duke what *you* really want? Do you even know what he is like?' he rushed on.

'Please, Lord Ethan, can't we just enjoy what is left of our time together and not talk of the Duke or of my future marriage?'

Ethan suppressed a sigh of frustration. He wanted to grab her by the arms, take her aside and give her a stern talking-to, to tell her she was about to make a mistake that she would regret for the rest of her life. But would that make him as bad as her mother? That woman was also telling Miss Cooper what she should do, what she should think and how she should feel. Just like Mrs Cooper, was he assuming he knew what was best for her? It all had to be Miss Cooper's decision, but she needed to make a decision knowing exactly what she was agreeing to. At present, she was blinded to the man's true character. Somehow, he had to make her see who Ravenswood really was and do so before it was too late.

Short of taking her to the Venus Gentlemen's Club and letting her see for herself the antics he got up to, or assembling a parade of maids and other vulnerable women the Duke had seduced and abandoned, he was struggling to think of how he would open her eyes to the man's true character.

But she was also right. This may be their last dance together. He should just enjoy it.

He held her closer, wanting to transfer his strength

to her. For a brief moment, her head lowered and gently rested on his shoulder. It was such a trusting gesture, one that sent warm affection surging through him.

'Miss Cooper,' he murmured softly in her ear, 'I want you to know I am your friend. You can always turn to me for help. If at any time you need me, do not be afraid to ask me for anything.'

She tilted back her head, her eyebrows drawn together as if she could not imagine a time when she would need to ask for help. 'Thank you, Lord Ethan, that's very kind of you.'

'Promise me you won't forget what I said.' It was vital to him she knew she could always escape from Ravenswood. That even if she married him, she had one friend who was on her side and would be her champion.

Her furrowed brow became smooth, and she smiled. 'Yes, I promise.'

It was not entirely what Ethan wanted. He wanted her to declare that she would never marry Ravenswood, but for now it would have to do.

'And always remember, you deserve to be loved, to be cared for and treated with respect, and let no one convince you otherwise.'

He looked down at her, at her soft, creamy skin, her blue eyes, her blonde hair, and for a moment wondered if he could be the man to love her, care for her and treat her with the respect she deserved. Then he dismissed that idea. His role as gallant knight didn't have to go that far. He did not want to marry Miss Cooper, or any other woman. And he certainly would not get married just so he could feel like some sort of Sir Galahad saving a defenceless young maiden. That would be as offensive as marrying someone to get a title or to settle your gambling debts with their dowry.

The waltz came to an end. He led her off the dance floor, back to her mother and, unfortunately, back to the waiting Duke.

'Remember what I said, Miss Cooper,' he murmured. 'I will always be your friend and if you ever need help, I will be there for you.'

Before she had a chance to respond, Ravenswood took her arm and without asking escorted her back onto the dance floor, where couples were lining up for the quadrille.

Ethan watched on helplessly, a failed knight in tarnished armour who hadn't even come close to saving his damsel.

As the Duke placed his arm proprietorially around her waist Ethan could only think of an innocent lamb in the arms of a butcher, one who had promised his charge that she had nothing to worry about and he was just taking her to play in a nice green field.

He had missed his opportunity. Possibly the only opportunity he would get this night. His attempts to warn her about the Duke had been too subtle, too guarded. If he was to save her from that man, he would have to ignore her innocence and spell out to her just how the Duke treated women. Then her blinkers would be removed, and she would know exactly what her marriage to Ravenswood would be like. It would be a shock, but perhaps a shock was what she needed if she was to avoid making a disastrous decision that would cause her immense suffering. If, once she knew all the facts, she still wanted to become a duchess, then he would have to, reluctantly, respect her decision.

'Lord Ethan, may I be so bold as to ask you to fetch me a glass of punch? It's so warm in here tonight,' he heard Mrs Cooper ask as he continued to stare at Ravenswood and Miss Cooper.

'Lord Ethan?' Mrs Cooper repeated.

'Yes, of course, Mrs Cooper,' he replied, giving the Duke and Miss Cooper one last look before moving through the crowd to the supper room. He paused at the doorway, considering what he would have to do. He didn't want to destroy the innocent way in which she viewed the world, but there was no option. As soon as he returned, that was what he would have to do.

## Chapter Six

Couples lined up for the quadrille, laughing and chattering together as they waited for the orchestra to play. Sophia's mind was not on the Duke of Ravenswood, as it should be, nor was it on the dance about to begin. All she could think of was Lord Ethan.

It was kind that he had offered to be her friend, and she appreciated his saying she could rely on his help any time she needed it. But why would he say such a thing? Was it an ominous warning that one day she would indeed need his help?

She looked over towards her mother, expecting to see Lord Ethan, but he had gone. Her gaze flicked around the ballroom. Was he dancing with another young lady? He said he had no wish to dance with anyone but her, but that was surely empty flattery. There must be other debutantes that would interest a man like him, and surely there were plenty of debutantes who would love to be led around the floor by such a handsome man.

Then she caught sight of him as he departed through

the doors leading to the supper room. She wasn't sure whether to feel pleased he was not paying attention to another, or bereft that he had abandoned her, or ashamed that she was even thinking about any man other than the Duke.

'My dear, your mother no doubt told you I would want a quiet word with you this evening,' the Duke said, interrupting her thoughts.

'Oh, yes, she did,' Sophia replied, looking up at him. He too was staring towards the doors and she hoped he did not know she had been watching Lord Ethan.

'I believe now would be an opportune time to do so?'

'Oh, but what about the dance? It's just about to start.' The moment those words were out, she knew she had already failed to follow her mother's instructions. He was asking to have a *quiet word with her*. This was what they had been waiting for. She should have responded with enthusiasm, with a modest smile, with a sign that she was amenable.

'My dear,' the Duke said, placing his hand on the small of her back. 'The quadrille can wait.'

Thankfully, her momentary lapse had not discouraged him, but she could not let that happen again. She had to keep in mind, at all times, everything her mother had said to her about the correct way to behave when in the Duke's company.

He steered her across the ballroom, through the assembled couples, and out onto the terrace. The glass doors shut behind them, muffling the laughter, talking and music from the ballroom.

'That's much better,' the Duke said. 'Now we can talk in peace.'

Sophia looked longingly towards the dancing couples moving almost soundlessly around the dance floor. Fighting to ignore the churning in her stomach, she held her breath and tried to smile at the Duke, hoping he could not see the tremor on her lips.

This was it. What she had been waiting for. The Duke was about to propose. She would return to her mother with such exciting news. She was about to become a duchess, to make her mother happy and honour all her father's wishes.

Remembering her mother's instructions, she forced her smile to be more amenable, as if there was no place she would rather be, then looked back at the ballroom, wondering whether Lord Ethan had yet returned.

'I believe we need even more privacy,' the Duke said.

She suppressed a gasp when he placed his hands on her waist and moved her to the stone wall beside the glass doors, where the light from the ballroom did not reach.

'That's better.' He stood in front of her, encasing her, his body cutting off even the subdued light from the full moon. Sophia gripped tightly on her fan, and moved back away from him, her retreat halted by the wall.

'Your mother has no doubt discussed with you my wish to court you with the intention of marrying you at the end of the Season, if we prove to be compatible and if we are both agreeable.'

Sophia placed her hand on her chest to still the thumping of her heart and nodded. 'Yes,' she said, her voice strangled, a sound she hoped the Duke would interpret as excitement.

'And are you agreeable with this arrangement? Do you want me to court you, Sophia?'

'Yes,' she repeated, her voice barely audible. It *was* what she wanted, what she'd always wanted. Her mother was right. She was so lucky that the Duke had picked her out from all the available debutantes.

'And I dare say your mother has also explained to you that I expect my future wife to be an obedient young lady.'

Sophia swallowed. He had moved even closer to her. She was now up against the wall, the hard stones digging into her back, his body almost touching hers.

'Well, has she explained that to you or not?'

Her mother's last lecture ran through her head, on how she had to be agreeable, modest but amenable. She still wasn't entirely sure what that meant, but her mother had also instructed her to follow the Duke's lead in all things, that he would know what was right and proper.

'Yes,' she whispered.

'Has she also explained that I am a man of the world?'

Sophia nodded. That was also something her mother had said, although she did not entirely know what it meant.

'And that I will expect to have a little sample of what you will offer me when you are my bride?'

Sophia slowly shook her head, wishing her mother

had explained things to her in less confusing terms. 'I'm not sure.'

'You are such an innocent.' He took hold of her chin and tilted up her head. 'That's what makes you so attractive. Your mother might not have told you exactly what I want from you, but I'm sure she told you to be obedient and do exactly what I tell you.'

'Oh, I see. Yes, she did say that.'

He released her chin and smiled, a smile that was almost a leer. 'Good girl. And to that end, first, I want you to kiss me.'

Her hands flew to her mouth to cover her shock. Her pounding heart thumped out the passing seconds as he stared down at her, waiting for her answer. 'But, Your Grace, we're not married,' she finally gasped out.

He laughed as if she had said something meant to amuse him. 'Not married *yet*. And need I remind you what your mother said about obedience?'

Sophia stared at him, her throat dry, her heart beating so loudly she was sure he must be able to hear it.

'Well?'

He leant down towards her, and Sophia turned her head to the side. 'But I don't want to kiss you. We're not married yet.'

He laughed again. 'You really are innocent, aren't you? But don't worry, I certainly won't be holding that against you. In fact, I rather like your demureness. It makes a refreshing change.'

He took a small step backwards. Sophia drew in a quick, relieved breath.

'I won't force you, Sophia. But if I am to marry you, I wish to know what I'm getting. I'll be giving

you a title. You must be aware of what an honour that
is. You'll be a duchess. I expect to get something in
return. I need to know that you are worthy of all that I
am bestowing upon you.'

He remained staring at her, as if expecting an answer. Sophia did not know what to say, so she merely
nodded.

'And a little kiss won't hurt anyone, will it?'

She shook her head, knowing that was the answer
he expected.

'By granting me a kiss, you will merely show me
how much you want to be my wife. That's not asking
too much, is it?'

She shook her head again as she continued to stare
up at him. He was a duke, so what he was saying must
be right, but it contradicted all that she had been told.
Her mother had not said he would expect her to kiss
him. Rather, she had always said never to kiss a man
before she married, and yet the Duke was saying he
wouldn't marry her unless she did kiss him. This entire courtship ritual was so perplexing, with the rules
seemingly changing constantly, and she hardly knew
what to think.

'Do you understand what I'm saying to you, Sophia?'

She shook her head slightly, then nodded and whispered, 'Yes.'

'You *are* an innocent, aren't you? Just as your
mother promised me. Even if you look like a tempt-
ress in that gown. That's going to make it even sweeter
when you do succumb.' He looked her slowly up and

down, his eyes lingering on her exposed décolletage. She resisted the temptation to cover her chest with her arms, certain that would not be what her mother meant by being amenable.

'Very sweet indeed.' His gaze returned to her face and his look hardened. 'But I won't wait for ever.' Once again, he took hold of her chin, more firmly than the last time, and lifted her head. 'I'm making allowances this time. I realise this is all new to you. That is part of your appeal. But next time I ask you to kiss me, I expect you to grant me my wish. Do you understand?'

Sophia nodded, hardly able to breathe.

'I'm not asking much. I just want you to express your gratitude for all I am doing for you and your family. Do you understand me?'

He waited for her answer.

'Yes,' she whispered, her throat dry.

He leant down and kissed her on the cheek, causing Sophia's body to go rigid.

'Think carefully about what I said, my dear. In future, if I want you to kiss me, I'll be expecting more than just obedience. I'll be anticipating some enthusiasm as well, otherwise I'll suspect you don't really want to be a duchess.'

He released her chin, took a step back and stared down at her. 'You are going to have to show me just how important it is for you to become a duchess and how much you appreciate what an honour it will be to marry a duke.'

With that, he turned and strolled down the stairs leading out into the garden and through to the street, where his carriage would be waiting, leaving a shaken and confused Sophia alone on the terrace.

Finally, Ethan made it back to the ballroom, glass of punch in hand. A quick trip to the supper room had turned into an ordeal. He'd been detained by one of the Duke of Ravenswood's friends, who had insisted on discussing an arrangement he had made with Ethan's brother for the repayment of a gambling debt. It was none of Ethan's business, but the man would not listen. In the end, Ethan had to all but push the man aside to get to the punch bowl.

Then, the moment he placed the ladle into the bowl, another of the Duke's boorish friends had upturned the table, sending the punch bowl, glasses and food crashing to the floor. Servants had sprung into action, removing the mat as quickly as possible, mopping up the spilled liquid, picking up shards of glass and setting the room to rights.

Another punch bowl had eventually been brought out, but it had all delayed his return.

'My apologies for taking so long, Mrs Cooper,' he said as he handed the lady the hard-won glass of punch.

'That's perfectly all right,' she said, placing the glass on a nearby table. 'It seems I'm no longer thirsty.'

Ethan suppressed a sigh of irritation. If she had known what he had gone through to get that damn punch, she would drink it with gratitude.

He looked around at the dancers.

'Where are Miss Cooper and Ravenswood? I can't see them on the dance floor.'

'The Duke escorted Sophia out onto the terrace. I suppose they wanted to get some air.' She smiled at him like a contented cat. 'Or perhaps to make a proposal.'

'And you left them alone together?' It was not Ethan's place to question Miss Cooper's mother, but such behaviour was surprising, to say the very least, particularly given the way Ravenswood had spoken about her daughter in front of Mrs Cooper. Had she forgotten the comments about not having to chase around town for what Miss Cooper could provide him, or his lewd references to elevated positions? Surely she knew her daughter was not safe with that man.

'Why should I mind them being alone together? He can hardly make his proposal in public, can he? And once they're married, they'll be alone together all the time.' She turned her back on Ethan as if his concerns for her daughter were of no consequence and began talking to a group of mothers.

'But they're not married yet,' Ethan mumbled under his breath. Blood pumping through his veins, his muscles tight, he rushed across the room towards the terrace doors. If the Duke was taking liberties with Miss Cooper, it would be the last thing he did. There would be no holding back this time. The man would feel the full extent of Ethan's rage.

He threw open the doors. The dimly lit terrace was empty. He looked back into the ballroom. Where had they gone? Where had the Duke taken her? Why had he been such a fool? He should have known that the Duke was up to something when his cronies waylaid him in the supper room. The mother and the Duke must be in on this. They must have conspired to keep him busy while he took Miss Cooper away to do heavens knew what.

Once again, he had let her down when she needed him.

'Lord Ethan.'

He turned his head and saw Miss Cooper, standing alone in a darkened corner.

He rushed to her and took hold of her hands. 'Are you all right? What happened? Where's the Duke?'

'I don't know where the Duke is. He left a few moments ago.' She pointed to the stairs leading off the terrace. 'And yes, I'm all right, thank you.' She stepped forward into the light. 'At least I think I'm all right.'

'What did he do to you?' he asked quietly through clenched teeth.

'He wanted to kiss me.'

'The bast…the blackguard. Believe me, he won't get away with this. I'll teach him a lesson he'll never forget.' He let go of her hands and turned to race down the stairs to find the Duke. Wherever he had fled to, Ethan would find him and unleash the full strength of his wrath on him.

She grabbed his arm to restrain him. 'No, really. It's all right. I'm all right. Please, Lord Ethan, calm down.'

*Calm down?* He turned to face her. What was wrong with her? Was she in shock? Had Ravenswood caused her to lose her sense of reason? He did not need to calm down. He needed to find Ravenswood and thrash the man within an inch of his life.

'Miss Cooper, I must…'

'You must do nothing,' she said, more firmly. 'The Duke did not hurt me. He wanted to kiss me, but he didn't force me. No harm has been done.'

Ethan stared at her, speechless.

'It is all right,' she repeated, her voice soothing, as if he was the one who needed to be comforted. 'As I said, I am perfectly all right. All that happened was the Duke told me he is considering asking for my hand in marriage so it would be all right if we kissed.'

'But he hasn't asked for your hand yet, has he?' Ethan was unsure what would be worse. That he had proposed and then asked for a kiss, or not proposed at all, but still expected her to kiss him.

'No, he didn't propose. He said he was considering it.' She drew in a deep breath and slowly exhaled. 'And that's where you might be able to help me.'

'Whatever you want I will do,' he said with relief. Finally, she was starting to see Ravenswood for who he was. Anything she wanted from him that would send that man on his way he would be more than happy about.

She drew in a slow breath, then looked up at him. Even in the dim light, he could see her cheeks were tinged with pink. 'After the Duke left, I had a chance to think.'

He nodded rapidly. This was good.

'I *do* want to become a duchess. It is what my father always wished for me, it's what my mother wants and it is what I want. But when the Duke asked me to kiss him, I must admit I was shocked.'

'Of course you were. The man is…'

'The man is a duke,' she said with some force, as if trying to convince a sceptical audience. 'And the man I wish to marry.'

'Miss Cooper. He tried to kiss you.'

'Yes. But he did not force me.'

How could she not see that he should not have even tried to kiss her at all, especially as he had not yet made a proposal of marriage? The man was beneath contempt.

'As I said, after he left, I had time to collect my thoughts,' she continued. 'And I've come to a conclusion that I believe would be the best solution to my problem.'

'Which problem? What solution?' Ethan knew exactly what the problem was—Ravenswood—and what the solution was. Get rid of the man. But he wanted her to say it. To tell him now that the Duke had revealed his true character, and she never wanted to see that odious man again.

She smiled, then bit her bottom lip. 'Well, the Duke tried to kiss me but I wouldn't let him.'

He exhaled, slowly and loudly, trying to control his temper. 'And quite rightly so.'

'He said next time he tries, he expects me to allow him, and he wants me to show a bit more enthusiasm.'

'Next time he tries you should slap his face.'

'No. I *do* want to marry the Duke.'

'Even though he...'

'Yes, even after he said he wanted to kiss me. As I said, he did not force me.'

She kept saying that, as if the lack of physical force

made it all right, but he should never have put her in this position in the first place, should never have made such demands of her. 'But, Miss Cooper…'

She held up her hand to stem his protests. 'Please, Lord Ethan. You said you were my friend, so as my friend I entreat you to listen to what I have to say.'

Anger still coursed through him, but she was right. His anger was not helping. He should listen to her. She had been through a trauma. She needed his comfort, his reassurance. He could deal with the Duke at a later time. So he reined in his fury and nodded to indicate she should continue.

She drew in another deep breath, then looked back up at him, her big blue eyes pleading for him to understand. 'I have decided that if the Duke asks me to kiss him, then I will. But there's another problem.'

Ethan stared at her as if she had lost all reason. Of course there was a problem. There were countless problems. More problems than Ethan could list, the biggest one being that Ravenswood was a cad of the worst kind and she should not even be thinking of kissing him.

'Don't look at me like that,' she said. 'I know this is rather forward of me, but you said you are my friend and I could ask you for help any time I need it.'

He took her hands once again. 'Of course, Miss Cooper. And I mean it. Anything. You can ask me to do anything.'

*If you want me to string Ravenswood up by the ankles, I will do it. If you want him to feel the force of my fists, I'll gladly do that for you as well.*

'I need to practise how to kiss, so I don't get it wrong. Lord Ethan, will you please kiss me?'

He stared at her, knowing he had heard correctly but doubting his own ears. 'You want me to kiss you?' His voice sounded as if someone was trying to throttle him.

'I know it's a strange request. But if I don't kiss the Duke back next time, he won't propose. Mother said I should do whatever he wants. She said that he would know what was right and proper, therefore, if I am to become a duchess, I have to do what he asks. I have to kiss him, but I need to practise first. This time he took me by surprise. Next time I must be prepared, know what to expect so I don't push him away.'

'Miss Cooper, if you want to push him away, then just push him away. You don't have to kiss him if you don't want to.'

'But I want to be a duchess,' she said quietly.

'If you want to be a duchess, then you can't kiss other men. If the Duke found out, it would give him good reason *not* to marry you.'

*Would that be such a bad thing?*

He looked down into her pleading eyes. If the Duke knew he had kissed her, would that taint her in his eyes? Most probably. It would certainly reduce the chance of his proposing. That had to be a good thing, and all he had to do was something immensely appealing. Take her in his arms, kiss those lush lips and save her from the horror of a miserable marriage.

He immediately dismissed that thought. Kissing her would also mean Miss Cooper would be less likely to get a proposal from any other man, and worse than that, if word got out, he would be the one expected to marry her. And that was something he most certainly did not want.

'No. This is wrong.'

'But, Lord Ethan, I feel safe with you. And you did say you were my friend. You said I could always come to you when I needed help. Well, I need your help now.'

This conversation was becoming ever more bizarre. No woman had ever wanted to kiss him because he was *safe*. Nor had he ever before found himself in the absurd situation of formulating arguments for not kissing a beautiful, available young woman.

'But what of your mother? She will be mortified if she finds out,' he continued, still struggling to find a reason to not do something he knew would give him enormous physical pleasure.

'Then I won't tell her. I didn't tell her about us escaping from my lady's maid when we were walking in the park, and I didn't tell her about getting caught out in the rain. What she doesn't know won't hurt her.'

She gave a small, embarrassed giggle and moved towards him. 'So, what do we do? Do I just let you kiss me or am I expected to do something in return?' She tilted back her head. 'How am I supposed to show enthusiasm? And what happens to our noses? Do they get in the way?'

Ethan looked down at her in the subdued light. She was so beautiful. Would it hurt to give her one little kiss? No one would know. No one would be hurt. His gaze lingered on those waiting lips, those soft, luscious, lovely lips. What would they feel like? What would she taste like? Just one kiss. That was all.

He lifted his gaze away from temptation and took a step back. No, of course he couldn't. She was an innocent, naïve young woman. She didn't know what she was doing. The mere fact that she was making this extraordinary request showed how innocent and artless she was.

'No, Miss Cooper. You should save your kisses for the man you marry.'

*Just make sure it is not Ravenswood.*

'But the man I want to marry is the one who wants me to kiss him, and I don't know how.' Her voice was taking on a petulant note. 'Please, Lord Ethan, I need your help. So, what do you do with your arms? Do we hold each other the way we did when we danced? Like this?' She stepped forward and placed a hand on his shoulder, close to his neck, tilted back her head and waited.

All the reasons why he should not kiss her jostled round inside his head like a turbulent cacophony of shouting voices, each one fighting for his attention. While his mind fought one battle, his body refused to listen to reason. He focused on those soft, waiting lips. She parted them slightly, and he failed to stop a groan of raw lust from escaping his own lips. He had never wanted to kiss a woman more than he wanted to kiss her. He had never wanted a woman more than he wanted Sophia Cooper.

She rose up on her tiptoes, her lips lightly stroking his. 'Is this what you do?' she murmured, her voice husky, her soft breath caressing his cheek. 'Show me, please.'

'God, help me,' Ethan murmured, knowing that no one could help him now, not even the Almighty. He was completely lost. He had to have her. Had to kiss her.

'Sophia, are you out here?' Mrs Cooper burst through the doors, bringing the noise of the ballroom with her and causing them to jump apart.

'Lord Ethan. What are you doing here? And where's the Duke?'

'I don't know, Mother. He left a little while ago.'

She looked around, as if expecting to find the Duke hiding in a dark corner.

'The Duke has gone, Mrs Cooper,' Ethan said, pleased that his firm voice did not betray the guilt he was feeling. 'But Miss Cooper should never have been left alone with a man.'

*Including me.*

Mrs Cooper gave a dismissive sniff and turned to her daughter. 'When did the Duke leave? I hope you did nothing to upset him, Sophia.'

'The Duke left just before Lord Ethan arrived.'

She looked Ethan up and down, her disdain unconcealed.

'And was the Duke happy when he left?' she asked, turning her attention to Miss Cooper.

'Yes, Mother.'

'There are more important issues here than Ravenswood's happiness,' Ethan said, hardly able to believe that Mrs Cooper was more concerned with how the Duke felt than for her own daughter's safety.

'Quite right,' she said, nodding vigorously.

Finally, the woman was seeing sense.

'You should not be alone out here with this man. It just won't do. What if the Duke was to hear? It would ruin your chances.' She scowled at Ethan, grabbed her daughter's arm and all but pulled her off the terrace and back into the ballroom.

Ethan's hands curled up in frustration. He paced up and down the terrace, while he mentally argued with Mrs Cooper. That woman was impossible. She was more than happy to leave Miss Cooper alone with that reprobate duke, and yet had dragged her away from Ethan as if her daughter's virtue was under threat from *him*.

*She's much safer with me than she would ever be with that pig of a man!* Ethan wanted to shout to Mrs Cooper's retreating back.

He stopped pacing. His fists released and his shoulders slumped. Was that entirely true? Could he really be angry with Mrs Cooper? He had been about to kiss her daughter. She was right to take her daughter away from him. He gripped the stone balustrade and stared out at the dark trees and shrubs, outlined by the light of the moon.

What sort of lowlife was he? He had been going to kiss her to prepare her for Ravenswood. He was despicable. Worse than despicable.

Miss Cooper wanted to marry Ravenswood. She had made that clear. She was even prepared to kiss another man so she could give Ravenswood what he wanted.

While he despised the Duke for putting her in such a

compromising position, Ethan was also no better than that reprobate.

He had wanted to kiss her, even though he knew it was wrong for so many reasons. His body had been craving the touch of her lips. He had been desperate to feel her soft body up against his. To taste her, to touch her, and that had overridden all sense of morality and decency.

No, he was wrong to think he was no better than the Duke. He was worse. At least Ravenswood was offering marriage. That was more than Ethan was doing. He had just wanted to kiss her, to caress her, and, if he was honest with himself, to do so much more, as much as that naïve young woman would allow him.

He had thought himself to be her saviour, her noble Sir Galahad. Instead, he had tried to take advantage of her trusting nature and inexperience to satisfy his own lust. She still needed saving, from her mother, from Ravenswood, and now, it seemed, from him.

## Chapter Seven

Sophia's mother kept a tight grip on her arm as they walked back into the ballroom. The orchestra was still playing, couples were still dancing, groups of mothers were still standing on the edge of the dance floor gossiping. Everyone was oblivious to the drama that had just taken place on the terrace.

Rather than release her arm, her mother continued walking, taking Sophia with her, out through the ballroom, up the stairs and into the corridor.

'Oh, are we leaving already?' Sophia said, looking towards the ballroom, from where the strains of a waltz could still be heard.

Her mother told a passing servant to retrieve their shawls and to arrange for their carriage to be ready to take them home.

'There's hardly any point staying now, is there? The Duke has left.' She sent Sophia a calculating look. 'And thank goodness for that. Hopefully, he won't hear that you were alone with Lord Ethan. Goodness knows what might happen if he did. He might give up on you altogether.'

For a moment, a strange sensation washed over Sophia, as if the tension gripping her body floated away. *He might give up altogether.* Would that be so bad? She shook her head to drive out that foolish notion. It *would* be bad, very bad. She wanted to marry a duke and be a duchess. She wanted to make all her dreams come true. It was what both her parents wished for her. If the Duke gave up on her, it would ruin everything.

'Your carriage is waiting at the front of the house,' the servant informed them with a bow as he handed them their shawls.

Her mother remained silent as they left the Wiltons' home and entered their carriage, but once they were travelling through the still crowded streets she turned to face Sophia, her eyes intense. 'Right. I want to know everything the Duke said and did, and I want to know everything you said to him.'

Heat rose in Sophia's cheeks. She had no desire to share such an uncomfortable exchange with her mother.

'This is no time for your blushes,' her mother said. 'You have a rival now. We need to secure a proposal from the Duke, or at the very least he needs to make it public that he is courting you, before that Lucretia Hawksbury and her family make their move.'

'That's not very romantic, Mother,' Sophia whispered.

'Don't be ridiculous. This is no time to get sentimental. Now, what happened out on the terrace? Did he propose? Will he be coming to visit me to ask for your hand?'

'No.' Sophia shrugged. 'He did talk about marriage, but he made no promises.'

'Damn.'

Sophia stared at her mother, shocked that she should use such language.

'I suppose it's good that he was talking about marriage, though. And I didn't see him take that Hawksbury girl out onto the terrace, so presumably he wasn't discussing marriage with her.' She nodded several times, as if to confirm this was a good sign. 'Nor did he dance with her, not even once. It's all looking very promising. So, if he didn't propose, what exactly did he say to you?'

The heat in Sophia's cheeks intensified.

'Well?' her mother insisted. 'Come on. Out with it.'

'He said he was considering courting me, and, if by the end of the Season we prove to be compatible, marrying me.'

'Excellent.' Her mother nodded rapidly, then sat forward on the carriage bench, her eyes fixed on Sophia, seemingly aware that she was holding back something. 'What else?'

'And he tried to kiss me.'

Her mother tilted her head, her eyes assessing. 'Tried? What do you mean, tried? Does that mean you didn't let him?'

'No. I told him we should wait until we're married.'

Her mother's lips pinched more tightly together, and she inhaled quickly and loudly.

'I'm sorry, Mother. I didn't know what to do,' she said in a hurry, desperate to assuage her mother's anger. 'I've never kissed a man before and he took me by surprise. And you'd always said I should never kiss a man before I marry.' She hated to see her mother so disappointed.

'Mmm, hopefully the Duke will realise your reticence was just coyness and good breeding. Was he angry with you? What did he say?'

'No, he wasn't angry. He said he would forgive me this time as my reluctance was due to my innocence, but he said next time I should be more compliant and show more enthusiasm.' She tried not to cringe at the memory. 'And that I must show him just how much I want to be a duchess.'

Her mother smiled and nodded slowly. 'That's excellent, Sophia. I believe you've played it perfectly, my girl. He's not angry, but he knows you are a sweet young thing who has never been kissed before. Plus, he's said he's still interested. Next time, let him. Do you understand?'

She swallowed down her discomfort. She knew she would have to kiss the Duke. He expected it of her, as did her mother, and it was the only way she was going to become a duchess and fulfil everyone's dreams.

The only person who didn't expect her to kiss the Duke was Lord Ethan. He was the only one who had said she should do what she wanted to, and no one should expect her to do otherwise. But he had to be wrong. Her mother would not make her do something that was wrong, nor would the Duke. After all, he was a *duke*. Men like him set the standard on what was right and proper. So it must be acceptable for her to kiss him before they married. And it should be something that she wanted to do.

'Well?' her mother asked.

Sophia nodded. 'Yes, Mother.'

She was sure she would not be so reticent about kissing him if she had practised with Lord Ethan. And if her mother hadn't barged in when she had, then tonight she would have had her first kiss. That little thrill coursed through her body again, the one that had possessed her when she had asked Lord Ethan to kiss her. And he almost had. He had been so tantalisingly close. His lips had almost touched hers. She had felt the roughness of his skin against hers, the warmth of his body, so near to her own.

'But don't be too forward.' Her mother's voice snapped her out of her reminiscence. 'Just follow his lead and let him do whatever he wants.'

Sophia's heart skipped a beat. If Lord Ethan had kissed her, the command to follow his lead would not have to be made. She would have done so happily, wherever it took them.

'But don't show too much enthusiasm to begin with, so he knows it's your first kiss.' She narrowed her eyes. 'It will be your first kiss, won't it?'

'Yes, of course, Mother.' Her cheeks burned brighter, and she moved awkwardly on the carriage bench. Once again, she wasn't telling the entire truth, but then, nor was she exactly lying. She may have asked Lord Ethan to kiss her, but it had not happened. Even if he had kissed her, she doubted she would have told her mother. As she had said to Lord Ethan, what her mother didn't know surely would not hurt her. And she only wanted to kiss Lord Ethan to prepare herself for kissing the man she was to marry. Her intentions had been good, hadn't they?

She bit her bottom lip, not entirely sure who she was lying to, her mother or herself.

'When the Duke kisses you, it would be best if you have a witness, just to be on the safe side. Someone of equal stature to the Duke. If someone else sees him kiss you, then he will *have* to marry you. Although I'm sure, as he is a gentleman of the highest order, he wouldn't expect a kiss without a proposal, a witness would definitely seal the deal.'

Sophia's mouth almost dropped open. Had she heard correctly? Did she really want someone to watch them doing something so intimate as kissing? It was bad enough that she had to let the Duke kiss her, but to have someone witness it would be mortifying.

'I don't think I can do that, Mother,' she whispered, surprised that she was contradicting her mother's wishes but knowing she had to. 'I don't think I can kiss the Duke while someone else watches.'

'All right, my dear,' she said, gently stroking her arm. 'You really are sweet. Just make sure you let him kiss you the next time he asks and let him know that you are doing so because he will be marrying you.'

They arrived home and Sophia made her excuses to retire. It had been a long, bewildering day, and she needed to be alone.

Her mother gently kissed her on the cheek. 'Yes, you get some rest, and dream of kissing your handsome duke and of your future life as a duchess.

Maggie helped her out of her gown and into her nightdress, then released her woven locks and brushed out her hair.

'Did you have an enjoyable evening, madam?' Maggie asked.

'Yes, thank you, Maggie, but I'll finish up.' She took the brush from her lady's maid's hand. 'You can retire for the night.' Confused and exhausted, Sophia had no energy left for maintaining a sense of excitement in front of her lady's maid, who was sure to report everything Sophia did and said back to her mother.

Maggie bobbed a curtsey and wished Sophia goodnight.

As she slowly stroked the brush over her long hair, she tried to make sense of the evening. She agreed with her mother that it was essential she kiss the Duke of Ravenswood should he ask again, and for her to do everything she could to please him. Too much depended on his wanting her to be his bride. And it was especially important she show him what a good wife she would be, now that she had a rival.

But how was she to show enthusiasm for something she was reluctant to do? Her mother had said it was only natural to fear the man you were to marry, but it didn't feel natural. And she didn't fear Lord Ethan. If her mother told her to kiss Lord Ethan, to show enthusiasm, she would not be so conflicted.

She had told Lord Ethan she needed to practise kissing as it would prepare her for kissing the Duke, but that was less than half true. The full truth was, she *wanted* to kiss him. She wanted Lord Ethan to be the first man to kiss her. It was so wrong, so very wrong. She intended to marry the Duke, but it was Lord Ethan she wanted to kiss. Everyone said she was an innocent young woman, but if they could see into her heart, read her thoughts, they would not think her quite so innocent.

And her claim that she felt safe with Lord Ethan had also been less than half true.

Safe was not what she felt when she asked him to kiss her. The fervent heat that had enveloped her was not safe, nor was the tingling that erupted deep within her. She had said she wanted him to show her how to kiss because he was her friend, but she did not want a friendly kiss. She wanted to feel his lips on hers. Her body had been calling to him, wanting him to touch her, to stroke her, to caress her.

And yet it was the Duke she intended to marry, a man she would rather not kiss. She placed the hairbrush on her dressing table, crossed the room and climbed into bed. It seemed there was a sinful side to her nature she had not known existed.

It was a side of her nature she would need to control.

'I want to marry the Duke. I want to be a duchess,' she told the empty room. As disappointing as it was, it was good that Lord Ethan had not kissed her. She had to save her kisses for the Duke. She did not need to practise. The Duke would teach her what to do, as was proper.

Her mind wandered back to dancing with Lord

Ethan, to being held in his arms, to feeling his body against hers, and that delicious tingling she knew she should not be feeling took hold of her body.

If only she could feel this way when the Duke danced with her.

Why she felt that way about Lord Ethan and not the Duke she did not know. They were both handsome men, but there was something about Lord Ethan that made him special, some quality that made it enchanting to be held by him. When she was dancing with the Duke, her body did not thrum with excitement, her skin did not feel alive. There was no temptation to lean in towards him and press her body against his.

Somehow, she was going to have to learn to feel that way about the Duke. Too much was dependent on his being pleased with her. As her mother said, he still might reject her. He might pursue the American heiress instead. That would disappoint her mother and be an insult to her father's memory.

She had to put Lord Ethan out of her mind. Hugging herself as she lay in bed, she fought not to think of him, not to imagine him kissing her, but even trying *not* to think of kissing him caused a delicious thrill to ripple through her.

*If only Lord Ethan were a duke. If only he wanted to marry me, everything would be all right*, was the last thought she had before she drifted off to sleep.

## Chapter Eight

'You? You're going to the opera?' Jake said, smirking, when Ethan entered the drawing room dressed in his formal evening wear. 'Who is she and when are you going to introduce this young lady to the family?'

'There is no young lady. I will be escorting Mother, and I believe some of her friends will join us.'

Jake looked him up and down, his eyebrows raised. 'So, you're going to the opera because you've suddenly discovered a love of high culture? I thought the music hall and the Gaiety Theatre were more your taste. What was the name of that little chorus girl you were seeing?'

Jake waited, that annoying smirk still distorting his lips.

'I don't remember.'

'Poor Annette,' Jake said, with mock concern. 'Has your new young lady driven all thoughts of her out of your head?'

Ethan scowled at his brother, annoyed that he was right. He had not thought of any other woman since meeting Miss Cooper, but that meant nothing. 'All right, yes, there is a young lady I'm expecting to see at the opera.' He looked towards the door, as if willing his mother to hurry so they could end this uncomfortable conversation.

'I knew it.' Jake's smirk changed to a satisfied grin. 'Luther now owes me twenty pounds.'

He turned to face his brother, shaking his head in disbelief. 'Is there nothing you don't bet on?'

'I only bet on sure things. And the way you've been acting lately, I was sure there had to be a young lady. When it comes to gambling, I rarely lose.'

'Isn't that what every gambler thinks? If they expected to lose, they wouldn't gamble.'

'Don't change the subject.' Jake stood up and poured himself another brandy. 'I want you to tell me all about this young lady and what your intentions are towards her.' He failed at keeping his face serious and that facetious grin reappeared. 'I certainly hope they're honourable.'

'Despite claiming you only bet on sure things, you are not entirely correct this time, so you'll be taking money off Luther under false pretences. Yes, there is a young lady, but it's not what you think.' Ethan had no idea what Jake thought. In fact, he didn't know precisely what *he* thought. All he knew was he thought of Miss Cooper more than he knew he should, and it wasn't just her perilous situation that occupied his mind. He frowned as an image of her waiting lips once again invaded his thoughts, then coughed and flicked his gloves against his thigh to drive out that memory.

'I'm merely trying to save a young woman from a love-less marriage.'

Jake laughed, nearly choking on his brandy. 'Then you're going to have a very busy Season indeed. Most debutantes end up making a loveless marriage.'

That was something he could not dispute. 'The mother of the young lady in question is trying to marry her off to the Duke of Ravenswood.'

'That cad.' Jake frowned and took a seat. 'Let's hope the mother isn't wanting to marry her daughter to him for his money. His gambling debts to me alone are all but immeasurable, and I'm not the only one he's in debt to. Apparently, he's in hock to moneylenders the length and breadth of the country, and I hear his country estate is mortgaged up to the hilt.'

'Her family has money.'

Jake nodded, aware that his brother's statement explained a lot. 'I take it her father has no title.'

'No, and unfortunately, the young lady has no idea what Ravenswood is really like. The mother does but doesn't care.'

'So, the Dukedom is the only attraction, then?'

'Hmm.'

'And I take it Ravenswood is interested in the girl?'

'Hmm.'

'Silly question. If the family's got money and they're after a title, then of course he's interested.' Jake took another drink from his brandy balloon, then placed it on the side table. 'Well, brother, it's not going to be easy. If the mother is chasing a title for her daughter, and she's got a duke on the hook, the only way you'll

save her is to replace Ravenswood with another duke.'
He gave a small laugh. 'Perhaps you need to have a
word with Luther and see if he wants to marry her.'

Ethan knew that could only be said in jest. Luther
was as reluctant to marry as Jake and Ethan were, but
his eldest brother knew his duty. Eventually he would
have to marry and father an heir for the Dukedom. But
when he chose a bride she would come from one of
the most distinguished families in England, one with
a similar lineage to his own. Unlike the Duke of Ravenswood, the Rosemonts did not need the money that
an heiress would bring with her.

Luther was also proving to be very fussy and had
not yet found his perfect duchess. Which suited both
of his younger brothers. Until the Duke married, none
of the Society mothers would be wasting their time on
either the spare or the spare's spare.

'But that doesn't explain your sudden interest in
high culture,' Jake said.

'I heard at my club that Ravenswood plans to escort
the young lady and her mother to the opera tonight. I
want to be present to keep my eye on them, and to ensure nothing untoward happens.'

'How very noble of you,' Jake said, looking at Ethan
sideways. 'And you have no interest in the young lady
yourself?'

'None whatsoever, but she does not deserve to be
forced into the arms of a man like Ravenswood.'

'I wish you good luck, although I suspect you're
fighting a lost cause. Debutantes tend to do what they're
told, and if a marriage has been arranged, then I don't

believe you or anyone else will be able to stop it.' Jake picked up his glass and downed the last of his brandy. 'And just to make you feel even worse, I should remind you that while you're fighting your losing battle and being bored out of your mind at the opera I'll be having the time of my life at Lady Sudbury's party. The Prince of Wales is expected to attend, so you know what that means—plenty of actresses and other young ladies looking for a good time. And if a young lady is after a good time, I feel it is my duty as a gentleman to provide it.'

Jake stood up, picked up his hat and gloves and patted his brother on the shoulder. 'When you've finished trying to save your damsel in distress, perhaps you'd like to join us. Lady Lydia Pearson was asking after you just the other night and I believe she will be there as well.'

'Yes, perhaps.' Ethan looked at the door once more, anxious that his mother hurry up. He was unsure if he was fighting a losing battle or not, but all would certainly be lost if they did not make it to the opera house in time.

'Did you not hear what I said?' Jake asked, his voice rising. 'Lady Lydia Pearson was asking after you. If that particular beauty had been asking after me, you wouldn't find me going to the opera instead of a party.'

'Hmm,' Ethan replied. 'What? Yes, enjoy yourself tonight and give my regards to… Who did you say? Lydia Sampson?'

Jake shook his head, still smiling. 'And you claim I only half won that bet. You're lost, little brother, completely lost.'

* * *

Sophia readied herself for the evening ahead. Her preparations did not just include dressing in another elegant gown. It didn't just mean sitting still while her hair was ornately styled. She had to prepare herself for what might happen tonight. It was all but inevitable that the Duke would try to kiss her again and this time she would have to respond in an appropriate manner.

She needed to show excitement, enthusiasm, girlish glee.

Suppressing another sigh, she stared at herself in the mirror. At the beginning of the Season Sophia had loved dressing up in such finery, had anticipated the dancing and flirting with such excitement. During her fittings at the dressmaker's, she had particularly loved this beautiful, swirling, pastel blue gown, with its delicately embroidered dark blue flowers winding their way down the skirt and onto the flowing train. The gossamer-fine lace straps that left her shoulders all but bare had seemed both feminine and just a bit risqué. But now it was as if she had been packaged up for the Duke's approval.

As her mother said, over and over, she needed to show the Duke that she was a better prospect than the stunningly attractive Lucretia Hawksbury. So, for tonight, her mother had selected a dress that revealed even more of Sophia's skin than the dress she had worn to Lord and Lady Wilton's ball. It was as if the gown was saying, look at what is on offer, look at what is yours for the taking.

She slowly released her held breath and tried to recapture the sense of anticipation she had so easily lost. Before her first ball, such thoughts would not have occurred to her. She would have seen this gown as a beautiful creation and would have been longing to wear it for the Duke. Dressed in such a manner, she would have been hoping that he would approve and admire her, would see her as a perfect duchess.

She practised smiling at her reflection, trying to keep the strain out of her expression. After tonight, she might be engaged to a duke, or at the very least officially be courted by him. She stood up and moved to the full-length mirror and practised what she had learnt in her deportment lessons. Head held high, shoulders back, chest out, just like a duchess.

She would soon be the Duke's betrothed and the envy of all. She would be a woman on her way to the very top of Society. It was the highest achievement for any debutante, and all the other mothers would envy hers. Despite having no title, despite coming from the provinces, both Sophia and her mother would be the biggest success of the Season, and no one would look down on either of them ever again. She had reason to be proud, reason to be happy.

'You *are* happy,' she told her reflection. 'You are about to achieve all your dreams, make your mother proud of you and honour your father's memory. Of course you are happy.'

The smile still held firmly in place, she picked up her gloves and fan and walked out of her bedroom, down the stairs, and joined her mother and the Duke in the drawing room.

They were deep in conversation, a conversation that immediately came to a halt at her entrance. The Duke stood and smiled at her. Her lips quivered, and she lowered her gaze. He was a duke, she reminded herself. She was the luckiest debutante of the Season. So many other young women would love to be in her situation. She raised her eyes and smiled back at him, repeating to herself that she was indeed grateful that it was her that he had chosen.

'You look stunning tonight,' the Duke said. 'Like a real duchess.'

Her mother beamed at her and Sophia wanted to feel pleased at the compliment. After all, what greater compliment was there than for a duke to tell her that she, little Sophia Cooper, looked like a duchess?

He took her arm and led her and her mother out through the door to his waiting carriage.

'Are you excited, Sophia?' her mother asked as they took their seats.

'Yes, Mother.'

Her mother's smile died, and she sent Sophia a quick glare of disapproval. What had she done wrong now? Had she shown too much enthusiasm, not enough enthusiasm? Been too modest or not modest enough?

Her mother had reiterated many times how significant this night at the opera was. She would be sitting in the Duke's box, where everyone would be able to see them. He would be sending out a message to everyone assembled that she was the young lady he was interested in. It was only a matter of time before he asked for her hand, and her mother believed there was a very good chance that tonight would be the night.

It must be the lack of enthusiasm her mother was objecting to.

'Oh, yes, very excited. Thank you so much, Your Grace, for the invitation,' Sophia added, causing her mother to once again smile in approval.

'My pleasure,' the Duke responded, lightly patting Sophia on the knee before tapping his silver-topped cane on the roof to signal to the driver.

Her mother continued smiling, either not noticing or choosing to ignore the overly familiar and decidedly inappropriate manner in which the Duke had just touched her. It was obvious that, unlike Sophia, her mother did not need to force her smile and kept looking at Sophia with such affection and admiration. She was making her mother so happy, and that alone should please her. Her mother had told her that raising a daughter who became a duchess would be such a momentous achievement for any woman. It would reward her mother for all the hard work she had endured, particularly since she became a widow two years ago.

Sophia forced her smile to widen and her lips not to quiver each time she looked at the Duke. In her mind, she went over and over her mother's instructions.

*'If he kisses you again, act coyly to begin with, as is fitting for a modest young woman, but do not object. Then gradually show more and more enthusiasm. Follow his lead and let him know with little sighs that you are enjoying what he is doing. And under no circumstances put up any resistance to anything he does.'*

Her mother hadn't said so, but Sophia knew, if she was to get through tonight, to endure his kisses, she would have to show no fear. Too much was riding on her pleasing the Duke.

Her mother and the Duke made polite conversation throughout the journey, but Sophia's stomach was too tied up in knots, her mind too baffled by what she was supposed to do, how she was supposed to act and what might happen this evening, for her to add anything to the conversation. Not that either her mother or the Duke appeared to notice or to care. It seemed all they required of her was to look pretty and to smile agreeably.

They arrived at the opera house, and the other drivers pulled back to allow the carriage bearing the Duke's crest through the crowded lane. The Duke helped them out of the carriage and took Sophia's arm while her mother walked in ahead of them, her head held high as if she was the one who was about to become a duchess.

Despite her nerves, Sophia gave a small gasp of genuine pleasure when they entered the building, and the Duke patted her hand in approval. A crystal chandelier lit up the foyer as brightly as any ballroom and sent light flickering around the marble walls and columns, creating an enchanting effect.

They made their way through the crowds of women dressed in an array of colourful gowns and men in formal attire of black evening suits, white shirts and bow ties. The crowds parted to let them through and some of the women gave quick curtseys as the Duke passed. With each acknowledgement, Sophia's mother's head seemed to rise higher in the air, until she was looking down her nose at everyone, including Sophia.

The Duke led them up the curving marble staircase, along the corridor and into his private box, which had an unimpeded view of the stage. Sophia looked around in wonder, but her mother took her seat with an air of nonchalance, as if such privileged seating was something she accepted as a matter of course and was no great honour.

'Are you happy to be here, my dear?' the Duke asked.

'Yes, Your Grace. The opera house is magnificent.' Sophia did not have to force a smile as she admired the luxurious auditorium, taking in the plush red seating and the sumptuous cream-and-gold walls painted with elaborate scenes featuring Greek and Roman gods and goddesses. The large ornate dome in the roof created the effect that they were in a house of worship, a place where the gods were about to perform for their entertainment.

She looked down at the stage, hidden behind voluminous maroon-and-gold velvet curtains, and anticipated the magic that was about to take place. Her glance swept around the audience. People were seating themselves in the chairs below, and many of them peered up to see which members of the nobility were occupying the boxes above them. She followed their eyes to see who else was lucky enough to have their own private box. Her sweeping gaze came to an abrupt halt. Across from them, in the facing box, was Lord Ethan, and he was staring straight at her.

Her breath caught, heat exploded on her cheeks and

her heart seemed to cease beating in her chest. She had not expected him to be attending the opera. Nor had she expected seeing him again would have such a profound effect on her.

Sophia did not know whether to be pleased or disconcerted by his presence. It was as if she now had an audience for her own performance, one where she had to play the role of a besotted young woman, one who was excited by the prospect of the Duke's courting her, one hoping with all her heart that she would one day be his duchess.

She drew in a slow breath and forced herself to look away. It was *not* a performance. She *did* want to marry the Duke. She *did* want to be a duchess. It had been her dream for many years. It was her mother's dream for her. It was what her beloved father had always wanted for her. Lord Ethan's presence made no difference at all. She flicked another glance in his direction. He was still staring at her. Did he disapprove of what she was doing? What she was about to do?

She lowered her eyes. Perhaps his presence had nothing to do with her at all, and it was a mere coincidence that he was here tonight. And anyway, she should not be thinking about another man. Not when she was seated beside the man she hoped to marry.

The orchestra struck up the overture, the crowd ceased their chatter and the curtain rose. Sophia tried to focus on the performers. She knew what she was watching was sublime, but she could not concentrate. Her attention kept being drawn to the man seated across the opera house, and he seemed to be spending more time watching her than the men and women who were singing their hearts out below them.

Why was he here if it wasn't to watch the opera? Was he acting as some sort of guardian angel, wanting to protect her from the Duke? But what was he trying to protect her from? From an eminently suitable marriage? From reaching the very pinnacle of British Society? From fulfilling all her dreams, and her parents' aspirations for her? She was so close to achieving them. He should be happy for her and not looking so worried.

She could only hope that neither the Duke nor her mother noticed how distracted she was. Her mother was focused on the performance below, looking down at the singers, her chin raised as if to demonstrate her superiority. The Duke appeared somewhat bored and restless, and several times he removed his fob watch from his pocket and tried to see the time in the dim lighting.

The curtain fell for the interval, the gas lights illuminated the auditorium, and conversation and movement erupted from the audience. From the volume of the babble and the smiles on the faces below her, it was obvious they had just witnessed something impressive. But Sophia had missed it all.

While her mother enthused to the Duke over the singers, the costumes and the scenery, Sophia sat quietly, unable to contribute any comments about a performance she had hardly seen. But once again, no one appeared to notice or care that she was quiet, presumably interpreting her silence as acceptable modesty. They would not know that she was too aware of the man watching her from across the theatre to take an interest in what they were saying.

'Perhaps you'd like to stretch your legs and join me for a drink before the performance begins again,' the Duke said, interrupting Sophia's thoughts.

'Oh, isn't the performance about to begin now?' Down in the auditorium, the patrons were returning to their seats in anticipation of the next act.

'Go, go,' her mother said, waving her fan at the door. 'You'll be back in plenty of time.'

The Duke stood up and held out his hand, so Sophia stood and allowed him to escort her out of the box. He placed his arm around her waist, holding her firmly against him, and led her along the corridor.

'Shouldn't we be going the other way?' She looked over her shoulder to where men in livery were still distributing glasses of champagne to the few remaining people milling around the foyer.

'No, we're going the right way, my dear,' the Duke said. 'We need some privacy for what I wish to do.'

'Oh!' she exclaimed as he pulled back a curtain and led her into an alcove.

'Has your mother had a word with you since we last spoke at the ball? Has she told you I intend to make you my bride?'

'Oh, yes, she has spoken to me.' Sophia was unsure whether he had just made a proposal and whether she had just accepted it.

'Good. And I believe she made it clear how you should behave. We're not going to have a repeat of that silliness at Lord and Lady Wilton's ball, are we?'

Sophia's heart quickened and her stomach clenched tighter. She closed her eyes briefly and tried to relax.

'Well, are we?'

She opened her eyes just as he closed the curtains, shutting them into the confined space. He stared at her, waiting.

She nodded and tried to send him a smile but had to bite her bottom lip to stop it trembling.

'Good girl.' He took a step towards her.

Sophia told herself not to be afraid. This was what she wanted. What she had always wanted. She just had to show the Duke how much she wished to be a duchess. Hadn't her mother told her repeatedly that it was a young woman's duty to be obedient to her father and when she married to be obedient to her husband? Now was the time to prove to the Duke that she would be a dutiful wife, that she would be exactly what he needed in a duchess.

'So, are you going to let me kiss you?'

Her body stiffened further. She swallowed to relieve her tight, dry throat, trying to remember her mother's instructions. Follow his lead. Do what he commands. Be compliant but show enthusiasm.

'You're nervous. That's to be expected,' he said, his voice quiet. 'But you don't have to be nervous. One day we'll be man and wife. You want that, don't you?'

She nodded. Of course she wanted that. She just wished she didn't have to prove it, right here and right now.

'Good girl. And you do look lovely tonight, Sophia,' he said, his gaze raking over her, then lingering on her breasts. 'I take it you dressed like that to please me, so I could see what a lovely, fresh young thing you are.'

Sophia swallowed again but said nothing.

He moved closer. She resisted the temptation to take a step backwards.

'I know you think this is all rather bold, but we are to marry, so we are doing nothing wrong.'

She looked at the flimsy curtain. He followed her gaze and laughed. 'Don't worry. No one will see us here, my dear, so you have nothing to worry about.' He looked her up and down once more. 'We are guaranteed privacy. I'm a duke. No one would dare interrupt us.' His gaze moved from her décolletage back to her face. 'I believe your mother has informed you there is nothing wrong with kissing a man if he intends to marry you and she has instructed you on how you should respond. I believe she has told you to do everything I ask of you.'

She nodded.

'And you wouldn't want to disobey your mother, would you?'

Before she could answer, he leant towards her. His lips touched hers, hard and dry. Hadn't her mother said it would be acceptable if she was coy and reserved to begin with? Thank goodness for that. Sophia's body remained ramrod straight, her lips tightly closed, her breath held, giving her no other choice but to be coy and reserved.

The Duke tilted back his head and smiled at her. 'That's better. You won't be pushing me away again, will you?'

Once again, he gave her no time to answer before pushing his body against her. His arms encircled her, holding her tight, pinning her against the wall. She had been instructed to show enthusiasm, to give little sighs of pleasure. But how did you do that when you were so numb you couldn't move? How did you sigh when you could hardly breathe?

One large hand took hold of both of her wrists, holding them firmly behind her back as he continued kissing her unresponsive lips. His other hand moved up her body, sliding over her waist, up her chest, and seizing hold of one of her breasts.

'No,' she gasped out, turning her head sharply to the side.

'Yes,' he said, his hands holding her wrists more tightly. 'This is what you want,' he murmured, his lips close to her ear. 'This is why you chose that gown to wear tonight, isn't it? So you could tempt me with what you have to offer. Well, you have tempted me, and you can't blame a man for succumbing to temptation.'

His hand moved from her breast, and she released a grateful sigh. He grabbed hold of her chin, turning her to face him.

'You promised me that there would be no more silliness. You promised me a kiss, didn't you? I'm not making you do anything you didn't agree to, am I?'

Sophia wanted to say she had not agreed to his touching her or grabbing her, but before she could formulate her objections his lips were once again on hers.

Releasing her chin, his hand slid down her body. She moved back, fearing that he would once again try to touch her breast, but instead he grasped at her skirt. She wanted to get away, but there was nowhere to move to. He had her pinned between his body and the wall.

'No,' she tried to say, the words unable to escape as he carried on kissing her.

His hand continued to grasp at her skirt, pulling it higher. The fabric rose above her ankles, up her legs, exposing her knees, then her thighs. This was intolerable. This should not be happening. She tried to free her hands, but he gripped them harder. She tried to wriggle away from him, but his body pushed more firmly against hers, while he continued to lift up her skirt.

She squirmed, trying to wriggle free. Deep shame engulfed her as he bunched her dress and petticoat up around her waist, exposing her stockings and drawers.

His hand moved between her legs, pushing inside the leg of her drawers and rising up her thigh. She tried to scream, but with his lips still pressed hard against hers, her scream was stifled in her throat.

This could not be happening. It had to be a nightmare. But even in a nightmare, Sophia could not imagine such a thing happening. He didn't just want a kiss, and if he didn't get what he wanted he was going to take it by force. How could she ever have thought she wanted to marry this callous brute?

Using all her strength, she managed to free one hand from behind her back and pushed at his chest.

Her attempt to repel him failed. His chest remained immobile as if he had not even registered her efforts, and his hand continued to move higher up her inner thigh.

She pulled back her foot and kicked him hard in the shins. It had no effect. Silk evening slippers were designed for no other purpose than to look pretty and feminine.

This was impossible. She had dreaded the thought of kissing him again but had never expected that he would treat her like this. All his kisses were doing now was holding her in place and stopping her from crying out for help.

And he could not possibly think she wanted this. He could not have failed to notice that she was objecting. But he was going to take what he wanted anyway. The man was a loathsome, predatory beast, and she was his defenceless, trapped prey.

He pushed his knee between her thighs, forcing them apart. She had to do something. She couldn't let this happen. She lifted her leg sharply, her knee making hard contact between his legs.

Her imprisoned wrist was freed. His hand dropped from her thigh and his knee moved from between her legs. He stumbled backwards, grabbing at the place where her knee had made contact, and doubled over.

She drew in several quick breaths, grateful that his lips were no longer on hers, that his body was no longer imprisoning her, and pushed down her skirt and petticoat.

'You little bitch,' he gasped out, glaring at her from his crouched position. 'You will regret this.'

Sophia doubted that very much. Right now, all she was feeling was intense relief.

'I'll ruin you.'

'I believe what I have just done saved me from being ruined,' she said, a small laugh escaping, either from fear, relief or because he certainly looked funny, bent over, his knees buckled, grasping his groin, his face a deep shade of red.

'You've ruined any chance that I will ever marry you. You'll never be a duchess now.'

'Thank goodness for that. As if I'd want to marry a despicable, despicable...' Sophia knew there had to be something despicable enough to describe a man like him, but nothing would suffice. Animal? Pig? Dog? Monster? None were insulting enough. 'You despicable duke,' she settled on instead.

'And no one else will want to marry you when I've told them what a little trollop you are.'

'Try to ruin my reputation and you'll once again feel the power of my knee,' she said, lifting her knee sharply to demonstrate what she would do to him. The Duke stumbled backwards, his face turning an even deeper shade, one closer to purple than red. Sophia couldn't stop herself from laughing again as she stared down at the now helpless man.

'No man will want you once I tell everyone that I deflowered you. Once I tell them how willingly you gave it up to me, you'll be an outcast,' he gasped in a few more breaths, his face the picture of pain. 'No decent man will want to be seen with you, let alone marry you, when I tell them you let me tup you in a public place like a common tart.'

Sophia glared down at him, her hands defiantly on her hips. 'Well, if you're an example of a decent man, then I'm obviously better off without one and I couldn't care less what you say about me and to whom you say it.'

He took a few mincing steps backwards. 'I'll make you regret what you've done. I promise you that.' His hand still clasping his groin, he slunk off through the curtain.

Sophia leant back against the wall and slowly breathed in and out to calm her racing heart. The Duke was a powerful man, one capable of exacting revenge, but despite that, right now, she could not feel more proud of what she had done.

## Chapter Nine

Ethan scoured every part of the theatre, becoming increasingly frantic with each passing minute. They had to be somewhere. The moment Ravenswood and Miss Cooper had risen from their seats, he had been out of the door of his own private box. In public she had been safe. But she was not safe now.

The Duke had her hidden away somewhere. What he was doing to her, Ethan hated to think.

But he had no time to think. He had to find her. He had already been to the foyer, had run along every corridor, had even checked to see if they had returned to the Duke's private box, hoping his fears were unfounded. Now he was retracing his steps, his desperation increasing.

He passed a curtain and heard giggling. Her giggling. Every muscle in his body tensed in preparation to manhandle the Duke, to rip him off Miss Cooper, throw him down the stairs and beat him senseless.

Without announcing his presence, he grabbed the

curtain and threw it open. He did not care if she was laughing. The Duke was a brute and had to be kept away from her.

She was alone in the alcove, her gloved hands over her mouth as she continued to giggle. With pleasure? How could that be?

She lowered her hands. 'Hello, Lord Ethan. How lovely to see you.' The giggling erupted again, and she covered her mouth as if it was the only way to stop its escape.

His body still readied for a fight, he stood at the edge of the alcove, gripping the curtain so tightly it strained at the rail, his breath coming in loud, fast gasps.

Was she hysterical? Had the Duke seduced and abandoned her, leaving her delirious?

'Hello, Miss Cooper,' he responded, eyeing her warily. 'You're alone?' The answer to that was obvious. What he wanted to know was, *Where is Ravenswood and what did he do to you?*

'Yes. I'm afraid the Duke of Ravenswood had to leave. Rather suddenly.' She gave another small giggle.

'Is everything all right?' He approached her, slowly, as if afraid any sudden movement would startle her.

'Yes.' She shrugged and shook her head. 'No. I don't really know.'

He took another slow step towards her. 'What happened?' he asked quietly. 'Did Ravenswood try to kiss you again?'

'Yes, he did.' Her smile faltered, to be replaced by a shudder.

Ethan stopped moving as he fought to keep his fury under control. He did not want to frighten her with the power of the rage surging through him. He had to try to rein in his anger, and not let her see how much he wanted to tear the Duke limb from limb.

'Well, at least he tried to,' she continued. 'But he won't be doing that again, I can assure you.'

He waited for her to explain.

'That man is despicable,' she said, shaking her head slowly from side to side. 'Just despicable.'

He closed his eyes briefly and dragged in a steadying breath. 'What happened?' he asked in his softest, most gentle voice.

'As I said, he tried to kiss me again and much more besides.'

He waited once again, worried that if he spoke he would not be able to hide the intensity of his anger and it would frighten her into silence.

'He really is despicable. The Despicable Duke.' She gave another nervous little laugh. 'That's what I called him.' She drew in a deep breath, then smiled at him, a smile that lit up her face and caused her eyes to sparkle. 'But I'm so pleased you're here with me now.'

Ethan fought not to be distracted by her evident joy in seeing him again. He had no reason to be pleased with himself. He had failed her. The Duke had obviously harmed her, then left her distraught and alone. If he couldn't save her from the Duke, the least he could do was make the man pay.

'Where is he now?' Ethan said, fighting to keep his voice calm.

'I don't know,' she said with a shrug. 'He hobbled off somewhere.'

'Hobbled?'

'Yes.' Her smile widened and she placed her hands on her hips, as if in triumph. 'When he was trying to force himself on me, I managed to get my knee between his legs. I lifted it up, hard and fast, and he doubled over.' She demonstrated what she meant, lifting her knee quickly and forcefully.

Ethan winced. One arm involuntarily flew across his groin in protection, although her knee came nowhere near his most vulnerable region.

'I see,' he responded, his voice stifled. 'I see,' he repeated, more decisively.

'When I did that, he lost interest immediately in what he was doing,' she continued. 'And then he left. I must say, it surprised me how effective my actions were.'

'Yes, kneeing a man in the groin does tend to stop him in his tracks,' he said, his knees still involuntarily crushed together. 'But are you all right? Did he hurt you?'

'Yes, I'm perfectly all right. And no, he didn't hurt me.' Her eyebrows drew together in a questioning frown as she took some time to think. 'In fact, I don't believe I have ever felt better than I do right now.'

She certainly appeared to be unharmed. Her chin was lifted, her shoulders squared, and her gaze was steady. She was not looking at him through lowered lashes, as she often did. Nor was that familiar shy blush turning her cheeks pink.

It was not the look of an innocent young woman who had been traumatised. Instead, she looked wonderful, like a victorious heroine, a Joan of Arc, or the warrior queen Boudica.

'I'm pleased you are unhurt. But you should never have been subjected to such barbaric treatment. I wish I had got here earlier. I'm so sorry I left you alone with him.'

She shrugged one shoulder. 'It's of no mind. I handled it all rather well, if I do say so myself, and now the Duke will know I most definitely will not make an obedient, compliant duchess. And thank goodness for that.'

She laughed again, and this time it was no nervous giggle. Ethan smiled back at her, revelling in her triumph. Then her smile turned to a sigh. 'I've been a fool, haven't I?' She shook her head as if amazed by her own gullibility.

'No, of course not. You didn't know what Ravenswood was like.'

'But you did. You tried to warn me, but I didn't listen. And I suspect my mother did as well, although instead of trying to warn me off, she encouraged me to be alone with him. She didn't care what he did to me.'

Her eyebrows drew together and she shook her head slowly. 'I have been a naïve little fool. I've been blind to the extent of my mother's ambitions and blinded by the Duke's title as to what he was really like. I thought because he was a man of such high status that he would be honourable. Deep down, I knew it was wrong to kiss him, but I thought whatever he did would always be the right and proper thing to do because he was a duke. What a fool I was.'

'No, you weren't to know. You weren't a fool. You were just too trusting.'

'I was more than just too trusting. I've let people use me for their own ends, manipulate me. Well, I won't be letting that happen ever again. I won't naively trust anyone ever again, especially men.'

'Not everyone's as bad as Ravenswood. I'm sure you'll meet someone else, someone kind and decent.'

She gave a small, dismissive wave of her hand. 'I don't want anyone else. Like you, I will not marry.'

She stared at him, defiant, determined. 'That's right. I'm not going to marry. I never thought I'd actually say that. But it's true. I don't want to marry anyone, ever. So those vile things that man said to me before he hobbled off will have no effect on me whatsoever.'

He took a step towards her, his fists once again clenching. 'What vile things did the Duke say?'

She flicked her hands once again, as if it was of no real account. 'Threats about how he was going to ruin me. How when he tells people he had me, here in the alcove of a public theatre, no one else will want to marry me.'

The fury bubbling under the surface once again surged up within him. The Duke would be doing no such thing. When Ethan got hold of him, he'd be saying nothing to anyone because he would not be able to talk again for some time. But Miss Cooper did not need to know any of that.

'As if I care,' she continued. 'Who cares if he does

say such things and my reputation is in tatters? I certainly don't care if no man wants to marry me. I'm better off without them.' She sent him another defiant look, as if daring him to challenge her.

'Not all men are like Ravenswood,' he repeated.

She gave a dismissive shrug as if this too was of little matter. 'Anyway, I want to go home now. Will you escort me, please, Lord Ethan?'

'Yes, of course. I'll get your mother, shall I?'

'No,' she said, her voice emphatic.

'But she will worry about where you are, where you've gone and whom you are with.'

'No, she won't. She'll think that the Duke has taken me away somewhere and is doing with me whatever he wants. If anything, she'll be pleased her plan has worked and that the Duke will have sealed the deal and be forced to marry me.' She gave an involuntary shudder. 'Let her think that. I'll disillusion her tomorrow and inform her that her dreams have all been destroyed and she will never be the mother of a duchess.'

She breathed in deeply and slowly exhaled, then smiled. 'But I don't want to think about that now. Let's not ruin what's left of this evening. From now on, I am determined to enjoy every moment, to live my life the way I want to and to hell with dukes, mothers, men, marriage and all that.'

Sophia wanted to dance, to sing, to laugh out loud. She was free. Free from the Duke. Free from her mother. And free from all the restraints put on her because she was a young woman of marriageable age with a substantial dowry.

While Lord Ethan returned to his private box to say goodnight to his mother, she paced up and down the corridor, unable to remain still for a moment longer. Emotion after powerful emotion surged up inside her, each one demanding her attention.

Despite claiming she did not want to think about the Duke or her mother, how could she not? She was both exhausted by her encounter and exhilarated by the way she had turned her fear into rage. And as for her mother, it was hard to know how she really felt about her, but she knew that anger and pain were in there, jostling for her attention.

The only person who did not elicit conflicting emotions in her was Lord Ethan. Unlike her mother and the Duke, he had wanted to save her, to care for her, to protect her. She smiled to herself, then that smile died. She was telling herself lies. Her emotions were just as conflicted when she thought of Lord Ethan, so much so that she could hardly name what they were.

When he returned, she smiled at him. At the sight of his handsome face all internal conflict evaporated. There was no confusion now. She was where she wanted to be and with the one person in the world she wanted to be with. Now all she felt was happiness and she all but skipped down the stairway and out through the now quiet, empty foyer.

They exited the theatre and walked out into the crisp night air. London was still bustling with hectic activity. Carriages rumbled along the cobbled stones, fashionable people walked along the well-lit streets, and the loud voices of drivers and people selling food and drink from carts filled the air.

Sophia took Lord Ethan's arm, as the glorious chaos of the vibrant city wrapped itself around her.

He held up his hand to hail a hackney cab, having left his own carriage for his mother and her friends, but she could not bear the thought of being confined. She needed to move, not sit still like the demure young lady she was determined never to be again. Where did being demure ever get you? It got you trapped in an alcove with a man who treated you like a possession, one he could use in whatever way he wanted.

No, she would never be that young woman ever again.

'Let's walk,' she said. 'It's not far, and it's such a lovely evening.' She looked up at the twinkling stars. Had they always shone so brightly? Did the moon always look so benevolent, shining over the people below with its soft white glow?

It was such a glorious evening she wanted it to never end, and with so much energy coursing through her veins she was sure she could spend the night walking the entirety of London, taking in all its sights and sounds, and enjoying the delicious night-time air, gentle on her skin.

'As you wish.' He sent her a curious look. 'You're different,' he said, as much to himself as to her.

'I feel different. I feel wonderful!' she exclaimed, as if announcing that fact to the entire world.

'I'd almost say you enjoyed kneeing the Duke in the bollocks.'

She laughed out loud, not caring whether such behaviour was considered unbecoming in a young lady. 'So what I did actually has a name?'

'Yes, while it was very effective in the circumstances, you aren't the first person to use that particular move. Although the Duke would never have expected it from you.'

She shuddered with revulsion. 'Good. He'll think more carefully before he grabs any other young woman.'

'Are you sure you are all right, Miss Cooper?' he asked, his voice solicitous.

'Yes, I'm fine.' She moved in even closer towards him. With him by her side she was more than fine.

They turned off the busy road onto a small street that led to her home. The bustling noise quietened as fewer carriages moved down the streets, and no other pedestrians were walking on the footpath. Gas lights were also less frequent, and once they passed out of each lamp's circle of light, they were almost in darkness. She was alone with him, in the dark, and yet she felt completely safe. She knew he would not grab at her, would not kiss her, would not touch intimate parts of her body. At least, not unless she wanted him to.

She smiled to herself.

Walking with him was perfect. His lovely body was warm beside her. She sighed and moved closer, loving his masculine scent of sandalwood and musk, loving his strength, and remembering their almost kiss.

'You really are a remarkable young woman.' Sophia could hear the admiration in his voice, causing pride to surge up inside her. Right now she did indeed feel remarkable, as if she could do anything, achieve anything, be anyone she wanted to be. 'But Ravenswood should be held to account for what he did,' he added, and she felt his body tense beside hers.

'I did hold him to account, remember? I kneed him in the bollocks.' She laughed again. 'As you said, he would never have expected that, nor do I think he will forget it any time soon.'

'On that, I am sure you are right,' he said, joining in with her laughter. 'The memory will be firmly printed on his mind, not to mention another part of his anatomy.'

'I'd like to think I taught him a lesson he won't soon forget.'

His laughter grew louder. 'I suspect you are right and he'll be feeling the effects of your raised knee for a while yet. It will certainly put a crimp in his lifestyle, of that you can be assured.'

'Good,' she said with satisfaction. 'But let's not waste any more time talking about the Despicable Duke. Let's just enjoy this glorious night, and our time together.'

He patted her arm and they walked slowly through the night, along the quiet, leafy streets of Mayfair, past the large, well-lit houses, until they eventually came to her home. Sophia had so enjoyed their time together she did not want it to end and was tempted to suggest that they continue walking endlessly through the night.

He opened the gate, escorted her up the path to the front door and lifted the knocker to summon a servant.

She reached out to still his hand. 'You never did

give me that kissing lesson, did you, Lord Ethan?' Her words were bold, but she felt bold, even if her thudding heart and held breath suggested otherwise.

He looked over his shoulder at the empty street. 'We can't. Your reputation. What if someone…?'

Refusing to listen to his objections, she took his hands and stepped backwards, leading him into a darkened area beside the porch, where a dense hedge of tall shrubs obscured their presence.

'No one will see us here. But even if they could, I no longer care. What good has my untarnished reputation done? Nothing. It merely attracted a man like the Duke of Ravenswood. I was exactly the sort of woman he wanted—obedient, innocent and with a generous dowry. Well, I am no longer that woman. And thank goodness for that.'

She gave a little laugh. 'All that's left is my dowry, and that's one thing no man will be getting his hands on.' She bit her lip to stop another laugh, realising how much truth there was in that. There were other parts of her she would happily allow Lord Ethan to get his hands on and she hoped that he would.

'Sophia, you've had a shock tonight. You're not thinking clearly.'

He took a step backwards towards the light, so she grabbed the lapels of his jacket to halt his movements.

Yes, she had experienced something shocking tonight. And yes, perhaps she wasn't thinking clearly. But that was no longer because of the Duke. Her thoughts were muddled because she was standing close to a man who was making her heart race, her skin tingle, and her body burn with excitement. A man who had just called her Sophia for the first time.

'You say you don't care about your reputation, but you should do nothing rash,' he continued, in that annoying rational manner.

'The Duke intends to ruin my reputation anyway, so I have nothing to lose in that regard.' She laughed, surprised at how little she cared. 'If Society's going to judge me, I might as well do some of the things I'm accused of.'

'This is so unfair, and the Duke must be punished for what he's done to you.'

'No. I've punished that man. And in one way, what happened was all for the best. If he hadn't behaved in such an abhorrent way, I might have actually married him. If it wasn't for what he tried to do tonight, I'd still be a naïve, trusting woman, blinded by the lure of a title.' Anger surged up inside her. She closed her eyes briefly, determined not to think of that man. 'But I'm not that woman any more, thank goodness. So, are you going to be a gentleman and do what I ask and kiss me?'

He stroked his finger gently along her cheek. She gasped in a quick breath, her head tilting towards that caressing finger.

'Sophia, are you sure?'

'I've never been more sure of anything in my life.'

'But are you really?' he asked, his finger still lightly stroking her cheek. 'You must know I do not wish to marry. I can promise you nothing.'

'Then it seems we have something in common. I

now know I will never marry either. And after the Duke spreads his lies, no other man will want to marry me. It would be cruel if the world saw me as damaged goods when I haven't even kissed a man yet.' Sophia discounted the forced kiss from the Duke. It did not count, and never would.

He gazed down at her, his eyes focused on her lips.

'Kiss me,' she whispered, her words holding a wealth of longing.

He leant down. His lips lightly stroked hers as if she was a fragile flower, as if he was afraid of hurting her.

She sighed gently. That was nice, very nice, but she wanted more, much more. She slid her hands round the back of his neck. If her words couldn't convince him, perhaps her actions would.

What on earth was he doing? Well, he knew what he was doing. The real question was, should he be doing this? And he knew the answer to that should be a resounding no.

He was supposed to be Sir Galahad, her champion, her defender. But this young woman did not really need to be saved, not by him, not by anyone.

Now he was proving himself to be an even more inadequate Sir Galahad, one who was moving quickly from seeing her as a damsel in distress to seeing her as a beautiful, enticing young woman. Surely a Sir Galahad would not be wondering what the damsel's lips tasted like. He was sure that noble defenders did not think about the damsel in distress's breasts, how creamy white those delectable mounds were, how they rose and fell above her gown as she breathed in and out, in almost hypnotic regularity. Would a champion imagine what it would be like to caress those breasts, to pull down the top of her gown and expose them to his view, to cup them, stroke them, to lick and nuzzle them?

He was sure that a heroic man would think no such things. But he was no hero, and she wanted him to kiss her. What he should do was step back into the doorway. That was what the gentleman he professed to be would do. Instead, he moved further into their darkened hiding place. Surely no harm would be done. After all, no one would see and it was just one kiss. One quick kiss. Nothing more.

His mouth lingered close to hers, so close he could feel her panting breath, so close he could almost taste her.

'Are you sure?' he repeated, still needing reassurance that what he was doing was not wrong.

'Yes. I want you to kiss me, really kiss me.'

Once again, his lips brushed lightly against hers. His body was screaming out to kiss her, hard and urgent, but his mind was telling him to go softly. Despite her behaviour tonight, despite her changed demeanour, despite the hands that were wrapped around his head, she was still an innocent young woman. He had to be gentle with her. Their lips connected softly, and he slid his arm around her waist.

She moulded into him, the length of her body touching his, those lovely soft breasts hard up against his chest. Be gentle, he reminded himself, refusing to allow his body to do what it wanted, forcing himself to take his time.

He lightly ran his tongue slowly along her bottom lip. As he hoped, her lips parted on a sigh, granting him entry. He deepened the kiss slightly. The part of his brain that could still function waited for an objection. None came. Instead, her tongue darted out, tentatively, exploratively. A groan of unfettered desire escaped from his mouth as his arms wrapped tighter around her waist, needing her with a ferocity that was almost frightening in its strength.

As if he had given his approval of her actions and shown her the strength of his desire for her, she pressed closer to him. Her lips pushed harder against his. Her hands gripped the back of his head, holding him to her lips. Her passion did not take him by surprise. She might be inexperienced, but he had seen a side of her tonight that showed she had a fire within her. A fire he wanted to flame, so he could burn in the full force of its heat.

He let his tongue enter her mouth, desperate to be inside her, to taste her, savour her. Slowly his hands moved over her gentle curves, loving her slender waist and the flare of her rounded hips. He wanted to cup her buttocks, to feel those soft, feminine mounds, but would that be going too far?

Under his caressing hands, she arched herself towards him, her body writhing seductively. There was no doubt now. She had told him with her words. Now her body was restating that demand, loud and clear. This was what she wanted.

His kisses moved to her neck, loving the feel of her delicate skin under his lips. She tasted so good, smelled so good, so fresh, like spring flowers after rain. He inhaled deeply, savouring that heavenly scent, before kissing her neck again, his tongue gently running along the silky flesh.

'Yes,' she murmured, her words as gentle as a sigh.

He moved up to her earlobe, and took the soft nub in his mouth, gently nuzzling it, loving the gasp that escaped from her parted lips as she once again murmured the word he so wanted to hear. 'Yes. Yes, Lord Ethan.'

'Ethan,' he murmured. 'Call me Ethan.'

'Yes, Ethan,' she responded, looking confidently into his eyes, meeting his gaze directly without coyness.

His lips returned to hers. This time he kissed her the way he wanted to, the way she wanted. Fierce, urgent, without restraint. Pushing her lips apart with his tongue, he entered her mouth again, deeper, as if claiming her as his own.

And she kissed him back, without reservation. Her fingers wound through his hair, holding him in place as her lips demanded satisfaction. She wanted him as much as he wanted her, and that thought unleashed a wild level of erotic need within him, its urgency greater than he had ever experienced before.

If he could, he would take her right here, right now, but he knew he would never do that. She had asked for his kisses, nothing more. That was what he was doing. That was all he would do.

\* \* \*

Sophia wanted more. His kisses were wonderful, but she needed to feel the caressing touch of his hands on her body, needed him to quell the wildness building up inside her, possessing her with its pounding insistence. Only his touch could free her, give her the release her body was demanding.

'Sophia,' he murmured, withdrawing from her lips, leaving her disappointed, but loving the way he said her name, with such passion, such demanding need. He nuzzled into her neck again, kissing the sensitive skin, and she felt as if she was being worshipped. She inclined her head, letting him know how much she wanted him to worship every inch of her body.

His hand moved slowly from her waist, over her hips and gently down to her buttocks, cupping them and bringing her body flush up against his. Now there was no part of her that wasn't touching him, but still, she wanted more. As if under an instinct over which she had no control, she rubbed herself against him, her back arching, trying to relieve the throbbing tension building up, higher and higher within her.

She moaned out a sigh, a sigh that was a plea, a demand, for what she wasn't sure, but for something she knew only he could give her.

His lips found hers again, crashing onto them with an urgency that was fierce and exciting.

Her kisses matched his. She ran her tongue along his bottom lip, just as he had done to her. He emitted a moan of pleasure, emboldening her further. She could feel his control slipping from him, and power surged through her. She wanted him to lose himself to her, the way she had lost herself to him. To need her as much as she needed him.

Her tongue explored his mouth, tasting and probing, loving the intimacy of what she was doing. As if under an instinctive command, her hands moved from behind his head and slid slowly down his back until they reached his buttocks. Following his lead, she cupped them, the muscles hard under her fingers. She pulled him in against her, relishing the sound of his wild, primitive groan of pleasure.

Holding her tightly, he deepened the kiss. Their tongues performed an exotic, tantalising dance. This was more than Sophia had expected a kiss would be like. She had not expected it to take her over so completely, to be so raw, to pulsate through her entire body.

'Ethan, oh, Ethan,' she gasped out as she lightly kissed his neck, loving the manly roughness of stubbled skin, so hard against her soft lips. She wanted to rip off his clothing, to run her tongue over his skin, to taste him, to kiss every part of his beautiful body.

His hands firmly on her waist, he moved her further backwards, placing her in the dark corner where the tall hedge met the wall of the house, and continued to kiss her lips and neck. His body was a hard, muscled wall in front of her, blocking out everything, even the dim light from the moon, and leaving them in complete darkness.

Excitement rippled through her. No one would ever see them here. He could do whatever he wanted and no one would know. He could do what she wanted, what she needed, what her body was crying out for.

Her heart hammering with anticipation, her body throbbing, a surging intensity gripping deep inside her, she parted her lips, and looked up at him in appeal.

His lips were once again on hers as his hand moved to her breast. The sensitive nub of her nipple tightened under his touch and she cursed the clothing that was separating her skin from his caresses. A deep, unrestrained moan escaped her lips, one she could hardly recognise as her own. Her desperation for him mounted. A desperation that was demanding he strip her of her clothing so he could fully explore her body, a desperation that he free her from this rising need for him, a consuming need that had taken hold of her, was possessing her.

His lips left hers and he kissed a tantalising trail down her neck, closer and closer to her aching breasts. His kisses reached her chest. He kissed a line along the exposed mounds. This was torture, exquisite torture. She wanted, needed, him to caress every inch of her, to release her from the demanding need building up inside her like a towering wave about to break on the shore.

His lips reclaimed hers as his hand moved inside her gown, cupping her breast, his thumb rubbing over the tight bud, sending shudders of pleasure rippling through her.

She placed her hand over his, pushing it harder against her breast, her breath coming in faster and faster gasps as he continued his tormenting caresses. But her breasts were not the only part demanding his touch. She wanted to feel his hands all over her body, her stomach, her inner thighs and on the most intimate part of her body, a part that was throbbing hard for him.

She had to tell him what she wanted, but all she could do was gasp out her pleasure, unable to form the words. She prayed that he would know what she needed, what she was demanding, even if she was incapable of telling him. And that he would give it to her right now.

## Chapter Ten

The muffled whinny of a nearby horse, and carriage wheels turning along the cobbled street, dragged Ethan's attention from Sophia. He took a step back to see what was happening in the street, but she grabbed hold of his jacket, refusing to let something as trivial as passing traffic distract him.

The sound of the carriage wheels stopped as the vehicle halted outside the house. Guilt surging through him, he took Sophia's hands and all but pulled her out of their hiding place. He quickly scanned her clothing. Everything was as it should be, although her heightened colour and swollen lips would signify what had just happened.

Mrs Cooper descended from the hackney cab and walked up the pathway, her arms swinging, beaming a triumphant smile. It was not the expression one would expect from a mother who had found her daughter alone, at night, on her doorstep with a man. Unless, of course, she was hoping that the man was the Duke of Ravenswood, the man she expected her daughter to marry.

He looked down at Sophia. She was glaring at her smiling mother, her lips pursed in disgust.

Mrs Cooper reached them, looked up and registered her mistake. Her smile dissolved, to be replaced with a contemptuous sneer.

Sophia stepped forward, her fury almost palpable, and he placed a restraining hand on her arm. He shared Sophia's outrage over the way this woman had behaved and her total disregard for her daughter's safety, but she was still Sophia's mother.

'Lord Ethan,' Mrs Cooper all but spat out, her nostrils flaring, her eyes narrowed. 'What are *you* doing here?'

Sophia took another step towards her mother, her hands firmly on her hips. 'He escorted me home after he saved me from the clutches of Ravenswood.'

Ethan looked at Sophia and raised his eyebrows. He hadn't actually saved her. She had saved herself. She raised one shoulder, as if to say now was not the time to quibble over the details.

'So where did the Duke go?' her mother asked. 'What happened to him? What did you do?' She glared once more at Ethan.

'I don't know, and I care even less,' Sophia said.

'Sophia!' her mother exclaimed, drawing the name out. 'How can you say such a thing?' She turned her enraged attention back to Ethan. 'Are you responsible for my daughter behaving like this? What have you said to her about the Duke?'

Ethan went to speak, but Sophia placed her hand on his arm, letting him know she did not need a man to fight her battles for her.

'Nobody has said anything to me. If I've changed it's because of Ravenswood and what he tried to do to me tonight. That man is a walking obscenity.'

A deep scarlet flush crept up Mrs Cooper's neck, then into her face, and her eyes bulged. 'How…how dare you speak like that about a duke?' she gasped out.

'Or are you the one who is the real obscenity, Mother? Rather than discussing my behaviour, should we talk about what you expected me to do tonight in order to secure a title?'

Mrs Cooper's mouth opened and shut, in a manner usually only seen on fish caught in a net.

'Get inside now!' her mother shouted, finally finding her voice.

'Don't raise your voice, Mother. Haven't you always said that ladies never raise their voices no matter what the provocation? And yes, I will join you inside when I'm ready, but first I want to say goodnight to Lord Ethan.'

'How dare you? You…you ungrateful girl.' She made a grab for Sophia's arm, but Ethan blocked her way. 'Get out of my way!' she screeched, her arms still flailing wildly.

'I think you need to calm down,' Ethan said, as Mrs Cooper's arms continued to make unsuccessful grabs in Sophia's direction.

'Yes, Mother. Go inside and calm down. I'll be in presently.' In contrast to Mrs Cooper's, Sophia's voice was level and composed. She turned and banged the door knocker. The door opened immediately, suggesting the footman had been standing behind it, possibly drawn by the unusual sound of angry voices on the doorstep.

'Please escort my mother inside, Charles,' Sophia said in a well-modulated voice, as if nothing was amiss. 'And you might want to give her a brandy to steady her nerves.'

'I'll see you inside, my girl, and you'd better have a good explanation for this behaviour,' Mrs Cooper said as she pushed past them. 'And you,' she added, pointing her finger into the footman's chest, 'stay where you are until this man leaves.'

'Yes, madam,' the footman replied. His gaze flicked between Mrs Cooper, Sophia and Ethan before he stood up tall against the door jamb, as if trying to make himself invisible.

Sophia watched with satisfaction as her mother bustled up the hallway. She had never stood up to her mother before, had never contradicted a word she said, but that time was now over. Too much had happened tonight for her to ever go back to being that compliant young woman who did as she was told. No one, including her mother, would ever manipulate her again. No one would ever use her to achieve their own ambitions the way her mother had used her. She had convinced Sophia she wished to marry Ravenswood, that he would make the perfect husband. She had blithely gone along with it, thinking her mother knew best and what she wanted was what Sophia also wanted. But never again. From now on she would be strong and would look out for herself. From now onwards, she would trust no one except herself.

She turned back to Lord Ethan, or Ethan, as he had asked her to call him, and smiled. Well, not everyone couldn't be trusted.

'Would you like me to stay?' he asked. 'Your mother is obviously agitated.'

They looked up the now empty hallway. 'Let her be agitated. It's no less than she deserves.' She turned to Ethan. 'Thank you for the offer, but if I can stand up to the Duke, I can certainly deal with my mother's temper tantrums.' She could hardly believe how composed she was. She had learnt some painful truths about her mother tonight, and about the way some men treated women. While it was a shock to know the truth, it was also liberating. She now saw the world as it truly was, not as the fantasy she had hitherto believed in. It was as if in one evening she had changed from being a trusting child to a confident woman.

'Yes, I believe you can. I rather like this new Sophia.' He smiled, that wonderful, enchanting smile, a smile that made her wonder whether she should suggest that he kiss her once again. She flicked a quick look at the impassive doorman and decided perhaps not.

'I rather like the new me as well,' she said instead.

'But unfortunately young women are always vulnerable and your mother has power over you,' he continued, no longer smiling, but staring into her eyes as if to make her understand the precariousness of her situation.

'Not this young woman. Once again, it seems I've been a fool. My father left me this house and a size-able fortune. That means I'm an independently wealthy woman. Until now, my mother has assumed control of my money, and if I marry my husband will get every-thing.' A surge of anger washed through her. 'No doubt my mother told Ravenswood of that fact and that's what he was interested in. That and my naivety, the fact that he would have a wife he could control completely.'

Ethan made no protest, confirming the truth of her statement.

Breathing deeply and calmly, she reminded herself that was all in the past. She had staved off a terrible fate. Instead of being angry about the past, she wanted to be proud of herself and look forward to her future.

'As my mother has no financial power over me, she can rant and rave about me being an ungrateful daugh-ter, or about the opportunity I've missed, or whatever she wants, but that's all she can do, rant and rave. She can't really hurt me, and she knows it.'

He nodded slowly, his brow still furrowed.

'Don't look so worried,' she said with a small laugh. 'I will be perfectly all right. In fact, I'll be better than all right. I am going to be magnificent.'

Slowly a smile curved the edges of his lovely lips. 'You are magnificent, Sophia.'

She wanted to say, *You're magnificent as well. And the way you kiss... My, oh, my, magnificent does not begin to describe it!* But for the first time since she had reduced the Duke to a hobbling, purple-faced joke of a man she was lost for words.

How did you tell a man that being kissed by him was indescribable? That your lips were still tingling, that your body was aching to feel his arms around it, that you were still burning for his touch? Instead, she merely gave a small sigh as they continued to smile at each other.

'So, what do you plan to do with all your new-found freedom?' he asked.

'I plan to enjoy myself,' she said with satisfaction. 'The Season is not yet over, so I intend to enjoy what's left of it without worrying about finding a husband. I shall experience all that London has to offer, without caring whether I'm seen in the right places or what impression I'm making on eligible men. I plan to have fun, lots and lots of fun.'

'And I wish you all the best in doing so. You deserve to enjoy yourself after everything you have been through.' He gazed down at her. Was he going to kiss her again? *Yes, please.*

He bent down and lightly kissed her cheek. 'Goodnight, Sophia.'

'Goodnight, Ethan,' she replied, her voice little more than a sigh.

They remained standing on the doorstep, still staring at each other.

'Goodnight,' he repeated and gently stroked her cheek. His gaze flicked to the footman and his hand dropped. 'Goodnight, Miss Cooper,' he said in a more formal voice, and gave her a quick bow.

It seemed *that* was all she was going to get tonight.
No more kisses. No more caresses. Propriety had taken
over. And so she bobbed a curtsey, said goodnight to
Lord Ethan and turned to walk into the house. Her
house.

The future was now open before her. She could de-
termine what happened to her, what she did, where she
went and whom she saw.

As she walked up the stairs to her bedroom, she
wondered what that future would hold. She knew it
would not include Ravenswood. Nor would her future
be about desperately finding a man to marry, and she
certainly would not be chasing after a title.

What she didn't know was whether her future would
include Lord Ethan Rosemont, a man who had made
her no promises.

Ethan walked down the now quiet Mayfair streets.
Some Sir Galahad he had turned out to be. His damsel
in distress didn't need his help, had never needed his
help. She had been perfectly capable of looking after
herself—she just hadn't realised it.

And he doubted a real knight in shining armour
would steal a kiss from the damsel he hadn't rescued,
then take it even further, take it too far.

He stopped walking and cringed at his behaviour.
He probably shouldn't have kissed her and he definitely should not have caressed her in the manner he
had. Thank goodness the mother had arrived when she
did or heaven knew what else he might have done that
he shouldn't have.

He could only hope Sophia forgave him for his transgression. Her words and manner did not suggest she thought he had behaved inappropriately—quite the reverse. When she had said goodbye, the way her breath had come in a series of quick gasps through her parted lips strongly suggested she expected him to kiss her one more time. And he would have, if it hadn't been for the presence of the witness. Mrs Cooper had done a lot of things for which Sophia had every right to condemn her, but placing a guard at the door was the one sensible thing she had done.

If she hadn't, Ethan was unsure whether he could have controlled himself. Looking down at her when they said goodbye, he had never seen a woman look more enticing. The need to take her in his arms one more time had been all but impossible to fight. Even now, he could still feel the imprint of her body against his, the touch of her soft breasts on his chest, the feel of her gentle curves under his caresses. He released an involuntary groan of desire as the memory of kissing and caressing her silk-like skin possessed him, of her reaction when he caressed her. Had a woman ever looked more beautiful as she gasped in pleasure?

He shook himself to drive out that image. He could not use her reactions to justify his behaviour. She was still a young, innocent debutante. That kiss should never have happened.

He commenced walking, shaking his head in disbelief at his own lack of gallantry. How he could have ever seen himself as a Sir Galahad was almost laughable. He hadn't saved her, then he had all but seduced her in a doorway. The fact that she had put up no objection was no excuse.

He came to another sudden halt. Was Sophia so responsive to his kisses because she now thought they were promised to each other? Did she think a marriage proposal would be imminent? As delightful as she was, as beautiful and enchanting, he did not want a wife, any wife.

She had said she expected nothing from him and had even declared that she did not want to marry anyone. He was unsure if he could believe such a claim from a debutante. Everything debutantes did and said was aimed at catching a husband. That was why he usually avoided them as if his very life depended on it. But then, Sophia Cooper was unlike any debutante—indeed, any woman—he had ever met.

And one thing he did know for certain. She had definitely not objected to his kisses, or his caresses. If she had, he'd be lying on the ground, writhing in agony and clutching his groin.

It was not an image that usually made one smile, but knowing that Sophia was such a firebrand, that she had reduced Ravenswood to that state in a way that few men would even dare to do, gave him immense satisfaction. He couldn't be prouder of his non-distressed damsel.

As for the knight in not so shiny armour, he could now get back to his old life. He was free. Although there was one last task he had to perform before he returned to enjoying his bachelor lifestyle.

To that end he visited the other side of London, a

side that couldn't be more different from the elegant balls and soirees attended by Society ladies. A seedy underworld that respectable women like Sophia and Mrs Cooper never got to see. Despite the late hour, the bawdy houses, gambling parlours and other places of ill repute were doing a brisk trade. Ethan pushed his way through the revelling crowds of men, and the scantily dressed women plying their trade, making enquiries of the Duke as he went. No one had seen him that evening. Several men stopped him, not to reveal Ravenswood's whereabouts, but to complain that the Duke owed them money for gambling debts which he kept promising he would soon be able to pay.

Ethan fought to keep his temper under control. He knew exactly how Ravenswood expected to pay those debts. With Sophia's money.

As he moved through each rowdy den of vice, with no sign of the Duke, he consoled himself. If Ravenswood was not in his usual late-night haunts, if he had gone straight home, he would not yet have had a chance to denigrate Sophia's good name to any of his cronies.

She claimed to no longer care about her reputation, but that was because she did not realise just what a damaged reputation could do to a young woman. She would be ostracised. The balls, soirees, picnics and other outings would all be closed to her. Society as a whole would turn its back on her, and the choice of whether she marry or not would be taken out of her hands. No man would want to marry a young woman whose reputation had been tarnished by the lies of a duke.

Sophia also claimed that Ravenswood deserved no

further punishment after what she had dealt out with her knee, but Ethan begged to differ. No punishment would be great enough for what that man had done to Sophia. He should be held accountable by the law and made to pay the price for his abhorrent actions, but that would never happen. He was a duke. No officer of the law would take the word of a young woman with no title and no connections against the word of the powerful Duke of Ravenswood.

It would be up to Ethan to try to redress some of that wrong.

Once he had exhausted the long list of dens of iniquity which catered to men like Ravenswood, he visited the Duke's Belgravia home. It was now the early hours of the morning, but that did not stop Ethan. He pounded on the door, letting everyone in the household know that he was not to be ignored.

'Tell Ravenswood that Ethan Rosemont demands to see him,' he told the footman when he opened the door.

'I'm afraid His Grace is not receiving at this time of night,' the footman said, closing the door.

Ethan's foot shot forward to stop the solid oak door from shutting in his face. 'He might not be receiving guests, but he will receive me.' Ethan pushed past the stunned man, and made his way down the corridor, opening every door. He found the Duke in the drawing room, still in his formal evening wear and nursing a whisky tumbler.

'What is the meaning of this?' the Duke said, attempting to rise from his chair, his face pinched with pain, and waving away the harried footman.

'I think you know perfectly well what this is about,' Ethan said, sorely tempted to take the Duke by the scruff of the neck and give him the beating he deserved. 'I'm here about Sophia Cooper.'

'That chit.' Wincing, he lowered himself slowly and carefully back into his chair. Good. Sophia's knee must have done considerable damage. Ethan suspected the man was suffering from some serious bruising. 'Come to defend her honour, have you?' He smirked and took a drink of his whisky. 'Bit late for that, old chap.'

Ethan swallowed his anger and forced himself to remain as calm as possible. 'What I've come for is to get your assurance that you will not carry out your threat and try to damage her reputation.'

The Duke huffed out his annoyance, then eyed Ethan, a sneer curling his lips. 'Fancy the little chit yourself, do you? Thought as much. Well, I've finished with her, so help yourself. But believe me, she's not worth the effort, especially now she's damaged goods.'

Ethan's hands tightened into fists at his sides. 'I haven't come here to *ask* for your promise to not spread lies about Miss Cooper. I'm here to *tell* you that you will *not* be spreading lies.'

'I'll say whatever I damn well like and to whomever I like about that little minx.' He flicked his hand in Ethan's direction as if dismissing him and everything he had to say.

Ethan's fists clenched tighter. His nails dug into his skin, reminding him he had to keep his temper under control.

'Surprised you're taking such an interest, Rosemont,' the Duke continued. 'She's hardly your type. I believe you like your women with a bit of experience, while me, I like them fresh and untouched. But I'm afraid that ship has now sailed.' He took a long, satisfied drink of whisky.

The temptation to drag the Duke out of his chair and shake him like a rag doll grew ever more intense. The man was an abomination. But beating him to a pulp would achieve nothing. The man was obviously trying to torment him, and he was here to save Sophia's reputation, not to satisfy his own need for vengeance.

'As much as I'd like to repeat what Miss Cooper did to you tonight…' He watched the Duke recoil in painful memory of Sophia's damaging knee. 'Hopefully, it will not come to that.'

Ravenswood huffed out his disapproval. 'You. I would have thought you would have more sense than to threaten a duke, unlike that little trollop, who deserves everything that's coming to her. I'll teach her to respect her betters if it's the last thing I do.'

Ethan breathed slowly and deeply, keeping his anger on a firm leash. 'What I would *like* to do right now is give you a beating you will never forget. But what I *will* do is inform you of what action I plan to take should I hear that you have uttered one bad word about Miss Cooper.'

Ravenswood looked over at him and sneered. 'And what can you do? What are you? A third son? You have no power, no authority. You are nothing, nobody.'

Ethan shrugged. 'Who I am is the brother of Jake Rosemont. A man to whom you owe a considerable amount of money in gambling debts. And Jake is a friend of many of the other men you are in debt to. It would just take one word from me for those men to call in their debts.'

The Duke raised his chin and stared down his nose at Ethan, as if he still considered himself untouchable, but his rapid breathing made it clear he was taking Ethan's threat seriously.

'You would be ruined, both financially and socially,' Ethan continued while the Duke glared at him. 'While Society is hard on a woman it believes has transgressed its strict moral code, it's even harder on a man who can't pay his gambling debts.'

The man had the audacity to shrug. 'I'm a duke. Even if Miss Cooper and her substantial dowry are no longer available to me, there are plenty of other heiresses who will do anything to get a title. There's that American chit. She looks tasty enough. There's no point threatening me. Once I'm married my debts will all be a thing of the past. In the meantime, I will make that Cooper girl pay, and pay dearly, for what she did to me.'

Ethan nodded as if seriously considering what he was saying. 'The problem is, if you spread lies that you seduced innocent Miss Sophia Cooper, do you think the parents of any heiress will consider you a suitable prospect? As you well know, England is full of impoverished aristocrats desperately needing the daughters of wealthy industrialists to bail them out with their dowries. There are all those other dukes, earls, barons and viscounts who don't go around seducing and abandoning sweet, innocent young women. Those other down-on-their-luck titled men would be much better prospects than a reprobate who forfeits on his gambling debts.'

'There's nothing sweet or innocent about that hussy,' he muttered, moving uncomfortably in his seat. 'She's nothing but a—'

'So, do I take it I have your word that you will say or do nothing to besmirch Miss Cooper's good name? I would say your word as a gentleman but after tonight's behaviour I don't think that is appropriate, do you?'

The Duke said nothing. Ethan waited until the man eventually saw sense and nodded.

'I want to hear you say it.'

'All right, Rosemont, you have my word that I won't ruin that chit's reputation.'

Ethan continued to stare at him.

'I promise I won't ruin Miss Sophia Cooper's reputation.'

'Nor will there be any snide innuendoes, lewd suggestions or hints that anything untoward happened between the two of you. Should her name come up in conversation and you can't avoid saying anything, then you will tell everyone what a delightful young woman she is.'

Ravenswood huffed again.

'Won't you?'

'Yes, yes, all right, damn you.'

'And in exchange I won't tell any of your cohorts that a sweet, innocent young girl reduced you to a blubbering mess who can hardly walk.'

Ethan suppressed a smile as the Duke's face turned an interesting colour, something akin to a boiled lobster, or perhaps the red of a coxcomb. Whatever it was, it looked suitably painful.

'Which is probably for the best,' Ethan continued. 'If word got out what she did to you, not only will you be a laughing stock, but everyone will wonder whether she's put an end to the Ravenswood line. I doubt if any heiresses or their families would then see you as a particularly attractive prospect in a potential groom.'

The Duke scowled, staring straight ahead.

'I'll show myself out, shall I?' Ethan could no longer stop himself from laughing as he walked out of the drawing room. It really did feel good to be a gallant knight after all.

## Chapter Eleven

Sleep would not come. After saying goodbye to Ethan, Sophia retired for the night, suddenly exhausted by all that had happened, only to find herself lying awake, staring up at the ceiling. Excitement, anger, contentment and pride all fought a war within her, trying to be her dominant reaction to a night that had been full of unexpected events. She was still furious at Ravenswood, but even more angry at her mother. She had been betrayed by the one person in the world she had always thought she could trust. Ravenswood's behaviour was abhorrent, but deep down, she knew that man meant nothing to her and her anger towards him would pass. And in a strange way, she was grateful for what the Duke had tried to do this evening. He had opened her eyes to his true character before it was too late. It would have been so much worse if he had waited until their wedding night before he revealed his brutishness. No, her anger was mainly directed at her mother. The Duke's vile behaviour had not only revealed the man's true self but had forced her to see just what her mother was prepared to subject her only child to in order to become a well-connected member of Society.

Until tonight, she had thought her mother cared about her. Well, maybe she did care in her own way. Perhaps she had assumed that, like herself, Sophia wanted more than anything else to take a high-ranking position in Society. That achieving such a goal mattered so much to Sophia that everything else could be sacrificed in order to achieve it.

But the days of doing what her mother wanted, without question, were over. From now on, Sophia would make her own decisions and live her life the way she wanted. She would not be that silly, naïve girl who did as she was told, who conformed to what Society and her mother expected of her.

Nor would she allow any man to treat her the way Ravenswood had. Men would soon learn they were dealing with a woman who knew her own mind, who was to be respected and not trifled with. All men, including Lord Ethan.

*Ethan.*

She repeated his name out loud, saying it softly, loving the sound of his name being whispered into the darkness of her bedroom. 'Ethan...'

This night had been full of revelations, and perhaps the greatest revelation were Ethan's kisses. She had never realised a kiss could be about more than just lips touching lips. That it could ignite a fire deep within you which consumed your entire body. When they had kissed, yes, she had felt it on her lips, but her entire body had also come alive, as if he was waking her up from a long, dreamless sleep.

Snuggling down into the warm blankets, she revelled in the memory. She doubted if kissing her had been quite so revelatory for him. She knew she would not be the first woman he had kissed. But for Sophia it had all but transformed her, from a woman who knew little about what happened between a man and a woman, to one who knew how astounding it could be.

At least, it could be astounding with a man like Ethan. She lightly drew her finger over her lips, remembering how his lips had gently caressed them, soft and tempting, like a feather-stroke. Then he had taken her fully in his arms, and the kiss had grown in intensity until all she was aware of was Ethan, and the surge of excitement building within her.

She had wanted him so much. If her mother had not arrived at such an inopportune moment, she knew she would have demanded more from him than just those impassioned kisses.

Sophia was unsure whether to thank her mother for that, or to add it to the growing list of grievances. But she would think of that another day. Now she needed to sleep, and she hoped she would spend the night dreaming of that kiss, and of nothing else that had taken place on this fateful evening.

Waking the next morning, Sophia stretched luxuriously in her bed. She'd got her wish. Despite being alone, a blush burned on her cheeks as she remembered all that the man of her dreams had done to her last night. Yes, her dream Ethan had kissed her, but those kisses had travelled far beyond her lips. She covered her mouth to stop an embarrassed giggle from escaping as the dream repeated itself in her mind. Was there any part of her she hadn't imagined him kissing? When he'd held her in his arms last night, she'd so wanted him to kiss and caress every part of her body. And now he had, or, at least, he had in her dreams.

But that was all it was. A dream. She threw back the bedcovers and called for her lady's maid to help her dress. Dreams were not reality. Only silly young ladies were deluded by dreams, fantasies and fairy tales, and she was no longer a silly young lady.

She entered the breakfast room to find her mother seated at the table, her back and face rigid as she glared up at Sophia. 'I believe you owe me an explanation, young lady. Not to mention an apology.' Her voice had the familiar reproachful tone that would once have immediately brought Sophia to heel, but not any more.

Ignoring her mother, she served herself her usual breakfast of toast with a scraping of butter and a small dab of jam, then thought better of it. Her mother had always insisted she eat small portions, saying that men like the Duke appreciated a slim, girlish figure.

Well, forget that. Sophia loaded up her plate with eggs, sausages, bacon, and muffins with lashings of butter. She was not a girl. She was a woman, and if men like the Duke didn't like that, well, who cared? Certainly not Sophia.

She sat opposite her mother and, with delight, watched her face become more pinched as she stared at the laden plate.

'Well?' her mother barked. 'Are you going to tell me what got into you last night, why you were acting like such an impudent child?'

Sophia poured herself a cup of tea, taking her time in responding. 'Where would you like me to start, Mother? Would you like me to describe what the Duke did when he escorted me out of his private box and into an even more private alcove?'

Her mother inclined her head and raised her eyebrows. 'What did happen?' She leant forward in anticipation. 'I don't need you to tell me the details, but will he be asking for your hand? Did he make you a promise first? Is that why you're acting so high and mighty? Is it because you're soon going to be a duchess?'

'*First?* What do you mean by *first*? What were you expecting the Duke to do to me *first*?'

Her mother waved her hand in the air as if the question was of no importance. 'Did he propose? Did he say he'd be calling on me to ask for your hand?'

'Well, yes, he did make a promise, a proposal of a sort, *first*.' Sophia gripped her teacup tightly, then forced herself to relax. She would waste no more energy getting angry with that man.

Her mother nodded, then took a contented sip of her tea. 'Good.'

'But I doubt if he will be asking for my hand.' She replaced the cup in the saucer. 'Not unless he is looking for a bride who will knee him in the bollocks when he tries to force himself on her.'

Her mother's teacup clattered to the table, missing the saucer and spilling its contents, the brown stain spreading over the white linen tablecloth. A footman rushed forward to clear away the damage. 'Leave it,' she shrieked, flapping her hands at the flustered servant. 'And leave this room. Now.'

The footman gave a quick bow and raced out of the door.

'What did you say? Do you even know the meaning of what you just said? Where on earth did you hear such language? Was it from that Lord Ethan?' Her mother placed her hand on her stomach and breathed in deeply, then smiled through gritted teeth. 'Obviously, you do not know the meaning of such words.'

'Believe me, I do,' Sophia said, spearing a sausage with her fork. 'When Ravenswood had me pinned up against the wall and was forcing my legs apart, I raised my knee hard. I believe that's the correct name given to that particular action.'

Her mother stared at her, goggle-eyed, her mouth opening and closing as if searching for words that would not come. 'You assaulted the Duke,' she finally gasped out.

'No. I defended myself from a man who was trying to assault me.'

'My dear,' her mother said, then paused, closed her eyes and drew in a shaking breath. 'My dear, the Duke was not trying to assault you. We discussed this before the ball. He had all but announced that he was going to marry you. He had taken you to the opera, shown you off to all of Society by sitting next to you in his private box. Then, as you said, he had made a promise, a proposal of a sort. If he kissed you, and perhaps took things a little bit further than he should, then he will most definitely have to marry you.'

Her mother nodded quickly and repeatedly, and Sophia could all but see the scheming taking place in her mind. 'All is perhaps not lost. I'll have a word with him. Explain about your innocence. After the way he has behaved, he is now duty-bound to make you his wife.'

Sophia lowered her knife and fork and placed them on her plate, no longer hungry. 'You will not be speaking to Ravenswood,' she said, her voice rising. 'I will not be marrying him. And how dare you think otherwise? You knew what he was going to do to me when he led me away, didn't you, Mother?'

Her mother shrugged. 'No, I didn't, not precisely. Yes, I knew the Duke was interested in you and thought he might try to take a few liberties, but if he did, it would all be for a good purpose and would make no difference as long as no one knew, and he would be honour-bound to marry you.' She smiled at Sophia as if all had been sufficiently explained away. 'When you become a duchess, you will have fulfilled all your father's dreams. He always said—'

'My father would not want me to be groped and grabbed against my will,' Sophia shot back. 'My father wanted me to be happy. That is what he meant by my becoming a princess.'

'You will be happy when you're a duchess.'

'I could never be happy married to a man like that. He's a degenerate.'

'My dear, he's a duke and dukes play by different rules than the rest of us.'

'In that case, thank goodness I've ruined any possibility of becoming a duchess. I'd never want to be married to a man who played by such dishonourable, dissolute rules.'

'Don't be too hasty, my dear. If I explain to the Duke that you didn't know what you were doing and that you promise it will never happen again, then I'm sure he'll forgive you.'

Sophia could hardly believe what she was hearing. '*He'll* forgive *me*? I've done nothing wrong. It is him that needs to be forgiven, and believe me, I won't be giving him my forgiveness.'

'Now, Sophia, my dear—'

'I...will...not...be...marrying...that...man.'

Her mother's condescending smile turned quickly to a scowl. 'I suppose you want to marry that Lord Ethan Rosemont. You foolish girl. You have a dowry that must be the envy of every other debutante. Why would you want to waste it on the third son of a duke? Marry him and you'll have no title at all and that's not how I raised you.'

'He might not have a title, but he is a far superior man to the Duke of Ravenswood.'

Her mother gave her a long, considering stare. 'You do have aspirations in that direction, don't you? You've become even more foolish than I thought. You do realise that he is no different from the Duke of Ravenswood, don't you?'

Sophia refused to answer her mother, realising she knew little about Ethan. All she knew was that he had been kind to her, and that his kisses were literally breathtaking.

'If anything, Lord Ethan has an even worse reputation than the Duke,' her mother continued, her expression almost gleeful. 'He's reputed to have had countless mistresses. Actresses, chorus girls, married women, you name it. They say he never goes long without a woman, and they are always women of a certain type.' Her mother's lips moved into a moue of disapproval. 'He's probably had even more mistresses than the Duke, and it wouldn't surprise me if they hadn't shared the same mistress at times. After all, they move in the same circles and frequent the same places…' She cast a glance upwards, as if searching for the right word. 'Places that cater to men with certain tastes.'

Her mother looked across the table and smiled, as a tense knot gripped Sophia's stomach and her head swam.

'Yes, that one has quite the blackened reputation,' her mother continued. 'I've heard the other mothers talking about him. That's the main reason they keep their daughters away from him. They don't want their precious girls seduced by a notorious rake, particularly one who has no interest in ever marrying.'

It had to be a lie. Ethan was not like that. But what did she really know about him? She knew he was handsome, charming, that he had tried to warn her about Ravenswood and that he was a wonderful kisser. The knot increased its grip on her stomach.

He *was* a wonderful kisser.

A man wasn't born with the ability to kiss like that.

It took practice. He needed to have kissed countless women to have perfected his technique. A technique that could make a woman surrender herself to him, give herself so easily, and do it with such gratitude. Was that not the very definition of a seducer?

If her mother hadn't arrived when she did, Sophia knew she would have let Ethan do whatever he wanted with her, would have all but begged him to do so. Was that really so different from what had happened with Ravenswood? They were both men who seduced women, but whereas Ravenswood lacked even the slightest finesse, Lord Ethan could do so in a manner where the young woman felt she was making the advances. And her mother was right. He had already told her he did not intend to marry her. He had done so just before he kissed her. Yet she had given herself to him freely, knowing he would never offer for her hand.

She shook her head as if to shake herself free of those tormenting thoughts. 'I do not plan to marry Lord Ethan and I very much doubt if I will ever see him again. He kindly escorted me home after Ravenswood assaulted me. That was all.'

Her mother eyed her for an extended moment. Sophia tried to drink her tea with as much nonchalance as possible, hoping her mother would not ask about what she had witnessed last night on the doorstep. Something that had been magical, that had awakened a sensual side of her that she had not known to exist, now seemed less special. She had become one more in the long line of women who had given themselves to Lord Ethan Rosemont. That was something she hardly wanted to think about, and she most certainly did not want to defend her actions to her mother.

'Good, at least you haven't fallen under the spell of that womaniser.' Her mother nodded with satisfaction. 'That's something, anyway. You may have lost the Duke, but there are other titled men still available.'

She stared at her mother in disbelief, anger replacing heartache. Had she not heard a word Sophia had said?

'You can put aside all thoughts of my going after another titled man, Mother, as I doubt that any will be interested in marrying me now.'

'Of course they will, my dear. You're a highly desirable catch. I'm sure there will be lots of other titled men who will be very interested in courting you. It might be hard to find another duke, but I'm confident you'll still be able to attract an earl, viscount or baron.'

'And I doubt if a single one of them will consider marrying a woman like me. The last thing Ravenswood said when he left was that he'll ruin my reputation in revenge for what I did. He intends to tell everyone that he had his way with me and that I am no longer chaste.'

Her mother's hands shot to her chest, gripping tightly as if she was about to have a heart attack. 'He did what?'

'You heard me, Mother. Or, more precisely, he said he'd tell everyone he'd tupped me in a public place like a common harlot. Are you still going to say that dukes play by different rules and we should forgive the—'

'But this is terrible. The Duke will not marry you and now no one else will. Sophia, how could you? Why did you not just give him what he wanted?'

Sophia stared at her mother, unable to believe what she had just said. Her hands clenching tightly, she chose not to answer, unsure whether she would be able to contain her temper.

'Now no one will marry you,' her mother continued, her face contorted as if she was the one who had suffered.

'Thank goodness for that,' Sophia replied through gritted teeth.

'You foolish, foolish girl. Of course you have to marry.'

'Why?'

'Why?' her mother almost screeched. 'Because if you don't, you'll be a spinster, an old maid. You'll be left on the shelf and pitied by everyone.'

'You mean, I'll be pitied by all those other debutantes who managed to marry and live a life of complete misery with a man who doesn't love them, their only compensation being the title their husband has bestowed on them. I'd rather be pitied than miserable.'

'You won't have a home of your own. You won't have children.'

Sophia's resolve wavered somewhat, but she would not let her mother get the better of her.

'A small sacrifice if it means I don't have to put up with a brutish husband.' She lifted her chin to signal that her mother's words had not affected her.

'You'll be an outcast with no one to support you. You'll end up living in poverty, because if you don't marry, don't expect me to give you a home or provide your keep. You'll have to become a governess or some elderly woman's paid companion, and believe me, you won't like either of those options. And with a sullied reputation, even those choices might be closed to you.'

'No, they are not my only options.'

'They are, and the only way you're going to avoid that fate is to apologise to the Duke and beg his forgiveness. Hopefully he'll be chivalrous and will marry you anyway, or if he doesn't, then at least he won't besmirch your name.'

'No. I won't be doing that. Instead, I'll remain single and live off the money my father left me, and, as I own this house, I'll never be homeless. So, you see, I don't actually need a man to support me.'

Her mother remained speechless, while Sophia resumed drinking her tea.

'You can't possibly mean that,' she eventually said.

'I can and I do.'

'Has that Lord Ethan put you up to this?' She narrowed her eyes. 'Has he suggested you become his mistress?'

*Become his mistress.* That was something Sophia had never considered. He had said he did not want to marry her, but he had said nothing about her becoming his mistress. Would that be such a terrible thing? Would it be so wrong to spend her evenings in his arms, in his bed? Would it be so dreadful for last night's dream to become a reality?

Surely that was something she wanted. She shook her head slightly to drive that thought out of her mind. She was not the type of woman to become any man's mistress, not even Lord Ethan Rosemont's.

'No one has put me up to anything. I shall be an independent woman who doesn't need anyone, including a husband.'

'You unnatural girl. I can hardly believe you are my daughter.'

Sophia smiled at her scowling mother. It seemed they had something in common. She too could hardly believe she was the same young woman who yesterday had gone along with her mother's schemes, with such docile obedience. That daughter was gone for ever.

Ethan was finally free. Sophia was no longer being courted by Ravenswood. Ravenswood had promised not to carry through on his threat to ruin her. Sophia could now find a more suitable man to marry, or, indeed, not marry at all, if that was her preference. She was not his responsibility any more, not that she ever really had been, but now he was truly free.

He could do anything he wanted with the day stretching out ahead of him. Perhaps take a ride in Hyde Park and watch the parade of pretty young ladies. Tonight he could visit one of his clubs, maybe the theatre, see if Annette would forgive him for his absence, perhaps find a party to attend. Whatever he wanted to do, he could do it.

Instead, what did he do? It was barely past midday when he grabbed his hat and coat and walked over to Sophia's town house.

After all, he wasn't really free, was he? Not yet.

Last night he had kissed her. He didn't want to marry her. He was sure he had made that clear before he kissed her, but there was no harm in restating the fact. Not that he expected her to insist he do the so-called right thing by her. She had also made it clear to him she wanted nothing from him. But he *had* kissed her. The very least he owed her was a visit. It would be the height of rudeness to do otherwise. Plus, he wanted to make sure she was indeed as un-traumatised by Ravenswood's behaviour as she had appeared last night.

Once this visit was over, then they could go their separate ways. All that was left to do was to reassure himself that she thought nothing of that kiss and was happy to carry on with her life without him in it.

Although, in all honesty, it had been more than *just* a kiss. He stopped walking, causing a young nanny pushing a perambulator almost as big as she was to nearly bump into him.

'Sorry,' they said simultaneously.

'Sorry,' he repeated, stepping out of her way and signalling for her to continue.

Sophia may have asked him to kiss her, but that was all. He had done much more than that. He had taken uninvited liberties. If Sophia expected him to offer for her hand, then she would be quite within her rights to do so. What on earth had he been thinking? Taking such liberties with a young debutante? It was not only wrong, but everyone knew where such behaviour led. Marriage. That was why he never got involved with debutantes.

Although, her behaviour last night was unlike that of any other debutante he had ever met. She had accepted that he did not wish to marry. But that was last night. She had now had time to think. Would she still believe his conduct was acceptable?

And as for the mother… Ethan released an exasperated huff. If the mother wanted her daughter married, she would now have Ethan caught, hook, line and sinker. He could only hope that she still had her heart set on catching a bigger fish than the untitled younger brother of a duke.

He commenced walking. Yes, there was a possibility he might have to marry Sophia, and the only way he could find out was by visiting the Coopers. His walking slowed down. Would marriage to Sophia be such a bad outcome? He shook his head as if answering his internal question. Yes, it would be. He hardly knew the woman. All he knew was she was pretty, delightful, was a sublime kisser and had a strong right knee.

His thoughts strayed back, yet again, to that sublime kiss. A kiss like none he had ever experienced. He had gone over and over it in his mind last night, unable to sleep and unable to come up with an explanation for why it was different. He suspected it had something to do with the strange reactions that had rushed through him when he had Sophia in his arms. Reactions he had not experienced before. It was more than lust. That was something he was very familiar with. There had been an intensity that was both unsettling and compelling. It was as if his heart were floating, had broken free from his chest and was encompassing them both with warmth and affection. Physical desire alone could not do that. For the duration of their kiss, it was as if he was exactly where he was supposed to be, and with the woman he was supposed to be with.

He smiled at his delusions, causing a passing young lady to smile back at him. Floating hearts? Ludicrous. It would have been lust, just good, clean—or perhaps not so clean—lust and nothing else. That was how he always felt when he had an attractive woman in his arms, and that was how he had felt with Sophia. Any other possibility was simply ludicrous.

That was another good reason for visiting her this morning. He was sure that after seeing her again, he would put all thoughts of floating hearts out of his mind. She would be consigned to his past, along with all the other women he had held in his arms. He would go back to living the life he had always lived. She would go on with living her life however she wanted to, and they would both forget he had ever embraced her, ever kissed her, that they had ever clung on to each other as if their very lives depended on it.

Presenting his card to the footman, he asked if Mrs and Miss Cooper were home to receiving guests. The footman departed and, a few moments later, reappeared to escort Ethan into the drawing room.

Sophia rose from her chair when he entered and walked towards him.

He halted in the doorway. Had he actually forgotten how beautiful she was? Dressed in a simple yellow-and-white-striped day dress, her hair in a simple bun at the back of her neck, she looked stunning. And like a dullard in the presence of a goddess, he was staring at her as if entranced.

'Lord Ethan, how lovely to see you again.'

He gave a small, formal bow, shaking himself out of this bizarre reaction to a pretty face and trying to ignore his racing heart and that strange feeling in his chest, as if he had been winded.

'Miss Cooper,' he said. It seemed they were now back to using formal titles. Perhaps he should take that as a good sign. Despite all they had experienced together last night, despite their kiss, she was not seeing them as being on informal terms. That was as he had hoped, he told himself, ignoring the illogical pang of disappointment. She did not see him as a man now expected to ask for her hand.

'Mrs Cooper.' He bowed to the mother, sitting beside the unlit fireplace. She looked him up and down, scowled, then went back to staring at the fireplace.

'Please sit,' Sophia said, sitting down on the sofa and indicating that he should join her.

Ethan glanced at Mrs Cooper, expecting her to put up some objection to such close proximity to her daughter, but she said nothing, merely flared her nostrils in silent anger, so he took the seat beside Sophia.

'I thought it best to visit you this morning to put your mind at rest.'

'About?' Sophia asked.

'About the Duke of Ravenswood.'

Mrs Cooper sat up straighter in her chair and turned to face him, as if the mere mention of the Duke's name was reason to act with greater propriety.

'I visited the Duke last night,' he continued, turning his attention back to Sophia.

'How is the poor man?' she said with a laugh. 'Is he able to walk upright yet?'

'Let's just say that he is as well as can be expected. And I have a promise from him that in the unlikely event that he ever mentions your name in public, he will be singing your praises, nothing else.'

Sophia raised her eyebrows. 'And you trust him to be true to his word?'

'I trust him to know what is in his best interests.'

Sophia laughed again and clapped her hands together, causing Ethan to smile.

'Well done, Lord Ethan.'

That duty completed, Ethan had no reason to remain in this drawing room. Sophia had obviously recovered from her ordeal last night. More than recovered. She seemed to be all but glowing. And her behaviour towards him was friendly but did not suggest she believed they were now a courting couple.

And yet, instead of saying his goodbyes, he stayed.

'I wasn't particularly worried about what Ravenswood threatened to say about me,' she continued. 'But it will make my life easier not having to deal with false rumours.' She stood up and rang the bell for a servant, and when the man arrived asked for tea to be served. Only yesterday, it would have been Mrs Cooper's decision whether a guest was welcome to stay long enough to take tea.

'So, what next for you, Miss Cooper?' he asked as she took her seat. 'Will you be going to Lord and Lady Stanmore's ball next week?'

'Perhaps. I haven't yet decided.' She gave a small

sigh. 'I think I've had enough of balls and the Season in general.'

Her mother's rustling in her seat drew their attention. Ethan expected her to express her disapproval and state that, for a young lady, attending balls was the whole point of the Season. It was the main place where she would be seen by prospective husbands. But instead of raising objections, Mrs Cooper merely crossed her arms firmly and continued to scowl at them.

'If you're tired of the Season, does that mean you'll be returning to Yorkshire?' Why this should concern Ethan he did not know, but he *was* concerned. Surely, that would be the best outcome for him. It would be proof that she expected no more from him and he was indeed free.

'No. I intend to remain in London, perhaps even after the Season has ended. London has so much more to offer than attending balls and chasing after husbands, something I will not be doing, ever again.' She sent a pointed look at her mother, causing the older woman to once again shuffle in her seat, and her scowl to become more pronounced.

Ethan was unsure whether to be pleased or worried. He had the assurance he wanted. She did not sound like a woman expecting a proposal of marriage. While he was pleased she had no expectations of him, he hoped she had not given up on marriage altogether. Hopefully, it was just a temporary reaction to Ravenswood's unforgivable behaviour. A woman as remarkable as Sophia deserved to find love with a good, respectable and steadfast man. A man who was nothing like Ethan.

The tea arrived. They waited while the footman poured and handed each of them a cup.

'So, what do you plan to do, then, if you're not going to attend balls?' There had been such a change in her, he could imagine her doing just about anything...taking to the stage, running off to the Americas, joining an expedition to Antarctica.

'Well, I did enjoy our walk home last night. Perhaps when we have finished our tea, we could go for another walk in Hyde Park.'

Ethan smiled with relief at her safe choice. 'I'd be delighted. Although I'm afraid I didn't bring my carriage.'

'Excellent,' she said, clapping her hands together. 'Do you know, we've been in London for several months now and apart from last night, I've only seen this neighbourhood through the window of a carriage? It will be lovely to walk the streets in daylight.'

Mrs Cooper sniffed. 'Respectable young ladies do not walk the streets.'

'Well, this young lady does,' Sophia continued, her voice still bright and cheerful. 'She doesn't care who approves or disapproves. In fact, if members of Society disapprove, to me that seems all the more reason to do something. Don't you agree, Lord Ethan?'

Ethan merely smiled and took another sip of his tea, not wanting to appear to be taking sides in the ongoing battle between mother and daughter.

'And I also want to see all of London's art galleries and museums.'

'Then I'd be honoured to escort you to them as well,

if you so wish.' The words were out of his mouth before he had thought about what he was saying. Wasn't he trying to regain his freedom?

'That will be wonderful. You must know all the best places.'

Ethan nodded, despite having never set foot inside a museum or an art gallery.

'And let's walk to them as well. I feel as if I've spent most of my life cooped up like a caged parrot. Now I want to spread my wings and take flight.'

He waited for Mrs Cooper's objections, but she seemed to have undergone as much of a transformation as Sophia and was now the meek and mild one. It was apparent that from now onwards Sophia would do whatever she wanted, and no one, not Ethan, and not her mother, could stop this vibrant young woman.

## *Chapter Twelve*

The moment they'd finished their tea, Sophia jumped to her feet, eager to get away from her disapproving mother and to be alone with Lord Ethan.

'Right. Let's go for that walk you promised,' she said, ringing the bell for her lady's maid.

Lord Ethan stood and said goodbye to her mother but received only another disapproving sniff in response. Despite Sophia's attempts to convince her that Lord Ethan had done nothing wrong, her mother still seemed to hold him at least partially responsible for changing her daughter's behaviour from deferential to defiant. Either that or she still feared that the untitled Lord Ethan would soon be her son-in-law, or worse, her daughter would become his mistress.

Well, let her worry.

Maggie entered and Sophia instructed her to bring her jacket and hat and to ready herself for a walk in the park.

'I don't know how long we'll be, Mother, but you're

not to concern yourself about what I get up to. And you know what an obedient, well-behaved young lady I am. I believe you often mentioned that fact to the Duke of Ravenswood,' Sophia said, unable to resist the temptation to tease her mother one more time. Her statement received the expected look of disapproval.

'We'll just be enjoying ourselves, but I won't be on the lookout for any dukes, earls, barons, viscounts or marquesses who are in want of a wife,' she added, taking pleasure in seeing her mother's mouth descend into a deeper scowl.

They exited the room and when the door closed behind them Lord Ethan turned to her, his lips curling into one of those slow, lazy smiles that made her insides flutter and her heart seemingly melt inside her chest.

'Your poor mother. You really are becoming rather wicked, aren't you?'

'Yes, I am. And it's rather wonderful.'

He laughed, causing her to smile with increased pleasure.

'So, shall we?' He extended his arm, which she gladly took.

They walked down the street, arm in arm, her lady's maid following several paces behind. Sophia tried not to react to having him so close and tried to ignore the thoughts whirling inside her head.

*Do not think of that kiss. Do not think of his hands caressing your body. Do not remember last night's dream. Think of something innocuous to talk about. Something. Anything.*

But nothing would come to her, so they walked

along the street in silence. It was hard to think about a polite topic of conversation when you were preoccupied with the warmth of the body next to yours, when your senses were reacting to that now familiar scent of sandalwood and musk, and your skin was tingling with the memory of this man's touch.

Other couples were out promenading along the leafy streets, and virtually every woman, young and old, cast a quick look in Lord Ethan's direction. Sophia had no choice but to forgive them. How could they not look at him? Few men were as handsome as the one on her arm. Few exuded that intoxicating sense of manliness. It was inevitable that such masculine beauty attracted the gazes of women, just as the warmth of the sun drew the faces of flowers. Despite that, Sophia was sure forgiveness was not what she'd be feeling if Ethan did anything to acknowledge their gazes. But fortunately he was oblivious to all that feminine attention, so her jealousy remained controlled.

Those women no doubt envied Sophia, and if they knew how he had kissed her last night, how he had brought her body to a state of sensual arousal she had not known was possible, she was sure every passing woman would turn a deep shade of jealous green.

But, she reminded herself yet again, she was *not* going to think about that kiss.

They entered Hyde Park and her mind was finally diverted from that kiss she wasn't thinking about. The park was full of young ladies promenading in the latest fashions, accompanied by their chaperones. The feathers, flowers and ribbons on their hats moved in the gentle breeze like the colourful plumage of exotic birds. And, just like the colourful birds they resembled, they were all trying to catch the attention of a potential mate. And if the plumage didn't do the trick, then the twirling of lacy parasols might draw the eye of the passing men.

Meanwhile, men were casually riding past them on horseback and in open carriages, observing what was on offer this Season.

And just one day ago, Sophia would have been part of that hopeful parade.

'It's so sad, isn't it?' she said, as much to herself as to Lord Ethan.

He raised his eyebrows in question.

'I was just looking at all those young ladies, showing themselves off in all their finery, and wondering how many of them realise what is really happening here? How they are being used by others in a game where they are unlikely to be the winners.'

He looked over at a group of giggling young ladies being escorted by their proud, smiling mother. 'Not many, unfortunately.'

'They're dressed up in their best clothes, looking so pretty and feeling like they're in a fairy tale.' She shook her head sadly at both her own previous naivety and the plight of so many other young women. 'Their families are trying to get the biggest return for the goods on offer. If she is pretty enough, has enough money, she might be able to move up the social hierarchy and elevate her entire family's social status. So much is riding on those young shoulders and they don't even know it.'

Thank goodness she was no longer part of that charade. Thank goodness her eyes had been opened to reality.

'Why, Miss Cooper, I believe you have become even more cynical than me.'

'Yes, I'm a changed woman.' She tilted up her chin and smiled. 'So changed that I wish you would call me Sophia.'

He frowned slightly and she wondered whether she had gone too far. Was he worried that she saw him as her new beau?

'I mean, we are friends, aren't we?' she asked, keeping her voice as light as possible. 'And surely friends call each other by their given names.'

His furrowed brow became smooth and he smiled. 'And you must call me Ethan.'

'Ethan,' she repeated, loving the sound of it, loving the feel of it on her tongue. She had called him Ethan when they kissed. It was such a lovely sound. Soft, sensual, yet masculine. Just like the man himself.

'So, Sophia,' he said, and they exchanged smiles. 'Would you like to walk across the grass? Perhaps it might rain again, as it did the first time we walked together. Then we can get away from your ever-present lady's maid.'

'On neither count do I believe we have anything to worry about.' She looked up at the blue sky, dotted with a few white clouds that appeared incapable of ever doing anything so dramatic as actually raining.

'The sky is going to stay a glorious blue, and we do not have to worry about Maggie.' She turned and looked over her shoulder at her lady's maid. 'Perhaps you'd like to take a walk by yourself, Maggie, and meet up with some of the other servants,' she called out.

Maggie nodded enthusiastically. 'Yes, madam.' She turned and headed off in a different direction towards a group of nannies sitting on a bench and slowly pushing their large black perambulators backwards and forwards as they chatted together.

'It seems your lady's maid has also undergone a transformation,' he said, looking in the direction of the departing chaperone.

'Yes. I informed Maggie this morning that the London home we all live in belongs to me, and that her wages come out of my money. That had the desired effect of changing her loyalty immediately from my mother to me. I very much doubt if Mother will get much out of Maggie about what I've been up to, no matter how hard she interrogates her.'

He laughed out loud. 'I was right. You really are quite wicked. I love it.'

Sophia joined in with his laughter. Pleased that he appreciated this new side of her and trying not to read anything into his use of the word *love*.

'I'm pleased you suggested this walk, because we need to talk,' he said, his voice suddenly serious.

She gave a small laugh, somewhat wary of his change in tone. 'Of course. Talk away.'

'We need to discuss what happened last night. Between us.' He drew in a long, slow breath. 'Our kiss,' he added on an exhalation.

'Oh, that.' She tried to keep smiling and ignore

her heart pounding hard against the wall of her chest. 'What is it you would like to discuss? Do you wish to give me instruction on my technique, or do you want to rate my performance compared to other women?' She laughed lightly, to let him know it was a joke, but he did not smile.

Perhaps she shouldn't have been so flippant. 'Ethan.. I don't want it to come between us,' she rushed on. 'It was just something that happened in the moment. It meant nothing. I don't want you to think that I expect anything more from you.'

He nodded slowly, and she was unsure if he believed her. Unsure if she believed what she was saying herself.

'My mother hoped that the Duke of Ravenswood would be compromised into marrying me. I just hope when I…' She did not know what to say. How did she explain that when she all but begged him to kiss her, she expected no more from him than just a kiss? 'I would be so upset if you thought I was trying to compromise you.'

He stopped, turned to face her and took her hands in his. 'Sophia, you are the most honest and open person I have ever met. Perhaps too honest for the sort of world in which we live. So, no, I did not think you were trying to compromise me.'

'Good.' She nodded. 'And rest assured I do not wish to marry you.'

His shoulders relaxed and he nodded again. A pang of disappointment clutched at her heart. Had she honestly expected him to object, to declare his love, to ask for her hand? No, of course she hadn't. She had only just found her independence. She wasn't about to surrender it so quickly. That pain in her chest was merely confusion over this unusual situation, and concern that he might think she was trying to trap him.

'But I do worry that if people see us out together, such as on this walk, or if I escort you to art galleries or museums, people are likely to get the wrong idea,' he said. 'They are likely to think that we are courting.'

The gripping of her heart intensified. 'Are you worried that it will ruin your chances of finding a suitable bride?' She attempted to laugh, as if merely teasing a good friend, and hoped he had not seen through her attempt at nonchalance.

'That is most definitely not something that concerns me, but if people do think we are courting, then your chances of marrying will diminish severely. You will not attract other men's interest if they think you are spoken for. I would not like to jeopardise your chances of making a good marriage.'

Sophia shrugged. 'As I said, I have no interest in marrying. At least not this Season. There is still plenty of time to think about that, but it is not important to me now.' She gave his hands a reassuring squeeze. 'So you have nothing to worry about.'

He patted her hand. 'As long as you are sure.'

She nodded, then bit her lip, daring herself to say it. 'But I still wouldn't mind if you did, you know?'

He frowned. 'You wouldn't mind if I did what?'

'Told me how I rated compared to other women you have kissed,' she said, and laughed more loudly than a young lady should. But it wasn't entirely said in jest. If her mother's claim was right, then he had kissed count-less women before her. She knew she was inexperi-enced, but she hoped he would remember her kisses as more than just a fumbling attempt at passion from a young woman who did not know what she was doing.

Still smiling, hoping he would see it as a jolly good jest, she waited. He didn't smile back. Instead, his eyes stared into hers, the intensity of which caused her breath to catch in her throat and her smile to dis-solve. She continued to wait for his answer, unable to breathe, as hope and desire swept through her. The way he was looking at her was the same way he had looked at her before he kissed her last night. A gaze that caused her to lose the ability to think, to only feel and to want, to want desperately.

His gaze left her eyes and moved to her lips. Unable to stop herself, even if she had wanted to, she parted them and ran the tip of her tongue along her bottom lip.

Was she sending him an invitation? Would he accept it? Would he kiss her again? Here, right in the middle of Hyde Park? With everyone watching?

His gaze returned to her eyes. 'Kissing you was wonderful,' he said softly. 'You're wonderful.'

She gripped his hands more tightly, sure she was about to swoon, like some love-struck maiden. Then realised the reason she was feeling so light-headed. She had stopped breathing. She dragged in a breath, hop-ing he wouldn't notice how gasping it was.

His unblinking eyes continued to stare down at her, their intensity holding her captive. 'I know you said you don't want to marry,' he murmured.

His words caused her to gasp in another breath, so loudly she was sure he must have heard. Was he going to propose to her after all? And if he did, what was she going to say?

'But you should,' he continued. 'You deserve to marry a good man, a loving, caring man. You are a lovely, unique woman. Now that you have realised what Ravenswood is really like, now you know there are men out there who will take advantage of a young woman's innocence, and that there are men who only want a wife for the marriage settlement she brings with her, you will be better placed to notice a good man when he comes along.'

*I think I already have.*

She swallowed. 'And what of you? Are you well placed to notice a good woman when she comes along?'

A smile transformed his serious countenance. 'I'm not seeking a wife, so it doesn't matter how well placed I am.'

*Fool. You little fool.*

Sophia had thought she had changed. She had been so proud of the new Sophia, the independent young woman who would never act like a silly, naïve girl ever again. But how much had she really changed? Instead of chasing after a reprobate because he had a title, now she was chasing after a rake who didn't want a wife, just because he was kind to her and was an accomplished kisser.

*He told you he doesn't want to marry you or anyone else. And here you are, expecting a proposal from him. Fool.*

She smiled back at him, determined that he would never know of her momentary lapse into a state of delusion. 'But even if you aren't looking for a wife, I trust you are looking for a friend,' she said, keeping her voice cheerful. 'And by that I, of course, mean me.'

'Yes. I hope we will always be friends.'

She wanted to add, *Very good friends indeed. Friends so good that maybe we could occasionally exchange passionate kisses in dark doorways.* He had claimed that she was the most honest person he had ever met. That was what she would say if she was really being honest. But it was certainly not what he wanted to hear, so she would keep such fanciful thoughts to herself.

He took her arm once more and they continued to promenade along the tree-lined walkway. Several gentlemen passed. They nodded to Ethan and tipped their top hats at Sophia.

'You seem to be attracting a lot of admiring glances today,' Ethan said. Was that a note of jealousy in his voice, or was it merely what she hoped to hear?

'Perhaps they know an heiress is back on the market, that the Duke of Ravenswood has been knocked out of prime position as first claimant on my settlement.'

'You sell yourself short, Sophia. You are a beautiful young woman, one that any man would be happy to call his wife, marriage settlement or no.'

*But that so-called list of many men does not include you.*

As she pushed aside that thought, they continued to walk around the park. And Sophia vowed to herself it would remain her secret that for one brief, foolish moment she forgot that Lord Ethan Rosemont was not, and never would be, a man in search of a wife.

Ethan had never had a female friend before. Lovers, yes, he'd had plenty of them, and he had good relationships with all the women in his life, even after they had ceased to be lovers. But a friend, never.

He did not know how a man and a woman behaved when they were friends, but one thing of which he was fairly certain, friends did not kiss each other passionately, they did not explore each other's bodies and they didn't constantly think about doing so.

Friendship was platonic. That much he did know. That meant he would not be kissing Sophia again. And her body would remain untouchable.

She looked up at him and smiled, that enchanting smile that lit up her face and made the world seem a brighter place. He smiled back at her, hoping his own smile was merely that of a good friend, and not of a man who was looking at a woman with lustful intent. Hopefully, his smile wasn't revealing to her how much he wanted to hold her, wanted to kiss her again, wanted to watch her lips as they moved from a smile to little gasps of passion, then pants of pure, frantic need. Just as they had last night.

He coughed to drive out that image. If he was a true friend, he wouldn't even think about such things. Friendship was all she wanted from him, and if he considered himself to be any sort of gentleman he would abide by her wishes, even in the privacy of his thoughts.

To do otherwise would make him no better than Ravenswood, a man who took what he wanted for his own gratification with no thought as to what the woman wanted or felt.

Yes, he would be her friend. That was all. He could do this. He wanted to do this. He wanted Sophia in his life, so they would be friends.

And he *did* want her in his life. He did enjoy her company, more than he'd enjoyed the company of any other woman, including the ones who made up that long line of women who had warmed his bed. So perhaps this friendship arrangement could work. If he was to spend time with her, all he had to do was keep the baser side of his nature firmly under control. Surely he could do that.

He'd just have to remember at all times that Sophia was a debutante. She differed from the women he usually mixed with, and she wanted a different sort of relationship with him.

He was sure he could make this work. Practising a bit of self-control wouldn't do him any harm whatsoever, and he had too much respect for Sophia to do otherwise.

'So, if you're not going to Lord and Lady Stanmore's ball, what does the new, free Sophia Cooper want to do next?' he asked in his new, good-friend manner.

'Do you know what I'd really like to do?' she said, smiling up at him, those big blue eyes sparkling.

*Do not hope she'll say* I want you to kiss me. *Good friend, remember.*

Ethan continued smiling, pleased that Sophia was no mind reader.

'I want to go to the opera.'

That took him as much by surprise as if she actually had said she wanted him to kiss her. 'Really? After… well, after what happened, I would have thought the opera house would be the last place you would want to go.'

'No, it's exactly where I want to go. That man will not ruin the opera for me. He won't ruin anything for me.'

She seemed to grow taller as she spoke. Her head was raised, her shoulders back, causing him to smile with admiration. She really was a remarkable woman, and he couldn't feel prouder of his new best friend.

'I missed most of the performance last night,' she continued, a defiant look in her eye. 'I want to see the entire performance next time and actually relax and enjoy it.'

'Then it would be my honour to escort you,' Ethan replied before he had fully taken in the ramifications of what he had said. Did escorting a young woman to the opera fit in with their being just friends? And it was hardly part of the plan to reclaim his freedom, something which he seemed to forget the moment he was in Sophia's presence.

She looked up at him, her head tilted. Was she wondering the same thing?

'When *that man* escorted me to the opera, Mother said he was sending out a message to all of Society that he was courting me.' She chewed the edge of her lip, seemingly less sure of herself. 'I wouldn't want to put you in a compromising position. I wouldn't want you to worry about what people will think if they see us together in your private box.'

'I'm not worried in the slightest about what Society thinks. Are you?'

She smiled, that delightful smile that always had the strangest effect on him, as if he was softening somehow. 'Not in the least. We'll just be two good friends enjoying a night at the opera together.'

'Although you will still have to take a chaperone,' Ethan added. He didn't want her throwing propriety completely to the wind and endangering her reputation. Plus, if he was completely honest with himself, he was not sure how much he could trust his own resolve to remain just friends. A chaperone would provide added protection. 'We might know that we are merely two friends enjoying the opera, but everyone else will see a man and a woman out together alone and tongues will wag.'

'Perhaps I'll ask Mother to join us because she has been so vigilant about protecting my virtue.' She gave a mirthless laugh. 'No, on second thoughts, I'll bring Maggie, as, unlike you and me, Mother has actually seen the entire performance.'

He heard a note of anger slipping into her otherwise cheerful demeanour and placed his hand lightly on her arm. 'I'm sorry, Sophia,' he murmured, knowing his words were inadequate to assuage the distress of what she had gone through.

She placed her hand over his and he fought not to react. *Good friends, remember.*

'It's of no matter,' she said, returning to her previously happy self. 'It's just a shame you're not a titled man or my mother would more than happily leave us alone and would be actually encouraging you to do whatever you want with me.'

Ethan gasped in a quick breath and looked out at the parkland, shame gripping him like a vice. It had been a joke, but if she could read his mind, if she knew what he wanted to do to her, she would not be finding it anything to joke about. Ever since that kiss, he had wondered about, fantasised about, what it would be like to have Sophia in his bed, to stroke and kiss her naked body, to make love to her and watch her writhe beneath him. He knew there was passion locked inside her, and he longed to release it, explore it, experience it. But that would not be happening. That could never happen.

She too was staring into the distance. 'That was a silly joke,' she said quietly, removing her hand. 'I know you're nothing like the Duke of Ravenswood.'

Ethan hoped that was true.

'For no other reason than I'd never want to be friends with *that* man,' she added with a laugh. 'I can't believe I thought he had to be a good man simply because he was a duke.' She gave a mock shudder.

'You wouldn't be the first young woman to be blinded by a title, and I doubt you'll be the last. Nor will your mother be the last woman to foist her daughter onto an inappropriate potential husband because of his position in Society.'

'I'm beginning to wonder about the members of Society. They have all these rules that women must live by and virtually none for men. A man like the Duke of Ravenswood can force himself on a young woman, and yet if people find out it is the young woman whose reputation is ruined.'

'Unfortunately, that is true. The man's a duke. People might gossip about him, even disapprove of him, but snub him—that virtually never happens. It's much easier to snub a young woman with no title or position in Society.'

'It is so unfair.'

Once again, Ethan cringed, as if he was personally responsible for this appalling situation. As a wealthy man from a well-established family, he could live however he liked, without care, without responsibility. Until now, he had never truly considered what it was like for a woman having to live under Society's strict rules and restrictions. While he'd always had sympathy for the debutantes and what they had to endure during the Season, and pitied the ones who made bad marriages, he rarely gave it much more than a passing thought, while he continued to indulge in his own hedonistic lifestyle.

He might transgress Society's expectations on an almost daily basis, but no one really condemned him for it. He was the third son. A man with no responsibilities. Society almost expected him to be a bit wild. But for a woman, the slightest transgression, even one over which she had no control, such as Sophia's assault by Ravenswood, could be devastating, socially and financially.

Until he met Sophia, he had never put himself in a

woman's place and truly understood how hard it was for them. Now he knew, and he could see how determined she was to never be the victim of Society's harsh rules. Even if she didn't think she needed him, he would always protect her from Society's judgements. In that respect, he knew he would always be her true friend.

'It is unfair,' he said, his words feeling inadequate.

'Perhaps I should be grateful to the Duke,' she said, surprising him with both her statement and the cheerful manner in which she made it.

He stopped walking and stared at her, lost for words.

'Don't look so stunned.' She smiled. 'I just mean, if he hadn't done what he did, then I'd still be that delusional girl, hoping for a fairy tale that didn't exist, thinking my handsome duke was going to sweep me off my feet and make me a duchess. Now I know that if he had married me, I would have been miserable. He made me realise I am better off just as I am.'

Ethan was unsure if that was something to be grateful for. Yes, he was pleased she had seen through the Duke and now realised what life would be like if she had become the Duchess of Ravenswood. But he wished she had come to that realisation without having to endure the Duke's repellent behaviour. And he hoped it had not put her off marriage altogether. Even though he did not want to marry her, he wanted her to be happy with a man that she loved, one who respected, loved and admired her in the way she deserved.

That was what a good friend would wish for her.

'Not all men are like Ravenswood,' he said. 'You might meet someone one day whom you want to marry.'

'I know all men are not like the Duke. You're not like the Duke.'

They stared at each other for a moment, neither smiling, then commenced walking again. Ethan could only hope she was right. He wanted her to be right. He wanted to prove to Sophia that he could be friends with her, that he was a better man than he had previously thought himself to be, and he could be worthy of this impressive young woman's friendship.

## Chapter Thirteen

'What is it today?' Jake asked Ethan over lunch several weeks later, or, in Jake's case, breakfast, which he ate in the middle of the day after rising late yet again. 'Another art gallery? Or will you be perusing the shops in Oxford Street so you can see the latest hats? I hear the French fashions this year are simply divine.'

Ethan didn't reply, merely threw a bread roll at his brother, surprised that despite a night of overindulgence Jake still had the reflexes to duck his head in time.

'For a man who is definitely not courting and not planning to get married, you seem to spend an awful lot of time with Miss Sophia Cooper,' Jake said with a laugh, reaching down to retrieve the bread missile.

Ethan wanted to object, but it was a question he had often asked himself. Why was he spending so much time with Sophia? She no longer needed him. If she ever had. Since they had decided they would just be good friends, the new, independent Sophia had joined several groups and was making other friends, ones who were much more appropriate than he would ever be. She had joined a reading society, several charitable associations, and even attended a literary salon frequented by authors and journalists. So why was he still offering his services as an escort? In anybody's eyes, that would look decidedly like courting. But thank goodness Sophia didn't see it that way.

'What will it be next? Sending bouquets of flowers that contain secret messages of love? Long walks in the park? The tentative holding of hands in the drawing room when the chaperone looks away, then breaking off before you're seen doing something so scandalous?' Jake laughed at the ludicrous nature of this image.

'We are not seeing each other today.'

Jake's eyes grew wide in mock surprise. 'What? You're going twenty-four hours without seeing the woman you're not courting?'

Ethan chose not to answer, merely ate some more of the game pie.

'Does this mean your non-courtship is all over?' Jake added, clasping his hands over his heart and fluttering his eyelashes like a music hall actress depicting heartbreak. 'Will that mean your path will never cross again with that fair maiden's?'

Another bread roll flew across the table, narrowly missing a laughing Jake.

'If it is all over, then you can join me tonight.' Jake took a drink of his black coffee and smiled with satisfaction. 'It's the last night of that new play at the Vaudeville Theatre, and you know how those actresses like to party on closing night.'

'I'm taking Miss Cooper to the opera tonight.'

Jake's laughter increased in volume and he almost spilled his coffee. 'I was right. You can't go twenty-four hours without seeing her.'

'We arranged this weeks ago and I have only just secured tickets. But we are not courting. Neither of us wants to marry,' he added, although there was no real reason he should explain his behaviour to his brother.

Jake tapped his chin and furrowed his brow, as if deep in thought. 'I'm just wondering what it is you're most deluded about. Is it that she doesn't want to marry you or that you don't want to marry her?'

'Both,' he replied. 'I mean neither. I'm not deluded, and neither is Sophia—Miss Cooper. After her experiences with Ravenswood, she's not interested in marriage, at least not yet, and certainly not to me. She knows what I think about marriage. No, she doesn't attend balls or any of those other places debutantes seek a husband.'

'Sensible woman. But that begs another question. Why are you still in her life? I can understand, I suppose, you wanting to play her gallant knight and rescue her from a marriage to Ravenswood. But haven't you saved her from that man?'

'Actually, she saved herself. The Duke tried to force himself on her and she dealt with him.' Ethan raised his knee in demonstration of Sophia's actions, causing Jake to cringe as his hands shot down to protect his groin.

'That would send a rather unambiguous message to Ravenswood,' Jake said, still wincing. 'I'm liking this Sophia Cooper more and more. Ravenswood hasn't been at any of his usual haunts lately and the ladies at the Venus Gentlemen's Club have been complaining about their drop in income, so she must have done him some serious damage. Good for her. But that doesn't answer my question. Now that you've saved her, or rather, she's saved herself, from Ravenswood, why are you still seeing her?'

That too was a good question and something Ethan had wondered about himself on numerous occasions. 'Her mother is still determined to marry her off to a titled man, any titled man, so she needs my guidance.'

Jake actually slapped his knee and nearly fell off his chair laughing. 'Your guidance? That really is a good one. When have you ever been capable of offering guidance to a debutante? What are you going to guide her in? Deportment? The art of polite conversation? How to entice a man's interest with a flick of your fan?'

'I can teach her which other men to watch out for,' Ethan replied, getting increasingly annoyed, either with his brother or with himself. He wasn't sure which.

Jake raised an eyebrow. 'Isn't that a bit like putting the fox in charge of the hen house?'

'Ridiculous. If you want to make comparisons, it's more a case of the poacher turned gamekeeper. I know what men are like and I can protect her.'

'Poor you,' Jake said with another mock frown. 'Personally, I prefer to remain a poacher for the rest of my life, especially after last night. I was at the Gaiety Theatre, and there's a rather lovely new actress there. I had dinner with her afterwards and have only just made it home. As long as there are women like her in the world, you won't get me acting like some poor gelding, protecting the virtue of a debutante. And I'm a bit surprised you have taken on that role. Are you sure it wasn't you whom Miss Cooper…?' He raised his knee. 'And dampened your enthusiasm for having a good time?'

Ethan's knees clenched tightly together but he made no comment. Jake was right. He wished he weren't, but he was. He was spending a lot of time with Sophia and had no real answer as to the reason why. She didn't really need him in her life. Did not need his protection or his guidance. She was perfectly capable of looking after herself, always had been and now even more so.

Nor did she need his friendship any more. She was making plenty of female friends. And as for protecting her from the judgement of Society, wasn't being seen repeatedly in his company *causing* people to make judgements? But he had promised to take her to the opera, so he would have to leave answering the perplexing question of why he was still in Sophia's life to a later time.

It was a night at the opera with her good friend. That was all. A good friend who just happened to be a marvellous kisser. A good friend who had the ability to turn her insides to jelly every time he smiled at her. A good friend she was forever imagining doing deliciously wicked things to her…things a young lady should not even think about.

He had kindly made good on his offer to escort her around London, to countless museums and art galleries. They'd had such fun together, laughed and chatted, just like the good friends they claimed to be.

She was sure that was not how he liked to spend his time. She had actually seen him suppress a yawn when listening to a lecture on Grecian artefacts at the museum. Although she couldn't blame him for that. The lecturer did have a rather monotonous voice, but still, it was unfair to make him sit through something he so obviously did not enjoy, just because she wanted his company.

She patted her hair, pleased with the way Maggie had styled it, and turned her head from side to side in the mirror, to see its effect from each angle, then sighed and lowered her hands.

Yes. She was being selfish. She was taking advantage of his good nature for her own ends. He said he was happy to accompany her, but was she unfairly monopolising all of his time? Every day she had suggested something new she wanted to do and asked him if he'd like to be her escort. She had even dragged him around the shops and asked his advice about hats. That really had been unfair, and she blushed at the memory of poor Ethan looking so out of place surrounded by hats bedecked with lace, ribbons and extravagant ostrich feathers. He'd even endured the sideways looks of shop girls and customers, all probably assuming that if they weren't courting, then Sophia had to be his mistress.

Her blushing intensified as she remembered how pleased she had been with that. She had wanted people to think she was his mistress, had even made a point of touching his arm repeatedly, as if they were on intimate terms.

And it was all just a charade. They were not courting. She was not his mistress, and the only time they were on intimate terms was during those fervid dreams that both delighted and tormented her sleep.

They were just good friends. And honestly, she wasn't even that. If she really was his friend, she wouldn't be so selfish. She would think about what he wanted, and she knew that would not involve visiting hat shops.

He had his own life and she should let him get back to it.

And yet, there was that kiss. How could she let him go when she still had the memory of that kiss lingering on her lips like an indelible imprint?

Staring at herself in the mirror, she gently ran her finger along her bottom lip.

Every time they were together, she wondered whether he would do it again. Each time they parted, it was with regret that he had not done so and hope that he would the next time they met.

Her hand dropped from her lips. It was clear all he wanted from her was her friendship, and friends did not kiss, not passionately, not in darkened doorways, not ever. That one kiss had been an aberration, never to be repeated, at least not with her.

This had to stop. She had to give Ethan back his freedom. Even if it hurt to do so, she owed it to him to let him live his life the way he wanted to, and that most certainly did not include looking at hat shops or listening to boring lectures.

She pulled on her elbow-length gloves, picked up her fan and reticule and gave herself one last inspection in the full-length mirror. She had dressed with such care tonight, selecting her most attractive gown, knowing the pale gold shade was flattering to her complexion, that the shimmering silver embroidery drew the eye to her curves, and the fine lace around the neckline and sleeves were like an invitation to admire her shoulders and the hint of décolletage.

Ravenswood had accused her of dressing to tempt a man, and wasn't that exactly what she was doing tonight, dressing to tempt a man to be more than just her friend? She released a long, slow sigh. And yet, she could not tempt him. That one kiss had happened because she had all but begged him.

How many times had she come close to begging him again? She had lost count. And it hadn't been just pride that had stopped her. Nor could she blame it completely on a fear that he might reject her.

She had not begged him because of the danger of where it might lead. If he kissed her again, she knew she risked losing herself completely, possibly even falling in love with him, and that would open herself up to more pain than she could possibly endure.

To fall in love with a man who wanted no more from you than your friendship, who would never marry you, would be a torture she suspected she did not have the strength to bear.

No, this had to change. She had to change. One more evening together, and then she would have to set him free. There would be no more suggestions that he escort her here, there and everywhere, no more invitations to take tea with her. No more walks in the park. No more anything. They would go their separate ways, live their separate lives.

After inspecting herself a few more times in front of the mirror, she strode down the corridor and stairs, then into the drawing room, where he was waiting for her.

Her determination faltered when she saw him again. She should have known that it would. Didn't she feel this way every time she saw him anew? As always happened, her heart did that strange leap, then increased its tempo, and the memory of their kiss invaded her mind like a physical presence.

She froze for a moment, and could almost feel his arms wrapped around her, his lips kissing a trail down her neck, his hands cupping her breasts.

Drawing in a quick, shaking breath, she forced herself to walk into the room, her head held high, and act as if she was not being tormented by those deliciously disturbing memories.

*Just friends. Just friends.*

She gave her friend a curtsey and smiled as brightly as she could.

'You look beautiful tonight, Sophia.'

Pleasure rippled through her. She wanted to be beautiful for him, and under his admiring gaze she did feel beautiful. But it mattered not what he thought of her appearance, she reminded herself.

'Thank you,' she responded briskly, as one would to a compliment from a friend. 'We should leave now. We wouldn't want to be late. Maggie, are you ready?'

she rushed on, adopting a nonchalant manner, as if her heart wasn't still beating at a fierce pace and her stomach wasn't tying itself into tighter knots.

They both looked over at Maggie, as if she was providing a much-needed distraction.

She had followed Sophia into the drawing room and was now standing quietly by the door, looking very pretty in a gown that Sophia had worn only once and had, as was the custom, passed on to her lady's maid.

'Yes, madam,' Maggie responded with a smile. She smiled a lot these days and claimed she had the best job in the world. Her role as so-called chaperone had taken her to many interesting places over the last few weeks and involved very little actual chaperoning. Sophia suspected tonight she would watch little of the opera, preferring to chat with the staff, particularly the waiters, and that was the reason for that smile.

And as for her mother, she had given up trying to control Sophia's behaviour altogether, knowing it was a lost cause. She wasn't even present to say goodnight to Ethan and her daughter.

'Shall we?' Ethan said, offering her his arm.

Sophia battled with her nerves as they walked out of the house and entered his carriage. She had been nervous the last time she attended this opera, but this time her anxiety was all about excitement and anticipation, not dread.

If she was being honest with herself, although she knew that this would be their last outing together, she was still hoping that tonight would be the night when he would kiss her again. Perhaps he might do more than kiss her. Would he suggest they leave his private box once the other patrons had taken their seats? Would he lead her to that private, secluded alcove and draw the curtain? Would he then…?

'You're very quiet tonight, Sophia. Is everything all right?' His question interrupted her thoughts, causing fire to erupt on her cheeks.

'Yes, perfectly all right.' She smiled at him, grateful that he couldn't read minds and grateful for the subdued lighting in the carriage that would hide her blushes.

'Going to the opera isn't bringing back bad memories, is it?'

'Not at all. I've all but put thoughts of Ravenswood out of my mind.' *And replaced them with thoughts of you.*

He patted her hand in what could only be seen as a friendly gesture. Damn it, his gestures were always only friendly ones. She sighed lightly, remembering that tonight she wasn't out to seduce Ethan. Not that she actually knew how one seduced a man, but even if she did, it would not do for her to behave in such a manner. Not because she thought a woman seducing a man was unacceptable behaviour—she was beginning to think that anything Society deemed unacceptable for women was exactly what they should do—but because tonight was all about letting him go. She would stop monopolising his time, stop expecting so much from him, stop chasing after something she could never have.

It was obvious he saw her as like a poor, abandoned kitten who needed to be looked after, but she was not that woman any more. She was an independent woman who could look after herself. She might want him in her life, but she did not need him. And she had to let him know this, so he could go back to living his own life, the way he did before he found her crying alone in the library.

They arrived at the opera house and he escorted her and Maggie through the jostling crowds in the foyer and up the marble stairs to his private box. Once they were seated, Sophia pulled her opera glasses out of her reticule and distracted herself by looking around the audience.

'That is so funny,' she said, handing her glasses to Ethan.

'What is?'

'Most of the women in the audience also have their glasses out and are looking at each other rather than at the stage. It makes me think most people come to the opera to be seen and to see who else is attending, rather than because of their love of music.'

He handed her back the glasses, as if needing no proof. 'And this surprises you?' They exchanged knowing smiles. 'Much of what happens in Society is designed so everyone can see what others are doing and wearing and whom they are courting. No one wants to miss out on the latest gossip, so they all have to attend every function to keep up.'

'I wonder what they will say about us?'

'That the lucky Lord Ethan Rosemont was seen at the opera with the beautiful Miss Sophia Cooper, the most sought-after debutante of the Season. Are they courting? Will there soon be a marriage, or will some other more suitable man capture her hand?' He laughed as if they were having a joke at Society's expense.

Sophia continued smiling, although her smile was now becoming strained. She knew the answers to all those questions. No, they were not courting. No, they would not soon be marrying, and as for another man, was there any other man she wanted? There should be, but after Ethan, would that ever be possible?

And there was an even more pertinent question she knew should be asked. When would a more suitable young woman capture Ethan's attention? He said he did not wish to marry, but her mother had said he was never without female company.

The opera house was full of attractive women. Was there a woman out in the audience that he would rather spend time with, instead of being stuck with his demanding friend? It was something she couldn't ask. She knew what his answer would be. He would deny it. Say he enjoyed her company immensely. Was more than happy to escort her to the opera or wherever she wanted to go. But would any of these answers be the truth?

The curtains parted and the stage revealed a garret in a poor district of Paris. Last time he had been to this opera, Ethan had spent the entire evening watching Sophia, thinking that he was protecting her from Ravenswood. Tonight, once again, he was missing the performance because he was watching Sophia. But he couldn't help himself. The spectacle on the stage might be magnificent, but so was she. How could he not watch her? How could he not take pleasure in her enjoyment?

He smiled as she leant forward, her hands on her heart, as if she was trying to contain the rapture inside her. Those lovely blue eyes glistened as she followed every line the performers sang, every action, every emotion.

Occasionally, she would look in his direction and they would exchange a smile. While she was smiling at the wonder she was observing onstage, he was smiling at the wonder that was Miss Sophia Cooper.

She was the most enchanting woman he had ever met. Beautiful, intelligent and passionate. The man she eventually married, and he knew she *would* eventually marry, would be fortunate indeed. His smile faltered. He looked around at the other patrons. The theatre was full of eligible men, many of whom he was certain would love to be courting Sophia. If it hadn't been for Ravenswood, he and Sophia would never have met and she would no doubt have found her Prince Charming. And that was what she deserved. Not all men were like Ravenswood, and not all men were like him. She deserved a man who wanted marriage, who wanted to make his life with her.

He swallowed down his anger. Who was he angry with? The man she would marry or with himself? Surely he was not angry that his lifestyle made him an unacceptable candidate for her hand. No, of course not. He enjoyed the life of a free-living man with no responsibility, one full of endless, equally free-living feminine company.

That was the life he would continue to live and Sophia would soon meet a respectable man who could give her a settled life of marriage and children.

And that would not happen if she kept being seen in public with him. She turned to smile at him once again and he smiled back, more with resignation than with enjoyment. He knew what he had to do. He would miss her, but there was no choice. It was the only kind thing to do. The only thing a true friend would do. He had to let her go so she could find a good man who would give her what he could not—love and marriage.

Initially, she might see it as a rejection, might even be hurt, but he knew that eventually, when she met the man she wanted to marry, she would forget all about her time with him.

He sat back in his chair and tried to appreciate the performance and enjoy the last time he would spend in Sophia's company. But how did you enjoy yourself when you had committed to an action that, even if you knew it was for the best, you didn't really want to take? He tried to take solace in knowing it was what a good friend would do. Or, if he wanted to still see himself in the role of a gallant knight, it was what a Sir Galahad would unselfishly do. But, if he was honest with himself, he much preferred being a selfish ass than either of those more noble types.

The interval arrived and she applauded with rapt enthusiasm.

'That was marvellous!' she exclaimed the moment the gas lights lit up the auditorium. 'I can't believe how much I missed last time and I don't just mean everything after the interval. I don't think I watched any of the performance that time, I was so nervous.' She closed her eyes briefly as if to dispel that unpleasant memory.

'Would you like some refreshments? I promise to get you back in time for the rest of the performance.'

She blushed slightly and he mentally kicked himself. That was not something he should joke about, even if she was making light of it. 'I'm sorry, Sophia, that was an appalling thing to say.'

She placed her hand on his arm. 'Not at all. As I said, I've all but forgotten about what happened between me and Ravenswood, and if we can turn that man into a joke, then all the better.'

He stood up, her hand still on his arm, still wondering why she had blushed if it was not due to being upset over what Ravenswood had done.

They walked through to the foyer. He escorted her to a seat, then made his way through the crowd to get the refreshments. When he returned, he found her surrounded by several young men and they were all talking animatedly together, discussing what they had just seen.

Ethan crushed down his irrational annoyance and joined the group. He'd met most of the young men before. They were all perfectly respectable gentlemen. Any one of them would make an ideal husband for Sophia, and, while none were dukes, several had titles, which would make her mother very happy.

Wasn't this what he wanted for her?

They continued to talk about the beauty of the soprano's voice, the evocative scenery and the passion of the tenor. To his chagrin, Sophia chatted away happily and merely took the glass of wine from his hand with a quick nod of thanks.

This was all for the best, he repeated to himself. This was what he wanted. When he first saw her crying in the library and had decided against his better judgement to help her, it had been so she would attract the attention of another man, one who he hoped would court her in the manner on which she had set her heart.

He wanted her to have that fairy-tale Season, to have the attention of men who would make good husbands. So why was he so irritated by their presence? Why did he want to tell those men to go away? Was it just because he knew this would be their final night together? Yes, that had to be the reason. He selfishly wanted to spend their last night together alone.

The bell rang for the end of the interval and they returned to their seats. Ethan forced himself to stop being so peevish. Sophia was enjoying herself. He should be happy for her.

One of the young men who had been talking to her waved at her from the box on the other side of the opera house. She waved back.

'What was that man's name again?' She nodded in the direction of the still smiling man. 'They all introduced themselves, but I instantly forgot everyone's name.'

'Simon Beaufort, the Earl of Burwood,' Ethan reluctantly informed her, deciding not to add that, unlike Ravenswood, Beaufort was fully solvent and was unlikely to have stepped into a gambling den in his life. Nor had Ethan seen him at the parties men like himself and his brother Jake frequented. In other words, unlike Ethan, he was the perfect husband for a young lady like Sophia.

'A bit of a bore, if you ask me,' he said instead.

'He knows an awful lot about opera, though.'

Exactly, Ethan would have added, but the lights were dimmed and the curtain was raised.

Once again Sophia became enraptured, and once again Ethan became enraptured by her lovely face and the range of expressions she displayed as she empathised with the lovers onstage. When the end neared and the leading lady was dying in her lover's arms, she actually gripped his arm, so entranced was she by the performance.

Ethan gently placed his hand over hers, telling himself it was just to comfort her, in case the scene they were witnessing distressed her.

When the final aria ended and the performers stood to take their bows, she released his arm, briefly clasped her hands to her chest, then applauded with great enthusiasm as she blinked away tears.

The clapping seemed to go on for an inordinate amount of time. He looked over at Beaufort, who was also applauding enthusiastically, but he wasn't quite as enraptured by the performance as Sophia, as he kept looking in her direction.

'Damn man,' Ethan muttered under his breath.

When the applause eventually died down, Sophia smiled at him. 'That was marvellous, Ethan. Thank you for taking me.'

'My pleasure.'

They exited the box and Beaufort was waiting for

them. The man must have run along the corridors to get there in time. 'Miss Cooper. I just had to ask you what you thought of the final act. Wasn't it magnificent?'

'Yes, it was perfect,' she said, clasping Beaufort's arm in much the same way she had clasped Ethan's during the performance. 'The power in their voices, the passion… It was transcendent.'

'Yes, that is the perfect word. Transcendent.'

Ethan tried not to roll his eyes.

'I'm afraid I have to rush off now,' Beaufort said, much to Ethan's relief. 'I do hope I will see you at Lord and Lady Preston's ball. Then we can discuss the performance further.'

Ethan waited for Sophia to inform him that she no longer went to balls.

'Yes, of course. I will see you there,' she said, taking Ethan's arm.

He escorted the still elated Sophia home, trying to make polite conversation while fighting off an absurd melancholy that was gripping him. This was what he wanted. He could hang up his metaphorical suit of armour and go back to living how he used to live. His damsel in distress had saved herself. Now she was all set to conquer the world and the heart of a man who would love and cherish her and make her his wife. A man who would not be him. A man who could not be him. The type of man he didn't want to be.

## Chapter Fourteen

A week had passed. He hadn't visited. Sophia did not know whether he would attend Lord and Lady Preston's ball and he had not asked to see her again. Had she said something wrong? Done something wrong? Sophia knew she was inexperienced in the ways of men, but she could think of nothing she had done or said that would have caused him to withdraw from her so completely and so suddenly.

She paced up and down her bedroom, tapping her hairbrush against the palm of her hand. Perhaps he was just busy or had gone away, visited his family estate in Somerset. But he had said nothing about being busy or leaving town when they had parted after their night at the opera. But he *had* been a little reserved when they said goodbye, and they had made no arrangements to see each other again. Sophia tried to put a halt to those agonising thoughts that were consuming her and making her miserable.

Wasn't this what she wanted? Hadn't she said she needed to set him free? That was why she had suggested no other outings. Well, he had set himself free and she should be pleased.

She placed the hairbrush on her dressing table and sighed. But what if she had said or done something wrong? She would hate for them to part on bad terms.

To put her mind at rest, there was only one thing for it. She must visit Ethan and ask him if there was a problem. If there was, she would have to try to make amends. Even if they parted company, as she knew they must, she wanted it to be on good terms.

It was against propriety for a young lady to visit a gentleman, but hadn't she already broken enough of Society's rules? Didn't she repeatedly tell herself that she no longer cared about such things?

With that determination in mind, she called for Maggie. Hastily dressing in a light brown skirt and jacket suitable for a stroll through the neighbourhood, they set off for Ethan's Belgravia town house.

This was all perfectly acceptable behaviour. They were just enjoying the delightfully warm day, she told herself as they walked along the tree-lined streets towards his home. If they happened to pass the Rosemonts' house, she was sure no one would think it strange if they dropped in briefly to exchange pleasantries.

She turned into his street and tried to ignore the fluttering in her stomach. Hesitating outside his imposing home, she looked up. The large white columns at the edge of the portico suddenly seemed intimidating.

She was being silly. The columns were merely an attractive feature of the house, as was the portico that covered the entrance. She took a deep breath, walked up the steps with as much determination as she could muster, then paused again. She looked down at the black and white tiles at the doorstep, then back up at the solid black front door, and tried not to see it as an impenetrable barrier.

Should she do this? Was she making a big mistake? It wasn't just Society's disapproval of a young lady visiting a man uninvited that was worrying her. It was the reception she might get. What if he did not want to see her? What if his attentions were now directed towards another?

Not that it mattered, of course. She lifted her hand to knock on the door. He could see whomever he wished, and if her mother's claim was true it was highly likely there would soon be another woman in his life, if there wasn't already.

She lowered her arm and gripped her hands tightly together. How would she react if that was the case? What if there was another young woman with whom he was now spending his time?

But she did want to see him again. She had to re-assure herself that she had done nothing wrong. Even if they never saw each other again, she wanted to know that he still held her in high regard. And there was only one way to find out. Before she could question her-self one more time, she lifted the brass door knocker and gave it several knocks that sounded more decisive than she felt.

'I'm Miss Sophia Cooper and I'm here to see Lord Ethan,' she told the footman when he opened the door. Did his eyebrows rise slightly in question? She was unsure. But he ushered her and Maggie into the hallway and signalled for them to wait, then disappeared into a drawing room.

Ethan emerged from the room, followed by two other smiling men, who introduced themselves as Luther Rosemont, the Duke of Southbridge, and his brother Jake Rosemont. Looking somewhat harassed, Ethan escorted Sophia and Maggie into the drawing room while the two brothers disappeared up the circular staircase.

Ethan indicated a sofa, and she and Maggie sat down. 'To what do I owe this pleasure?' he asked, seating himself in the opposite chair.

'Maggie and I were just out walking. It's such a lovely, warm day. We passed your house, so we thought we would stop in and say hello.'

He gave her a studied stare and she hoped he could not see through her subterfuge, but he nodded as if accepting her lie. 'I'll call for tea, then.' He stood up and approached the bell pull to summon a servant.

'No, please don't go to any trouble. We don't plan to stay.'

'As you wish.' He sat back down.

She tried not to be disappointed. Surely she had not expected him to argue with her, to insist that she take tea, that she not rush away.

'I also wanted to thank you for taking me to the opera.' She had already thanked him several times. That was not why she was visiting him but could think of no way to discover the answers to the questions that had been nagging at her.

'It was my pleasure,' he answered politely. 'I'm pleased you enjoyed yourself.'

He was being so formal, so stiff, as if they were mere acquaintances. Something had definitely changed. He was never like this. Even when they had first met in the library of this town house, he had not been so formal. So what had changed?

She looked at Maggie, not wanting to reveal anything personal in front of her lady's maid, but what choice did she have? She had to know. 'Ethan, what has happened?'

He frowned slightly. 'Happened? Regarding what?'

'Us.'

He raised his hands, palms upwards. 'What do you mean, *us*?'

'Well…' She thought for a moment. 'We are still friends, aren't we?'

She waited for him to give her his assurance, even to rush across the room, take her hands in his and tell her not to be silly, to stop worrying, that of course they were friends, the very best of friends. Instead, he looked out of the window, as if something in the empty street had captured his attention, then turned back to face her.

'I believe, Miss Cooper, that friendship between a man and a woman is not feasible.'

She stared at him, unsure whether she had heard him correctly. 'Not feasible?'

'Exactly. I believe it would be better if we no longer spent time in each other's company.'

Her body tensed, as if suddenly numbed by the cold. 'But why? What have I done?'

He rose from his chair, and she hoped now he was going to come to her, to tell her it was some sort of trick he was playing. Although why he should play such a cruel trick, she did not know. But instead he moved towards the marble mantelpiece and stood looking down at her.

'You have done nothing wrong, Miss Cooper. You are a lovely, delightful young woman. You should be enjoying the rest of the Season. I am confident you will soon meet a young man who is suitable for you. But you have less chance of doing that if you and I are spending time together. No matter what we think, other people will assume we are courting. A friendship between us is not possible.'

'But you know I don't care about that,' Sophia said. She should be embarrassed that she sounded so pitiful, but she didn't care about that either.

'You say that, but that is just because of your experience with Ravenswood. There are many eligible men who would make ideal husbands for you. Men with whom you could have a fulfilling life.'

She swallowed, her throat suddenly tight and dry. 'So, are you saying you don't want to see any more of me? That we won't walk out together, won't be attending the theatre, visiting art galleries or museums?'

'That is exactly what I am saying.'

She stared at him speechlessly, her breath held, her stomach and heart aching. She knew she had no right to be so aggrieved. She wanted him to have his freedom. At least, that was what she had told herself. Hadn't she claimed she did not want to monopolise his time, his attention? Hadn't she promised herself that she would stop being so selfish? But she wanted to be selfish. She wanted him, but she couldn't have him. And he didn't want her.

'Sophia,' he said, his voice softening. 'Miss Cooper, there are other young men who I am sure would wish to escort you to the theatre or to walk out with you. The Earl of Burwood being one.'

'Who?' Sophia asked, trying to make sense of what he was saying.

'The Earl of Burwood, Simon Beaufort, the man who introduced himself at the opera. And there were those other men at the opera who were equally eager to make your acquaintance. They are the men you should spend time with, not me.'

He drew in a long breath. 'You need to get on with your life, and I need to get back to my life.'

'I see,' she said, her voice coming out in a ragged gasp. 'Yes, you are right,' she added, standing up, pleased that her voice had become stronger. 'Well, Maggie and I won't keep you any longer. I have many other things I wish to do today, and I have to get organised for Lord and Lady Preston's ball tonight. Will you be in attendance?' she asked, keeping her voice as uninterested as possible.

'No, I am afraid I have other plans for tonight,' he said, pulling the bell for a servant to show her out.

'Yes, of course. Well, goodbye, Lord Ethan,' she said, walking to the door, her head held high.

'Goodbye, Miss Cooper.'

Had she heard a note of regret in his voice? Or was

that something she conjured up in a desperate attempt to save the last shreds of her dignity?

It was over. The moment she left, Ethan collapsed back into his chair. This was what he had wanted for her the moment he had first seen her, crying alone in the library. She was now free of Ravenswood, free of her mother and free of him. She could make her own choices and he knew she would choose wisely. Soon he would hear that she was engaged to the Earl of Burwood or another equally suitable young man who would give her the life she deserved, love her in the manner she deserved to be loved.

Yes, he had done the right thing. It was strange how doing the right thing felt so bad.

Luther and Jake returned to the drawing room and he waited for the inevitable ribbing. None came. Had they registered that he was not in the mood? It wasn't like his brothers to be so sensitive.

'So that was Miss Sophia Cooper,' Jake finally said. 'She seems rather lovely.'

'Hmm,' was the only response Ethan felt up to giving.

'And is everything all right?' Luther asked, his voice uncharacteristically cautious.

'Everything is perfect,' he responded with more cheer than he felt. 'She was out for a walk, passed this house, so decided to pay a quick visit to thank me for escorting her to the opera.'

Jake and Luther exchanged looks, the meaning of which Ethan had no energy to discern.

'Are you still friends?' Jake asked, without a hint of teasing.

He looked up at his brothers. They had not believed it was possible for a man to be just friends with a young lady, and it seemed they were right.

'No, we have decided that such an arrangement is not a sensible one. Society and all that.' Ethan waved his hand in the air as if that explained everything.

'I see,' Luther said, although Ethan doubted he saw anything at all.

'We have parted ways,' Ethan said, to give further clarification to a situation that was anything but clear.

'I see,' Jake echoed his brother.

'Being with me can't be good for a young lady's reputation.' *And it's not good for my state of mind.*

Both brothers nodded, as if that was something they understood to be true, causing Ethan to frown. 'People will think we're courting, which may put off potential suitors.'

The brothers merely stared at him.

'Don't look so grim.' Ethan gave a small laugh. 'It's all over. No more art galleries, museums or sitting through tedious operas. And I will never, ever, visit another hat shop as long as I live.' He forced himself to laugh again. 'No more worrying about a debutante who should mean nothing to me. I can go back to doing what I do best—enjoying myself completely and living a life with no responsibilities whatsoever.'

He expected lots of backslapping and approval from his brothers, even a bit of merciless teasing about one actress or another, or Lady Lydia Pearson, who was supposedly still asking after him. But instead they looked at him, with matching expressions of…of what? Confusion…concern…whatever it was, it was an expression they should not have been wearing.

He rubbed his hands together in an exaggerated display of excitement. 'And tonight will be the first night of my regained freedom. I can hardly wait to make full use of it.'

He would no longer mope about the house as he had for much of the last week. He would stop wondering about Sophia, what she was doing, whom she was seeing, whether she was happy, or, most foolishly of all, wondering whether she was thinking of him.

No, that was all over. He was back to being himself, and not some half-baked knight in shining armour.

'I intend to spend tonight indulging in every vice I can think of.'

The brothers nodded, but not with the enthusiasm Ethan would have expected. Had they detected some false bonhomie in his voice? If they had, it was an aberration. Yes, he might feel less than joyful right now, but that would pass. He would soon put Miss Sophia Cooper out of his mind. He would enjoy himself tonight, indulge himself, even overindulge himself if need be.

Meanwhile, Sophia would be out at a Society ball, also enjoying herself. In time, she would meet another man, marry, have children and well and truly forget all about him, just as he was determined to forget all about her.

## Chapter Fifteen

Lord and Lady Preston's ball was all that Sophia would have once wished for. The ballroom looked magical. The orchestra's romantic music filled the air and once again Sophia was wearing a beautiful, floating gown designed by a top French fashion house. This was the fairy-tale Season she had dreamt of, so she should be happy.

Accompanied by her mother, she entered the room, and several men instantly surrounded them, eager to write their names on her dance card. Simon Beaufort was the first to claim a dance, and he led her around the floor with the expertise one would have expected from a well-schooled member of the aristocracy. Sophia made the required small talk about the opera they had both seen, and she had to admit he was a very pleasant young man.

When he led her off the dance floor, her mother could not have been smiling more brightly.

'He's an earl, you know,' her mother twittered, once the young man had departed. 'And the next man on your dance card is a viscount. This is wonderful, Sophia. I'm so pleased you've put that dreadful Ethan Rosemont behind you. I always knew you would eventually come to your senses. I know that one day you will make me proud and marry a suitable man, one with a respectable title.'

Sophia swallowed down her anger. She would not ruin the ball by arguing with her mother. And anyway, she was partly correct. She was here tonight to put Ethan Rosemont behind her. Although she could never describe him as dreadful. The only dreadful thing about knowing Ethan was the pain she was trying to suppress now he was no longer in her life.

'And it looks like being associated with Lord Ethan has done your reputation no harm,' her mother continued, exchanging a polite smile with another mother. 'No one appears to see you as the type of woman he usually associates with. If they did, they wouldn't talk to you. No, everyone appears to realise you're respectable and not *that* sort of woman.'

Sophia's simmering temper started to come to a boil. If her mother said one more word, just one more disparaging word about Ethan, she would explode. She would forget where they were and expose her mother to the full force of her wrath.

But her mother was saved when the next man on her dance card approached, bowed low and guided her towards the dance floor.

Sophia forced herself to make polite conversation, trying to ignore all that her mother had said about Ethan, and about the type of women he usually associated with, and to just enjoy the dancing, the music and the pleasure of finally having the Season she had always wanted.

And she almost succeeded. Once that dance was over, another man escorted her onto the floor, then another, every one of them equally eligible young men.

As she smiled and danced, she was sure no one would suspect the pain and turmoil that was churning inside her. She even indulged in a bit of flirting, flicking her fan in the way she had been taught, laughing at the men's jokes and taking part in light-hearted conversations.

In many ways, it was just as she had imagined her Season would be. If only her heart was truly in it.

And perhaps her heart would truly be in it, and her Season really *would* have been everything she had hoped for, if the Duke of Ravenswood had not shown an interest in her before her first ball. If the Duke had not staked her out as his possession, perhaps other men would have danced with her. Maybe the next day they would have sent her flowers and left their cards. She would have had a choice of beaus. Then she would have chosen one to walk out with, to be courted by and to eventually marry. It would have been the fairy tale she had longed for, and she would have felt like the princess her father had wished her to be.

Instead, that arrogant man had claimed her as his, then all but ignored her. He had assumed that an untitled heiress would be so grateful that he did not have to make any effort, that he could treat her any way he wanted, and she would tolerate anything, as long as he made her a duchess.

As much as it now shamed her, he was almost right. If his behaviour hadn't been so obnoxious, perhaps she might not have seen through him.

And if he hadn't been so arrogant as to neglect her at her first ball, she would never have met Ethan.

She closed her eyes. Ethan. Ironically, she had the Duke to thank for bringing Ethan into her life. If he hadn't found her crying in the library, she would not have experienced such heights of joy as she did in his company, would never have discovered the ecstasy of being in his arms, the rapture of being kissed until she forgot herself, forgot how to think and became capable only of feeling. But then, she would also not have experienced the depth of loss, the anguish of knowing he would never again be in her life.

'Miss Cooper, what do you think?'

She looked up at the man with whom she was dancing, the man who had interrupted her thoughts. The man whose name she could not remember. Hadn't her mother said he was the eldest son of an earl, but what his name and titles were she didn't know.

'Yes, I'm sure you are right,' she responded, which caused him to smile and continue talking about whatever it was they were supposedly discussing.

This would not do. She was being rude. She needed to concentrate. With Ethan, her mind never drifted off. She heard every lovely word he said, and she knew he also listened to what she had to say. He did not treat her as someone who should hang on his every word of wisdom and merely agree when that was called for, the way this man did.

And he could make her laugh. Laughing with Ethan was such a precious gift. She smiled to herself, remembering all the times they had laughed together. Visions of them running through the rain entered her mind, of his arm around her shoulder as they sheltered under his jacket. She had felt so safe that day, so protected, so pleased she had met him, even if she had still foolishly thought her heart belonged to another.

Then she remembered walking home with him after she had dealt with the Duke. It had been wonderful to share that moment of elation with him. And then he had kissed her and she had been lost.

She sighed lightly. Would she ever feel about another man the way she felt about Ethan? Would another man cause her temperature to rise every time she looked at him? Would another man make her feel so alive, as if colours were brighter, flowers smelled sweeter, and even grey, rainy days were a delight?

Damn it all. She wished he were here tonight. Despite her attempts to convince herself otherwise, he was the man she wanted to be with. If he were here, she would really be enjoying herself, not just going through the motions. She wanted Ethan. Wanted to dance with him, laugh with him, and more importantly she wanted to be held by him. But that would never happen now.

She swallowed a sigh.

He had made it clear. He did not want her in his life. One thing she was certain of, he would not be moping over her. As her mother had said, he was not a man to go long without a woman, and it was a certain type of woman he spent his days and nights with. A type of woman who was not a respectable debutante.

And she *was* a respectable debutante, for all the good it did her. If she was *that type of woman*, as her mother disparagingly described them, perhaps he would not have turned her away. If she really did not care what Society thought of her, as she claimed, she could be *that sort of woman*. She would be with him now. In his arms, maybe in his bed.

But she wasn't. She was a debutante who went to balls and made polite conversation with men whom she would never even kiss until her wedding night. Meanwhile, Ethan was enjoying himself with a different type of woman.

A surge of anger rushed through her, all directed at that unknown woman.

Well, if he had forgotten all about her, she would do the same. If he was happy in his world, she could be happy in hers.

She circled the room on the arm of a young man who was exactly the type a debutante looked for as a husband. He was friendly and presentable. If she hadn't met Ethan, then this man could easily have captured her heart. She just needed to forget about Ethan, not think of him and certainly not imagine him with any other woman.

*Or you could become his mistress.*

She stumbled over her feet, shocked at that inappropriate thought, which had invaded her mind.

'I'm so sorry, Miss Cooper,' her partner said, graciously taking responsibility for something that was obviously Sophia's fault.

She smiled up at him, her mind a whirlwind of confused thoughts.

How could she possibly think that? She was not the type to become a man's mistress. As much as she despised the way Society made one rule for men and one for women, could she ever transgress that far?

If she became his mistress, she would destroy her reputation. Once he moved on to the next woman, she would be left with nothing and no one. A good man, like the one she was now dancing with, would never want to be associated with her.

And yet, did she really want any other man than Ethan? Could any other man make her yearn for his touch the way Ethan did? Would any other man occupy her thoughts so completely? Would any other man cause her heart to soar with pleasure every time he smiled at her?

The dance came to an end and her partner escorted her back to her waiting mother, who simpered and chatted with the young man, whose name she still could not remember.

At least her mother was happy. When Sophia had announced she wished to attend this ball, her mother had immediately reverted to her old self. Plotting and planning which titled man they should set their sights on.

Sophia sighed lightly. Nothing had really changed, and perhaps it would not be long before she married one of those aristocratic gentlemen, and fulfilled her mother's dreams, if not her own.

Another man asked her to dance. She smiled politely and allowed him to lead her back onto the dance floor.

He was handsome, he was titled, he was polite, everything she should want in a husband. But he wasn't Ethan Rosemont. No matter how accomplished a dancer he was, Sophia couldn't stop wishing it was Ethan who was holding her close and leading her round the floor. It seemed she had been lost from that first dance on the night of her first ball. At the time she had tried to convince herself that she wanted to marry the Duke, but she had never really wanted him. From the moment she had seen him, there had only ever been Ethan. And now she was trying to convince herself she could be happy with one of these other men.

As she jumped and pirouetted and tried to enjoy the polka, that unwanted thought re-entered her mind once more. Could she, should she, become Ethan's mistress?

Could she defy Society's rules that much? Once she took that step, there would be no going back. Society would shun her. But did she care so much for Society's opinion that she would deny herself the chance of true happiness?

Society would have shunned her if the Duke had spread his malicious lies. Becoming Ethan's mistress would have the same outcome, but at least she would experience a level of sensual pleasure that those respectable women who looked down on her would never know.

And she was no longer that wide-eyed debutante she had been at the beginning of the Season, the one who thought she was living in a fairy tale. She was no longer the sort of naïve woman who believed a man was honourable just because he had a title. She no longer thought that every man would automatically act like a gentleman and treat a woman respectfully.

But had she changed enough to become the sort of woman a man took as his mistress?

Sophia shook away those thoughts. If Ethan didn't want to be her friend, then he certainly did not want her as his mistress. He wanted to move on, and that was what she too should be doing.

She should be happy. She would be happy. She had to be happy. It would be foolish to waste her time pining for a man she could never have.

She looked up at her partner and smiled. 'Will I be seeing you at the next ball?' she asked, determined to put all foolish notions out of her mind.

He smiled back at her. 'If you are going to be there, Miss Cooper, then I most certainly will be.'

She tilted her head and fluttered her eyelashes. This was what she should be doing. Flirting with eligible men, not thinking about throwing away her life and her reputation for a man who didn't even want her.

Freedom. It had eluded him for months, but now he had it back. He could do whatever he wanted, with whomever he wanted, whenever he wanted. And yet here he was again, at home, alone, nursing a brandy, wondering what to do with himself.

How could you want something so desperately but feel so empty when you finally got it? That was a question Ethan had plenty of time to ponder. Too much time to ponder. And he needed to stop thinking and start enjoying himself again.

He could go to one of his clubs. He dismissed that idea immediately. He'd been to his club earlier in the week. Rather than having the expected fun, the high jinks of the other members had failed to amuse him. They had seemed childish and he had returned home almost at once. He could go to the theatre. Annette had sent him an invitation to dine with her after she finished performing. He should take her up on the offer. Only a fool would not. But right now he was being a fool.

He could join Jake at one of London's many illegal gambling dens. While gambling did not appeal to him the way it did to his brother, the licentious nature of those clubs had always held a certain attraction in the past. But whatever it was that had once drawn him in was lost on him now. Parties also seemed loud and pointless.

He swirled the amber liquid round his brandy balloon. Alcohol also failed in its promise to numb the sorrow that possessed him. It was ridiculous. This was not like him. Enjoying himself was the one thing he always excelled at.

Sophia could not have changed him this much. Had her innocence tainted him, so he now saw his own life as decadent?

Ridiculous. It was how he lived and how he intended to continue to live. He just needed more time to put her out of his head. She might have changed from the young woman he had seen sitting in the library, tears streaking her face. She might no longer be naïve enough to think Ravenswood was a good man and would make a perfect husband just because he was a duke, but she hadn't changed that much. She was still an innocent young debutante, albeit an innocent young debutante who could kiss a man until he lost all sense of reason. But she was still a respectable young woman. And respectable young women all eventually wanted a husband, and he was not, never had been, and never would be, husband material.

The women who shared his life all did so knowing it was a temporary arrangement, something which they too were content with. Sophia would never accept such an arrangement, and he would never expect it of her. She wanted a husband, respectability, and that was something he could never give her.

He drained his glass and stood up to pour himself another, then paused, the decanter poised above the glass.

Sometimes he actually wished he had never met her.

He filled the glass and smiled to himself. That was not true. If he hadn't met her, he would never have known the pleasure of her smile. Would never have delighted in her laughter or that cheeky side to her otherwise shy and polite personality. And he would never have experienced that kiss. That kiss had taken him by surprise. Had left him reeling, as if he were the naïve one who was kissing someone for the first time, who was experiencing something new and ecstatic.

He walked back to his chair and slumped down. If he was to get himself out of this funk, he would have to forget about that kiss and forget about Sophia.

He should go away, leave London and leave Sophia behind.

And that was what he would do. But, unfortunately, his departure would have to wait till the end of the Season.

The Season started with a Rosemont ball, and a Rosemont ball ended it. His mother would never forgive him if he did not stay until then. Once he'd got that duty over and done with, he would leave England. Perhaps spend some time on the Continent, away from everything that was familiar to him. New surroundings would clear his head. Then he could get back to being the man he really was, back to enjoying himself the way he had before he had met Sophia.

With that decided, Ethan was determined to stop thinking about all that had happened. All this introspection was not like him. He just had to get the final ball of the Season out of the way, then he could pursue all those pleasures that had been eluding him since that first ball five months ago.

## *Chapter Sixteen*

It was the last ball of the Season, and Ethan was desperate to escape. As with every ball his mother hosted, he was attending this one under sufferance. But his mother insisted that all three brothers be present, and she expected them to at least try to look as if they were enjoying themselves.

This final ball provided her with one last opportunity to interest Luther in one of the still available debutantes. Ethan, Jake and Luther all knew that she would fail in her quest to find the next Duchess of Southbridge, but their mother would not be deterred.

Usually, Ethan had mixed feelings about the final ball. While any ball was a trial, at least this one was the last for a while. He could take comfort in knowing it would be seven glorious months before he had to endure another.

But tonight's ball was different. Gone was the expected boredom. Instead, what he was experiencing was more akin to a form of torture. He had not expected

Sophia to be present. If he had, even his mother's re-monstrations would not have been enough to drag him into this ballroom.

Only a martyr would remain to endure this agony of watching her in the arms of other men, and he was no martyr.

He looked longingly at the doors that would lead him out of the ballroom. But tonight, it wasn't freedom that was calling to him. It wasn't the desire to be with a pretty chorus girl. It was a need to save himself from the torment of watching Sophia being whirled around the dance floor by a succession of eligible young men.

As if he really was a martyr longing for greater pun-ishment, his gaze moved back to her. She was dancing with the Earl of Tilford, yet another perfectly accept-able man. He was respectable, would make a good husband for Sophia and would satisfy her mother's need for a title.

He released a despondent sigh, then mentally chas-tised himself for his mean-spiritedness. She looked beautiful tonight and she was finally getting her fairy-tale Season. Men were flocking around her. Her dance card had to be full, judging by the number of part-ners who had taken her hand and led her out onto the dance floor.

He should be taking pleasure in her success. Instead, he released another grunt of annoyance.

The dance came to an end and she glanced in his direction as Tilford led her off the floor. He quickly looked away. He had no desire to ruin her happiness with his gloomy countenance. She was having a good time. That was exactly what he had wanted for her when they had first met. He should leave her to enjoy herself, leave her to find a man who would make her happy.

He looked over at his mother. Her attention was focused on Luther, and the fruitless task of trying to find him a bride. Fortunately, his mother had not tried to introduce Luther to Sophia, or if she had, Luther had possessed enough sensitivity to put his foot down. That would be a torment too far.

As if the gods were listening to his thoughts and were taking pleasure in torturing this mere mortal, Luther excused himself from the gaggle of young ladies surrounding him and crossed the floor to Sophia. He wouldn't. He couldn't. Would he? He did.

Luther bowed low and introduced himself to Sophia's mother. The young man waiting to take Sophia's hand for the next dance was hastily brushed aside by Mrs Cooper in favour of the Duke of Southbridge. In horror, Ethan watched as a smiling Luther led Sophia onto the floor for the quadrille, while her mother beamed with pleasure.

This was too much. He could almost cope with other young men dancing and flirting with Sophia. Almost. But his own brother...

He had to get away. No longer caring whether his mother noticed his exit, he strode across the ballroom and out through the doors.

He passed the library and halted. It was hard to believe it was a mere five months ago that he had found

Sophia in that room, bundled up in a chair, tears running down her face.

So much had changed in those five short months.

Now she was a vibrant, confident young woman, the belle of the ball, who would never again allow a man to treat her the way Ravenswood had.

And he too had changed, but not for the better. He had gone from a man who cherished his independence and enjoyed every moment of it to a man who didn't know what to do with himself, a man who no longer knew who he was or what he wanted from life.

As if drawn by an irresistible force, he entered the library and sat down in the same leather chair he had sat in so he could comfort the crying debutante. He smiled to himself, remembering how terrible she had looked that night.

With red-rimmed eyes, a swollen face wet with tears, she had looked dreadful. Even after her attempts to repair the damage to her appearance in the ladies' retiring room, she hadn't looked much better. And yet, even with a blotchy face, there had still been something captivating about her, a quality that was beyond physical beauty. That elusive quality had been apparent from that moment, and he had been further entranced by it the more he got to know her.

He smiled at the memory of discovering that naughty side of her nature, when they had run through the rain together, defying her stern lady's maid and the expected reprimand from her mother. Even then, there had been a hint of rebellion under that well-behaved facade. And she had looked so beautiful that day, her hair coming loose from its carefully constructed coiffure, her cheeks flushed from exertion, her face damp from the rain.

His smiled turned to a laugh when he remembered how she had looked when he found her alone in the alcove at the opera house. After that, there had been no doubt that she possessed an underlying strength that was magnificent.

Instead of the expected distressed damsel, she was like a Valkyrie, a vanquishing warrior queen, energised by her victory. She had taught the Duke a lesson he wouldn't soon forget, and she had looked majestic, as if she could take on the world and teach every man who had ever mistreated a woman that he would be wise to never do it again. He would love to have witnessed Ravenswood crumpling before her, would love to have seen the Duke's face when he realised that Sophia had a mind of her own, that she wasn't going to bend to his will or the will of her mother.

And then everything changed. His smile died. She didn't need him from that point onwards. Had never really needed him. He had convinced himself he had to be her protector because she was a vulnerable young woman who couldn't look after herself, but there was nothing vulnerable about Sophia.

And didn't his present misery show how unworthy he was of her? He should be celebrating her triumph, not wallowing in self-pity, alone in the library.

He slumped further down in the chair and placed his head in his hands, wishing he could be happy for her. But, damn it all, he couldn't.

\* \* \*

The quadrille finally came to an end. Ethan's brother escorted her off the floor, bowed to her mother and with a wry smile departed.

Now was Sophia's chance. She needed to move fast before the next man on her dance card took her hand.

Too late.

'Miss Cooper, I believe this dance is mine,' the Earl of Linwood said with a bow.

'I'm so sorry,' she said, ignoring his extended hand. 'I'm afraid I must sit this one out.' She patted her hair as if indicating it needed some urgent repair.

He bowed graciously. 'But will you promise me a dance as soon as you return?'

'Of course,' she replied and rushed off towards the door, as if fixing her hair was something that could not wait a second longer.

She all but ran along the corridors, hoping and praying Lord Ethan had not yet left the house. She needed to talk to him again. This might be her last opportunity.

What she would say, she had no idea. All she knew was she had to be honest with him. She had to tell him what she felt, what was in her heart.

She ran past the open door of the library, then stopped and retraced her steps. There he was, sitting alone, looking so sad and dejected.

'Ethan,' she murmured.

He looked up. They stared at each other, neither smiling. Then he sat up straight and sent her one of his glorious smiles. A smile that always made her melt inside and forget who she was and what she was doing.

Then that smile disappeared and he frowned, as if he had been caught doing something he shouldn't.

He stood up. 'Sophia.' His voice was merely a whisper.

She took one step into the room. 'I had wondered where you had gone. I thought you would ask me for at least one dance before you left.'

'You hardly need my assistance any more. You seem to have all the male attention you could possibly wish for.'

'Not all the attention I could wish for,' she said quietly, taking another step forward. She breathed deeply and slowly to give herself courage to continue. 'And I wanted to talk to you.' She took the seat across from him, sure that her weak legs would be unable to support her for much longer.

He remained standing, as upright and rigid as a soldier on parade. 'You do?'

'Yes.' She looked down, took in another deep breath, then looked up at him, forcing her gaze to remain steady. She needed to be brave now. Braver than she had been when she confronted Ravenswood. Braver than she had been when she stood up to her mother. 'I miss you, Ethan.'

He continued to stare at her, not speaking. She bit her bottom lip, waiting for him to say something, anything.

'And I miss you, Sophia,' he finally said. 'But you will soon meet a man you want to marry and then you will forget all about me.' He gave a dismissive laugh, as if forgetting him was something and nothing, and she did not need to worry herself about it.

She shook her head. How could she ever meet a man she wanted to marry when all she could think about was Ethan Rosemont?

'And what about you, Ethan?' she asked, holding her breath while she waited for his answer.

He gave another laugh, which sounded fake. 'As you know, I do not intend to marry, so I won't be meeting any such women, soon, later, or ever.'

She stood up and took a tentative step towards him. 'But is there anyone in your life at the moment? Any other woman?'

He looked down but didn't answer.

'I'm sorry,' she said quietly. 'Perhaps that is none of my business.'

His dark brown eyes returned to stare into hers, and then they softened, along with his rigid posture. 'You never have to apologise to me, Sophia,' he said.

'It's just, I know it is not my concern, but even though I know you aren't the type to marry, I also believe you are not a man who is likely to go any length of time without a woman in your life.'

He dragged in a slow, ragged breath. She had probably gone too far, but she did not want to stop now. She both wanted to know and didn't want to know the answer to her painful question. Was some other woman experiencing the rapture of his kisses, the ecstasy of being in his arms? Was she wasting her time?

'No, there is no one else.'

She slowly released her held breath. They continued to stare at each other, neither speaking. There was so much Sophia wanted to say to him, so many emotions she needed to express, so much she needed to tell him.

*Be brave. Take a risk. Tell him what you want, what you have thought about constantly, what you have dreamt about.*

She closed her eyes briefly, to gather in all her reserves of strength. 'There could be.' Her heart pounding fiercely in her chest, she opened her eyes, looked up at him and waited for him to take in the meaning of her words. But he said nothing, just stared down at her, his brow furrowed, his lips a thin line.

'I know you don't wish to marry,' she rushed on, trying to fill the uncomfortable silence. 'But…' She paused, breathed slowly and told herself yet again to be strong. She would never forgive herself if she did not take this last opportunity to tell him what she wanted. She would always wonder, for the rest of her life, what might have happened if only she had been honest and open, if only she had been brave enough to expose her longing to him.

What she was about to say was hard, but it could be no harder than trying to live without Ethan in her life. Drawing in another deep breath, she continued. 'I know you don't want to marry, but perhaps I could become your mistress?'

The words seemed to hang in the air between them. Sophia's body remained taut, tensing in expectation of his reply. He said nothing while her heart thumped out the passing seconds.

'No.'

Blood rushed to her ears, pounding loudly, as if to

drown out that devastating word that had destroyed all her dreams. While her mind and heart remained numb, as if unable to accept the shock of what he had just said, her body reacted immediately. She turned and fled the library.

## Chapter Seventeen

What had he done? How many times had he fantasised about having Sophia in his bed? How could he
have turned down such an offer? He had never seduced
a debutante. In fact, he never seduced any women.
Every woman who had ever shared his bed came there
knowing exactly what he was offering and was more
than happy with that arrangement. They were merry
widows or actresses or other women who cared nothing for social conventions and took pleasure in defying
the rules that Society imposed on them.

Sophia was a debutante, but wasn't she now becoming the sort of woman who defied convention? She was
now an independent young woman who knew her own
mind. She had been the one to ask him. He would not
be seducing her. And yet he had said no. What on earth
was wrong with him? And worse than that, he had
insulted and upset her. That alone was unforgivable.

He released his tight grip on the edge of the desk,
left the library and returned to the ballroom. Sophia

was now dancing with the Earl of Linwood. A waltz. A smile was plastered on her face, but even from this distance he could see it was fake. Her body, which usually moved in time to the music with such grace and elegance, was held stiffly. She was in pain, and he had caused that pain. How could he hurt someone he cared about so much? How could he hurt the woman he loved?

Loved?

That word hit him like a physical blow. Love. He loved Sophia Cooper.

That explained everything, why he couldn't sleep, why he couldn't eat, why he could think of nothing except her. He was in love. In love with the bravest, most beautiful, most magnificent woman he had ever met. And like a fool, he had nearly let her slip away from him.

Not waiting for the dance to end, he moved through the circling couples. He needed to make this right. No matter what, he could not hurt the woman he loved.

'Excuse me, Linwood. This is my dance.'

Before the startled man could respond, Ethan took hold of Sophia's hands and moved her away from the flustered earl. Her body still ramrod stiff, he placed her hand on his shoulder and slid his arm around her waist.

'You don't have to say anything, Ethan,' she said, not looking at him. 'You don't have to explain or apologise.'

'I plan to do none of those things.' He pulled her in close to him and was pleased to feel her body soften under his touch. Hadn't he dreamt about holding her again, so many times? And yet the dream did not come close to the reality.

She placed her head gently on his shoulder. 'Then perhaps we should just enjoy this dance together, one last time.'

'No, I don't want to do that either.'

She lifted her head and looked at him, her brow furrowed in a questioning frown, those lovely lips turned down.

'I was telling you the truth when I said I don't want you to be my mistress.'

The hand holding his clenched tightly and her bottom lip trembled slightly. He was doing this all wrong. He was hurting her more and that was the last thing he wanted to do.

'I said you don't have to apologise, and I meant it,' she said while he scrambled to order his thoughts so he would do no more damage. 'I know you see me as an innocent debutante, and I know you would not want to ruin my reputation. You are an honourable man, it's just…'

'I'm not that honourable. Sophia, I've dreamt about having you in my bed. Or at least, I've spent countless sleepless nights fantasising about it. Believe me, nothing I have thought about doing to you is particularly honourable.'

She looked up at him, her eyes growing wide, then she smiled and a delightful shade of pink tinged her cheeks. 'Well, I've had a few dishonourable dreams about you as well. So what's stopping us from making those dreams come true? If you're worried about my reputation, I don't care about that. If you're worried no one will want to marry me, well, I no longer care about that either. I know what I'm doing. I want to be your mistress, and if I'm hearing you correctly, then you want that as well.'

'No, Sophia. I don't want you as my mistress. I want you as my wife.'

They stared at each other, both unsure he had actually said those words.

'You want me to be…but you said you wouldn't… you would never…'

'I know what I said, but I was wrong. I've been so wrong about so many things. I want to marry you. I want you to be my wife, not my mistress. Will you marry me?'

Her wide eyes lost their shocked expression and a cheeky smile curved the edges of her lips. 'What are you saying to me? You won't let me have my wicked way with you until I put a ring on your finger?'

He laughed loudly, his arm wrapping tighter around her waist. 'Yes, it seems that is exactly what I'm saying.' He stopped laughing, and gazed down at her blue eyes, imploring her to understand how serious he was. 'I can't live without you. I have tried but I have failed. I want you in my life. I want to spend my days and nights with you. I want to know that we will always be together, that we will grow old together, that we will watch our children and our grandchildren grow up. And that cannot happen if you are my mistress. It can only happen if you are my wife.'

He smiled, realising just how true his words were.

'I love you, Sophia, and I want the world to know it. I want you to be my wife.'

'You do?' she said, still smiling.

'Yes, I do. I can't believe it has taken me this long to realise it.' He shook his head slowly in disbelief. Why was he such a fool? Why had it taken so long to discover such a simple truth? 'In the past, I never wanted to marry for one reason—because I had never been in love. But now I am. I love you, Sophia.'

He paused and drew in a few steadying breaths. 'Will you marry me?' he asked, happiness sweeping over him, a happiness that was so strong he was sure everyone else in the room must be able to feel it. 'Sophia, will you marry me? Will you be my wife?'

She paused, her face serious as she considered his proposal. The bubble of joy inside him deflated. Was she going to say no? Did she want to be his mistress but not his wife? Did she not want to spend the rest of her life with him? Was she going to destroy his happiness? How was he going to live if it was without Sophia by his side for ever?

'Yes,' she finally said, that cheeky smile returning. 'Yes,' she repeated. 'Yes, yes, yes!' Her voice became louder with each word.

He spun her around, sure that they could almost take flight he felt so light. But he needed to do more than dance with his beautiful Sophia to give this moment the significance it deserved.

Not caring where they were, not caring who was looking, he wrapped her tightly in his arms and kissed her. Her lips were just as he remembered them, just as soft and tasting just as sweet. She moulded herself into him, and he pulled her closer, pressing her curvaceous body against his. He had wondered whether his fevered mind had exaggerated how good it was to have her in his arms, how glorious it was to hold her. But it had been no exaggeration. If anything, his memories had shown a severe lack of imagination.

He forced himself to withdraw from her tempting lips, certain that if he did not, he would be unable to restrain the passion that had been desperate for release over the time they were apart.

'But you deserve a proper proposal,' he said, her lips still a few enticing inches from his. 'I'm not Prince Charming but you deserve as much of the fairy tale as I can provide.'

She opened her eyes and was about to speak, but before she could do so he took hold of her hand and dropped to one knee. The swirling dancers came to a halt, all staring at the man making a spectacle of himself in the middle of the dance floor. Even the band stopped playing, seemingly realising there was no point if no one was dancing.

'Miss Sophia Cooper,' he said, looking up at the beautiful, vibrant woman he loved so much. 'Would you do me the greatest honour by consenting to be my wife? I can't offer you a title, but what I can offer you is my undying love and devotion. I can promise that every day of my life I will try to be worthy of you and to prove to you the depth of my love for you. Sophia, will you marry me?'

'Yes, oh, yes, I will,' she said, her eyes dancing with joy, those beautiful lips smiling.

The surrounding couples broke into spontaneous applause, all smiling as if infected with his joy, and as if on cue the orchestra struck up the marriage march, causing the applause to increase in volume and the smiles to grow wider.

While everyone was still clapping, she bent down and whispered in his ear. 'If I can't be your mistress, then I suppose I'm going to have to be your wife.'

'I don't see why you can't be both,' he replied with a laugh.

'In that case, you said I deserved a proper proposal, and I now have one worthy of a wife. But I think I also deserve a proper kiss, one worthy of a mistress.'

'Then you shall have one, my darling.' Ethan stood up, took his bride-to-be in his arms and kissed her without restraint. They were no doubt causing a scandal to do so in such a public place with everyone watching, one that would be talked about for many Seasons to come, but who cared? Certainly not Ethan, and, by the way Sophia was kissing him back, certainly not his future bride.

With his lips on hers, his arms holding her tightly, her body pressed hard against his, Ethan knew he was exactly where he was meant to be. This was the woman he was meant to be with, now and for ever. This was the woman who completed him. The woman he loved with all his heart and soul.

Finally breaking from the kiss, he stared down at her, hardly able to speak his heart was so full. 'I love you,' he whispered, those three words containing so much meaning.

'I love you,' she said back, her words causing his heart to soar even higher.

Slowly the surrounding couples came back into focus, and on the side of the dance floor his two brothers and his mother were smiling at him, his mother clasping her hands to her heart.

He took Sophia's hand, lightly kissed it, then led her across the floor to meet her future family. They surrounded them, congratulating Ethan and giving Sophia kisses on the cheek. Even Mrs Cooper joined them and kissed her daughter lightly and mumbled her congratulations.

A group of debutantes surrounded Sophia, all talking at once, and Ethan turned to his smiling brothers, expecting some inevitable teasing.

'Looks like this time you owe me twenty pounds,' Luther said, slapping Jake on the back.

'Money well spent,' Jake laughed, shaking Ethan's hands once again.

'Twenty pounds?' he asked Luther.

'I bet Jake that I could force you into finally doing what you wanted to do and ask the girl to marry you. And I did. Nothing like jealousy to make a man open his eyes to what he really wants.'

'That dance…you deliberately…I was so angry I…'

Jake and Luther's laughter grew louder, drowning out his spluttered reprimands. Sophia turned to look at the laughing brothers, and any consternation he felt towards Luther and Jake evaporated.

Their mother also watched his brothers and smiled. 'I knew hosting the last ball of the Season would result in one of my boys marrying,' she announced, still clasping her hands to her heart. 'Hopefully, next year my other two sons will also find brides when the Rosemont ball opens the Season.'

Jake and Luther instantly stopped laughing and looked around the room, as if their mother must be talking about two other sons and her expectations had nothing to do with them.

Other guests approached them, all expressing their joy at seeing a couple so in love and wishing them every happiness for their future life together.

When the excited chatter finally died down, Ethan took Sophia's hand and led her back onto the dance floor so he could waltz with his future bride. Once again, her cheeks were streaked with tears, just as they had been on the night they had met, but this time they were tears of happiness.

That night he had been in search of freedom, but he had been chasing an illusion. Real freedom came when you opened up your heart and loved without restraint. With the woman he loved in his arms, the woman he would spend his life with, he finally knew what true freedom was.

\* \* \* \* \*

*If you enjoyed this story,
be sure to read the other books in the
Those Roguish Rosemonts miniseries
Coming soon!*

*And whilst you're waiting for the next book,
why not check out her other miniseries,
Young Victorian Ladies*

Wagering on the Wallflower
Stranded with the Reclusive Earl
The Duke's Rebellious Lady